DO OVER DAUGHTER

MARRIAGE SURVIVORS CLUB
BOOK 1

ANNETTE NAURAINE

BEASLEY PUBLISHING

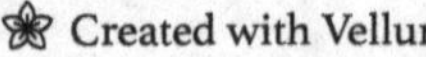 Created with Vellum

This book is dedicated to my wonderful husband, Peter, who has encouraged me throughout my writing journey, and to my two sons, Lincoln and Ulysses, who understand what my writing means to me.

This series is a Valentine to St. Paul's on the Green and all the people I've met who've become my friends.
Remember: if you don't want to see yourself in a book,
don't be friends with a writer.

CONTENTS

FRANKIE CARTER

Frankie Carter can build anything--a house, a family, and a life without the alcoholic mother who abandoned her when she was eight. When her mother, Doralee, reappears after forty-seven years, Frankie finds herself yearning for her mother's love and admiration. Even though Doralee breaks Frankie's heart at every turn, indomitable Frankie fights for the love she grew up without.

Frankie is elbow-deep in establishing an LGTBQ+ youth shelter in a house that holds painful memories of her childhood with Doralee. Real estate developer, Cam Simpson, demolishes her dream when he snatches the house away. Charming Cam wants to develop a relationship with Frankie, but the house will always be a barrier between them.

With all her plans collapsing, Frankie is devastated to learn she will soon lose Doralee forever. Frankie's best friends in the Marriage Survivors Club remind her all mothers—herself included, are imperfect. If Frankie can find the courage to forgive, she might be able to accept what love her mother can give before time runs out.

MARRIAGE SURVIVORS CLUB PRAYER

Marriage Survivors Club Prayer

From the Ionian Church Community

Dear Lord,
Please give me a few friends who understand me and remain my friends.

Addendum by the Marriage Survivors Club:
And who will tell me when I'm full of bullshit.

CHAPTER 1

Hope

For hope is a breathing thing
Living against odds or logic
Burning bright when all common sense
Means to drown it
The beating of a well-intentioned heart
Foolish, hurling itself against the sky
Sun and Moon
Look down in pity

Sofia Barrow

In the darkness, Frankie Carter drove her spade into the weed-choked, spongy side yard of the house at 61 East Avenue. She dumped the spade full of dirt onto the mounting pile. The scent of spring, loamy soil, worms, sprouting grass, and rain hung in the cool air. Soon, the lilacs would bloom and fill the air with a fragrance that only ever reminded Frankie of her childhood. Tonight, hope and possibility swung through the night sky like a pair of birds.

Olivia Maxwell, Frankie's business partner, stood by, bossing her. Peering into the hole, Olivia said, "A little deeper, and we should be good." She looked around furtively. "I hope we don't get caught."

"Nobody cares that we're digging a hole in the yard of an abandoned house. Why are we doing this anyway?"

Frankie wore her hair in tiny silver and black braids. Her sienna-brown skin and pugnacious chin were her father's, but her green half-moon eyes—so her father told her—were her mother's.

Olivia checked the ground around her feet, wary no doubt, for snakes, spiders, scorpions, ticks, or bugs of any kind. "I asked the Marriage Survivors Club to bring things to represent all their hopes, prayers, juju, karma, or whatever, so you'll win the house at tomorrow's auction. We're all behind you on turning this house, or maybe another one, into the LGBTQ youth shelter."

The Marriage Survivors Club was a diverse group of six 50-something women who had weathered divorce, widowhood, or dodged the bullet of marriage. Never-married Frankie was a founding member of the Marriage Survivors Club because she'd successfully avoided marriage. She'd considered some contenders for the husband position, but in the end, she couldn't convince herself that marriage was a good proposition for a strong woman. Her father was a long yardstick against which to measure any man.

"So we all bury our stuff, and then what?" Frankie asked, resting her foot on the shovel.

Olivia lifted her chin authoritatively. "We each drop in our item, say what we're contributing, and why. I'll have you know this is an ancient Celtic ritual passed down from my great-great-great-grandmother. Burying stuff is good luck."

Frankie laughed but hoped the magic, or whatever it was, would work. "And I quote the Marriage Survivors Club motto to you, 'One for all, and no bullshit for any,' and if I ever heard bullshit, that was a big load."

Across East Avenue, the carillon bells of St. Paul's Episcopal Church chimed the melody for the hymn "All are Welcome."

The church had decided to buy this house because St. Paul's took everybody. Once renovated, the house would be a safe place for queer kids who needed a home because everybody deserved to belong. Frankie wanted to turn the house into a safe, warm, loving place full of life and laughter, the kind of home her alcoholic mother had never been able to provide.

"I don't know why St. Paul's agreed to buy this broken-down relic. I know you want this house, but wouldn't it be cheaper to tear it down and start over?" Olivia put her hands on her hips. "And we wouldn't be doing this if we'd have taken the house on Maplecrest. It wasn't as big, but the layout was better."

Olivia, an itty-bitty White widow on the near side of fifty, who wore her blond hair in a sleek, short ponytail and only weighed about a hundred and five. With her classic clothes, porcelain skin, and flawless beauty, Olivia reminded Frankie of a tiny, menopausal Barbie doll with an indomitable spirit and a radar for the emotional center of others.

Still, Olivia's doubts raised Frankie's hackles. "The Maplecrest house had no character. It wasn't the right house for a shelter." Frankie kicked a soggy lump of dirt off the shovel. "That neighborhood would have gone all NIMBY on us."

Olivia frowned and tilted her head in question.

"You know, *not in my back yard.* This house has more bedrooms, is right across the street from St. Paul's, and is in a mixed-use zone. Besides, this house has great bones; you said so yourself."

"Broken bones, if you ask me." Olivia slapped at a mosquito. "I'll probably get Zika standing around out here."

"Deep enough?" Frankie jerked her chin toward the hole.

Olivia shined the flashlight into the hole. "No, keep going."

"We diggin' to China? I'm not as young as I used to be, you know. Maybe we should have rented a backhoe." Frankie paused to lean on the shovel and gaze up at the house.

In the blue arch of the sky, a kind of magical starlight shimmered through gauzy clouds. The full moon gleamed like a Christmas ornament, casting a cool, white luster on the grass. At the corner of the house, contorted and twisted with age, was a lilac bush. Frankie and her mother, Doralee, used to cut blooms from that very bush. Even though it was still too early for the lilacs to bloom, Frankie still recalled the heady scent which had filled every room in their house. "Isn't she beautiful?" Frankie sighed.

In her mind, the Catrambone house was still as elegant and warm as she remembered from her childhood. Darkness shrouded the unloved, long-abandoned, three-story Colonial, squatting amidst knee-high weeds. Paint peeled off her nearly two-hundred-year-old clapboards, and a few remaining black wooden shutters hung crookedly. The once spacious wraparound wooden porch sagged like an old lady's bosom. The porch railing had gaps from missing pickets. Her chimney, made of fieldstone, rose steeple-like against the night sky.

Frankie mused aloud. "Just think of all the family dinners that were eaten, all the Christmases and birthdays were celebrated in this house, all the summers spent rocking on the front porch. We can make those things happen again."

"That porch is a termite buffet," Olivia said.

"Exterminators."

"The peeling paint looks like a third-degree sunburn."

"Sanding."

Before Olivia could make a counterargument, a car pulled up. Carolina Singh, another member of the club, had arrived. Olivia shined the flashlight beam to light Carolina's way as she picked through the weeds.

Carolina had wavy, chocolate-colored hair skimming her shoulders, an inquisitive nature, and a serene attitude. She was the devout one of the group, and even in the dark, her eyes shone as if she carried a candle within.

Carolina hooked her arm through Frankie's. "This house is going to be beautiful. Think about how many kids we can help, all because of you."

Frankie ducked her chin. "Oh, it wasn't only me."

"Of course, it was," Olivia said. "You're always so self-depre-cating. We've waited long enough for it to come up for auction. I'm excited to see your dream come to fruition."

"You persuaded the church to follow your dream, Frankie," Carolina said. "Everyone will be praying for you at the auction tomorrow."

"Good, because I feel like we may even need to sacrifice a fatted calf to get this house," Frankie said and heaved a sigh.

"Do you want one of us to come with you? You don't have to do it all by yourself, you know," Carolina said.

"Thanks, but I don't want to impose on anybody," Frankie said. "And besides, Father Gabriel is coming with me."

Carolina laughed. "That will be like one of those take-your-kid-to-work days."

A painful metallic scraping noise announced Frederica 'Flicka' Cole Williamson Strada Kolinsky Whitehall's arrival as her BMW Boxster hit bottom on a driveway. She climbed out, unruffled, and minced her way through the weeds in her ever-present stilettos.

"Good God!" Flicka shuddered. "This place is bad enough in the light. In the dark, it's like being in a Stephen King novel. I feel like something's going to jump out and drag me under the porch."

The plunging neckline of Flicka's clingy black cocktail dress displayed her enhanced cleavage like fresh rolls in a bakery shop window. She had a poof of flaming—dyed—red hair, long beauty-queen legs, and a figure maintained through fanatical exercise and an addiction to plastic surgery.

Olivia eyed Flicka's dress. "You didn't have to dress up for this."

"I didn't. I have a date," Flicka said.

Carolina said, "After four husbands, I think you'd be ready to give up."

"I like men," Flicka said with a shrug. "I just don't want a permanent one. I get bored easily."

"You hittin' Tinder again?" Frankie teased.

"I wouldn't think of using Tinder," Flicka said with feigned haughtiness. "Match dot com."

Olivia said, "Does your profile say you're fifty-two?"

Flicka cupped her breasts and gave them a bouncy lift. "I can pass for forty-two."

"Only if he's blind," Frankie said.

Flicka laughed. A dirty, suggestive sound that made the birds rise out of the trees. "I've done that, too." She squinted through the dimming light. "So where is the rest of the Marriage Survivors Club?"

As if on cue, Bianca Treviso galumphed up the sidewalk carrying a shopping bag that said, "Afraid of sharks? You should meet my divorce attorney," and below that, her name and phone number.

Bianca had expensive teeth, the blue eyes of her Northern Italian ancestors, and a pudgy figure that came from spending more time watching than participating in sports. Tonight, she smelled like fries, Philly cheesesteak, and beer. Her appearance, always slightly disheveled, had made many opposing attorneys mistake her for a pushover when she would have been good at guerilla warfare.

"I was over at DeLuca's watching the Red Sox trash the Yankees. I left my car there and walked over." Huffing and puffing a bit, she dropped the bag in the weeds. It landed with a clunk. "Lord knows I need the exercise. Am I late?"

Carolina said, "You're only late if you come after Hélène."

Bianca stepped closer.

Carolina put out a hand to stop her and pointed. "Look out. Don't fall in."

Bianca stared down into the foot-deep hole. "That's one big groundhog."

"It's not groundhogs." Olivia said, "This is where we're going to bury the stuff we all brought."

They heard Hélène Charbonneau's radio cranked up full blast to a classical music station before they saw her.

She pulled into the driveway, climbed out of her car, and waved. "Sorry I'm late!" she called in her fluty voice.

The standing joke was that Hélène would show up late to her own funeral.

Paris-born Hélène had enormous dark eyes and—due to multiple Mallen streaks—black *and* white hair that gave her the look of an exotic bird. She moved with a sensuous grace in the way, Frankie imagined, music moved through air. Hélène was divorced, but that was as much as anybody knew.

Hands on her boyish hips, Hélène looked up at the house and squinted. "I think it's leaning a little to the left. Have we met to pray for this house not to fall down?"

"Oh, ye of little faith!" Frankie chided with all seriousness.

"No, we of safety concerns," Olivia said dryly. She waved her flashlight across the front of the house, and, for a moment, light seemed to come from inside the black windows, staring out at them.

She glanced around. "Since this was my idea, I'll go first." From her pocket, Olivia withdrew a can of pepper spray. The can, one of many, belonged to her daughter, Ariel, twenty-two, who had Down syndrome. Olivia believed that Ariel would *never* be safe if she left home.

"This so the kids will be safe here as they grow up." Olivia shined the light on Bianca. "You next."

From her bag, Bianca pulled a brass-colored, metal statue of Lady Justice, blindfolded and holding scales. She dropped it into the hole, where it landed with a definitive thud. "I brought this so these kids will one day have the justice and equality God intended them to have."

Carolina produced two note-card-sized flags, mementos which she kept in a vase on her mantel. "This flag is from my father's country, Guyana. The other one is, of course, for the U.S., my mother's country. When Poppy came here, he found a place where he could thrive."

She bent down and reverently laid the flags in with the other items and stood. "These flags are so the kids who live in the shelter will find family and home wherever they go." She paused to look around at the Marriage Survivors Club. Her voice caught. "Like all of you are my family."

Olivia hugged her.

"My turn," Hélène said.

Olivia's flashlight reflected off the mirrored, silvery surface as Hélène tossed a CD into the hole.

"This is some random recording—not a very good one, sorry —of Liszt's *La Campanella,* which means *bell* in Italian. When the church bells rang in medieval times, they called people together, like our bells at St. Paul's call us together. It represents how we are all coming together to make a place for kids who need a home."

Flicka slipped off her Rolex watch and dangled it high above the hole. The diamond-encrusted face and gold wristband sparkled in the beam of Olivia's flashlight. Flicka tossed it nonchalantly into the hole, where it clinked against Bianca's brass statue.

Frankie was aghast. "Your Rolex? That's worth a fortune! Get it back. We can sell it."

"Nah, it's fake," Flicka said. "Rhinestones. Bought it on the street in New York."

"You're throwing in a fake thing for Frankie?" Olivia asked.

Flicka said, "I'm burying what's not real. So the kids who live here can be who they were meant to be."

Frankie was last. She took a pair of her mother's sterling silver earrings from her pocket. Her mother had left the earrings and matching bracelet behind when she disappeared. The jewelry was part of Frankie's collection, which she kept hidden in a shoebox in the back of her closet. That was where she hoarded everything that remained of her mother: photos, costume jewelry, a barrette, a green headband, hand-written notes, and postcards. From these bits and pieces, Frankie kept alive the memory of the woman who had abandoned her.

Frankie tipped her head back and gazed up at the stars winking in the blue-black sky. In one of his sermons, their priest, Father Gabriel, once said the stars were the souls of the departed, watching over their loved ones. Her mother might be one of those stars watching Frankie. Or maybe her mother was at the bottom of a bottle.

Which was better: dead or dead drunk?

The metal earrings were cool in Frankie's palm. Was this the right thing to bury? Should she have brought something else? But if parting with the earrings still had the power to break her heart, wasn't that powerful? It would be ironic if her part in the ritual caused the whole thing to fail.

Frankie opened her hand, and the earrings, as though in slow motion, twinkled and tumbled end over end into the hole. When they landed in the bottom, they caused the most frightening, lonely sound Frankie had ever heard. "These earrings belonged to my mother." She paused and got her emotions under control. "They're so all the kids who live in the shelter will be supported and cared for."

"Now, we each put some dirt in the hole." Olivia handed the flashlight to Bianca.

Olivia grunted as she tugged the shovel out of the ground. Too small to lift a shovel load, she had to settle for scraping dirt into the hole.

Bianca passed the flashlight to Carolina and easily slung a spadeful of dirt into the hole. Then Hélène, Flicka, and finally, Frankie each cast soil into the hole. Frankie stamped down the dirt when the dirt mounded over their buried treasure.

"Okay, now what?" Flicka said into the night.

Olivia said, "Let's join hands."

"And dance around whooping our heads off," Flicka crowed.

Bianca elbowed her.

"I'll say a prayer," Carolina said.

They joined hands, bowed their heads, and Carolina prayed. "Lord, help Frankie win the auction. Let her know we love her and remind her we have her back, no matter what. Amen."

Together, they raised their hands and gave the rallying cry of the Marriage Survivors Club. "One for all and no bullshit for any!"

CHAPTER 2

Let us Build a House, Hymn No. 301

Let us build a house where love can dwell
and all can safely live
a place where saints and children tell
how hearts learn to forgive.

Marty Haugen

Frankie pushed her cart through the scrum of shoppers clogging the front entrance to Stew Leonard's grocery. It annoyed her that the place was like a tourist destination at 9:10 a.m. People came to gawk at the animated talking cow, see the mechanical chicken poop out an egg, or hear the mangy robotic dogs sing bad country western songs.

Her maternal sense of being perpetually late shot through her stomach like a flaming arrow. Being a mom and trying to meet the onslaught of demands was like swimming up a waterfall. She checked the time on her phone. She was cutting it close, but if she did self-check-out, she could pick up the things on her dad's list for dinner and get to the auction at Town Hall on time.

Her phone pinged with a schedule reminder. *AUCTION! Don't be late!* Buying 61 East Avenue had been her sole focus for the last two years. She couldn't blow it over a rump roast. One hiccup, and everything else went sideways.

Frankie flexed her grip on the handle of her cart and gave herself a pep talk. *She* was the sort of woman who Got Things Done. Whatever anyone needed, *she* would fire up her inner pisser and get it done.

Hit it with a hammer!

Stew's—as it was known in local parlance—was arranged in a maze that forced shoppers to walk past everything to get back to the checkout. She pushed forward with singular purpose, past dairy, cutting through at the pasta, cornering at the cheese counter, weaving past the shiny fish laid out on ice. At the butcher's counter, she took her place at the rear of a customer pile-up and pulled a pink tab out of the number machine.

"Seventy-eight!" the butcher called out.

Frankie had number eighty-seven. She groaned inwardly. She was far enough down in the queue that, if she hurried, there was time to grab the vegetables and make it back in time for her number. Holding her ticket, she left her cart in the traffic jam, wriggled between carts, and hustled to the produce maze. She grabbed a bunch of kale, a bag of carrots, and a head of celery and pawed through the potatoes until she found a perfectly round one for Javier—because that was the only shape he would eat—and a few more for the rest of them. Arms loaded with vegetables, she turned back towards the butcher's counter. She dumped the produce in the cart and rocked her cart back and forth as if preparing for take-off. Frankie checked the time again, willing the other customers to evaporate.

A prickling sensation ran up the back of her neck to the top of her scalp. She turned around to see an old White lady staring intently at Frankie across the sea of carts. Crimson spider veins laced the woman's sunken cheeks and bulbous nose. With her strangely plump stomach over spindly legs and wispy white hair, she reminded Frankie of a chubby, molting bird. She wore a raggedy, flapping navy overcoat. A beat-up black patent-leather purse hung from one stooped shoulder, and she leaned on a cane.

Something about the woman's gaze struck Frankie as familiar. The woman had green half-moon eyes just like Frankie's.

Recognition slugged Frankie in the solar plexus. Everything moved as though in water. Sounds receded. The light seemed thin and foggy. A shivery astonishment spread through Frankie.

After all these years, it couldn't be her mother, and if it was, why didn't she call Frankie's name? Was Doralee still so disappointed in Frankie that she didn't want anything to do with her?

Frankie had recently called her Aunt Evelyn and left a message, which, like always, wasn't returned. When Frankie was younger, she'd called her aunt once a month. Now, she only called a couple of times a year, hoping for word about Doralee. She always assumed Evelyn didn't know any more than Frankie did.

Could this woman really be Doralee? Was she still alive after all these years?

The old lady turned away, leaving her cart, and melted into the crowd. For an old lady with a cane, she moved fast, but maybe it was because Frankie couldn't move her feet. Her voice caught in her throat: *Don't you recognize me? It's me, Francine.*

A hatchet-faced woman banged Doralee's abandoned cart

out of the way with her own. "I hate it when people dump their stuff," the woman complained.

Frankie stared at the contents of the cart: sugar, a half-gallon of 2%, a bag of slick, uncooked shrimp, and a box of Zatarain's gumbo mix.

Hot, spicy flavors flooded Frankie's mouth. Her nose filled with the aroma of rice, shrimp, onions, tomatoes, and okra, cooking on the stove. She heard the spit and sizzle of oil in the pan. Zatarain's had once been her favorite, but after Doralee left, Frankie could never again look at a box of the stuff.

She remembered Doralee's feet stomping to Cajun music, the way she tucked her face against Dad's collarbone, laughing. The glow in his eyes, the lovesick grin on his face.

The smell of the *stinky stuff*.

"Eighty-seven!" the butcher cried out.

Her phone pinged again. Frankie glanced at its message. *AUCTION! Don't be late!* How could she forget?

Frankie shook her head to clear her mind of what she assumed was just another of her mom illusions. A ghost image imprinted on the eye of her heart. For years after Doralee left, Frankie often thought she saw her mother and had crept up behind women, peering into their faces, only to feel the embarrassment that came from looking into the eyes of a stranger. The women would smile and ask if she was lost. Frankie would slink back to her dad and squeeze his hand until she felt safe again.

"Eighty-seven! Eighty-seven!" the butcher called out.

The number echoed somewhere in the periphery of Frankie's consciousness. Everything was happening at light speed, but time had stopped.

"That you? You going to order or not?" the hatchet-faced woman demanded.

Frankie stood, unmoving, blinking, trying to sift something

logical out of the near encounter. *Why is she running away if she is my mother? If she isn't my mother, why's she running away?*

Frankie left her cart with the vegetables and the one perfectly round potato behind and wove her way out of the cart jam. If she hurried, she could catch the woman and ask if she really was her mother.

As Frankie maneuvered through the clog of shoppers, dread and hope slugged it out in her chest. Did she truly want to see the woman who'd walked out of her life forty-seven years ago? Frankie couldn't change how her mother felt about her, and no apology from Doralee would scratch the surface of Frankie's years of loneliness.

Of course, Frankie knew her mother was an alcoholic, but all the *ifs* smacked into Frankie's brain:

If I had been smarter.

If I had been a better daughter.

If I had been Blacker or Whiter.

If I had been prettier.

What was it that had made her mother leave? Why was booze more important than Frankie and her dad? Frankie didn't expect or even want a relationship, but she did want answers.

Customers spooned wings, mac-n-cheese, and roasted potatoes at the hot bar into take-home tins and blocked Frankie's path to the registers. She stood on tiptoe and strained to see. A drop of sweat trickled down her spine. What was she going to say to Doralee? *Did you forget something? Like you had a daughter?*

Her phone pinged *AUCTION! 10 minutes.* She wanted to throw the dang thing against the wall.

Frankie spotted her passing the customer service desk. She called out, "Wait!" when what she wanted to call out was, "Mom!"

Doralee turned, and across the crowd, her green half-moon

eyes met Frankie's gaze. Doralee tipped her chin up and gave a slight shake of her head. Then she headed out the door.

That reproving gaze walloped the breath out of Frankie. She froze for a moment, then charged ahead.

But Doralee had disappeared in the crowd.

Church bells chimed on Frankie's phone: Father Gabriel's ringtone. She stopped to dig the phone out of her pocket.

"Hello, Frankie, it's Father Gabriel. I'm at Town Hall, but I don't see you. Are you here? The auction's about to start."

She'd never heard a hint of anxiety in his voice, but he sounded on the verge of hyperventilation. If she rushed, she might catch Doralee and ask her all the questions which, up to now, Frankie had convinced herself didn't matter. But now all those questions gnawed at her like hungry mice, more voracious than ever.

If she didn't speak to her mother now, she might never have another chance. She might disappear and return to wherever she had been hiding for the last forty-seven years.

If Frankie went to the auction to buy the house for the LGBTQ youth shelter, she might help save the lives of dozens of kids.

She could follow that dream or chase down the woman who had left her when she was eight.

"Frankie?" Father Gabriel asked.

"Can you possibly just bid on the property without me?" she said.

There was a deep silence on the other end. "Your name is registered for the bidding. The Vestry authorized you and you alone to bid on the property." She thought she heard him moan. "If we have a prayer of getting this, you have to do it."

Frankie's heightened sense of responsibility kicked into high gear. "I'll be there in a minute."

"We don't have much time."

"I'm coming." She pocketed her phone and dashed out to the parking lot.

A car was driving away with Frankie's mother in the passenger seat. Her mother had come back and run away from her.

Again.

CHAPTER 3

Past

I held your hand
Trusting and absolute you were
Certain of me and my love
Was it ever enough
That flimsy garment I tried to hide behind?
Were you ever fooled?
It was not what I intended
But the best I had to offer.

Sofia Barrow

In Doralee's mind, Frankie was still the little girl with missing teeth, long dark hair tamed back in braids and barrettes, all knobby, scraped knees, and a dedication to her daddy, Vic Carter, that was tight as Fort Knox.

Evie, Doralee's younger sister, was driving. Evie's curly hair, cut short, was grayer than Doralee remembered. Evie's arms were still stout, her build sturdy as a workhorse and she had the ability to stare right through other people like they weren't there she'd had as a kid.

Doralee couldn't remember where they were, but she was pretty sure they were in the town where she once lived.

But she knew Francine the minute she had seen her because it was like finding a missing limb that Doralee herself had chopped off, leaving a bloody stump. Even from a distance, there was a glory in looking into her daughter's eyes, seeing something of herself not yet ruined. Francine's autumn-leaf skin was Vic's, but Francine's eyes, with their hot spark of light, were the eyes of Doralee's younger self.

She reached back in her mind and saw little Francine, Vic, a lilac bush, a small house, and a big church. There had been happiness. The first safety she'd ever had. No one pawing, no locking herself behind doors.

Or maybe those things weren't real, either.

"There she was, right in the grocery store, my daughter, a beautiful, middle-aged woman. It was a pure marvel." Doralee was still awed by seeing the daughter she had forced herself to love from a distance. It was as if Francine was real again after having been imaginary for years and years.

"That was her, all right," Evie said with her characteristic dryness. "I saw her come out of the store."

Hardly anything moved Evie, a hard, practical woman. Since they were kids, she'd put one foot in front of the other, never letting anything stick to her, walking away from everything except Doralee. Evie had lived her life with no connections, and after what their mother had put them through, Doralee couldn't blame her. Francine had always been in Doralee's heart and the idea that maybe Francine still loved Doralee kept her from dying. She never imagined laying eyes on her daughter again, but a long invisible thread had always somehow linked them together.

Doralee struggled to keep her voice from breaking. "Even though I seen pictures of her, I never thought she'd be so grown up."

"You've been gone for years," Evie said. "She's not a kid anymore."

How many years have I been gone?

When they arrived at the house, Doralee organized her body to climb out of the car. Directing her decrepit, matchstick legs took concentration because they didn't behave the way they were supposed to. Slowly, leaning on her cane, unable to feel the ground beneath her feet, she shuffled to the front door. Evie unlocked the front door, and they went in.

Are we at the right place? Have I been here before?

Doralee pressed her purse tightly under her arm. It made her feel safe, this purse. If she had her purse, things would be all right. Used to be when she could get one, she carried her bottle in it. Her mother didn't carry the bottles the men brought her. They didn't last long enough to carry anywhere.

Evie said, "If she saw you, she'll come after you here for sure. Frankie's tough."

Doralee flapped her hand. "Why the hell would she want to see me anyway?" Catching sight of herself in the entryway mirror, she turned away, disgusted. "God, I can't even face myself." She was too ashamed for Francine to see what she had become.

Fingers of icy fear circled Doralee's throat. How long had she been this sick? Old man death was waiting on her, for sure. Seventy-eight years was a long enough life. Not that she could remember most of it. What she did know for sure was that she had been too weak to quit, even when she tried. Most of her life, she'd lived only for the next drink.

Evie took Doralee's jacket and hung it in the closet, but Doralee kept her purse tight under her arm. Evie turned and examined Doralee in a way she hated. "You know where you are?"

Doralee snorted at her and turned away. "'Course." But not really.

She'd been confused a lot lately, but she wasn't about to admit it, even to Evie. Nothing stuck in her mind: ideas were like stepping on an oil slick, and memories twisted so she wasn't sure if they'd happened or not. But she knew Francine was her daughter, and when she started not knowing, the end was near.

Had their mother remembered them when she died? Had she ever once thought of what she was doing to them? *Who ... who was their mother? Wha ...* and the idea was gone.

"Why'd I come here?" Doralee asked, trying for an easy tone that would mask the fact that she couldn't remember when she'd come and why.

Evie stared at her. "Because the Lafayette police had found you wandering around. They knew you, so they called me. Said you were a danger to yourself. I bought you a bus ticket, and you came here to Connecticut to stay with me."

"Oh, yes, now I remember," Doralee said, but she didn't.

"I wish you'd think about seeing Francine. She needs you."

"No, she don't." Doralee dropped into a chair. She couldn't even remember how long it had been since she'd seen her daughter.

Frankie would be rightfully furious that Doralee had left her. What woman leaves a child? *A complete and total drunken shit, that's who.* At least she'd left Frankie, unlike their own mother. That woman kept picking them up wherever they landed until she couldn't because she was dead.

"You can't face her, can you?" Evie said accusingly.

"Not without a drink anyway. How about it?" Doralee rested her hands on her plump stomach. She hardly ever ate much, so why was she getting so fat?

"No," Evie said. "Doctors say your liver can't take any more abuse."

"What the hell do they know?" Doralee said.

Damn! Evie was a bossy know-it-all. Doralee shifted in her seat, trying to ease the fire in the upper right side of her stomach. Booze gave her the courage to get up, to live with herself and what she'd done. "If I could have a drink, just one, maybe two, or a bottle even, then I could face Francine, tell her why I had to leave."

"Why are you so hard? You don't have a lot of time, you know."

To Doralee's surprise, a sob escaped Evie. Doralee begged her sister, "Promise me. We always kept our promises to each other. Promise me this."

Evie's eyes were wet when she nodded. "Promise."

"It's okay, Evie. I done lived my life the way I wanted to, and I'm not about to stop now."

It had taken every ounce of her strength to keep her distance from Francine, to protect her. Doralee wasn't about to hurt her daughter now.

CHAPTER 4

Let us Build a House, Hymn No. 301

Built of hopes and dreams and visions,
rock of faith and vault of grace;
here the love of Christ
shall end divisions.
All are welcome, all are welcome,
All are welcome in this place.

Marty Haugen

At Town Hall, Frankie pulled into a parking space and hopped out. She tried to push the scene at Stew Leonard's grocery out of her mind, but questions hammered her concentration.

She couldn't believe she'd seen her *mother*. It was pure malice that Evelyn hadn't let her, and her dad know Doralee was in town. Maybe Doralee would call them herself. Frankie's throat tightened at the idea of answering a call from her mother.

Inside Norwalk City Hall, Frankie ran into the concert hall where the auction was being held. She was panting when she reached Father Gabriel's side.

He gave her a silent nod of greeting, which set her back a second. Ordinarily, he would greet her with a jovial toothsome smile that reminded Frankie of her Goldendoodle, Beasley, without the tail wagging.

His baby face was in direct opposition to his lanky, six-foot-six frame. He stood a head above the rest of the crowd, and in his clerical collar and charcoal grey suit, he was even more of an oddity. Today, tension strained his boyish, prayer-smoothed face, and anxiety transformed his brown eyes. He'd tried to plaster his curly chocolate hair to his head, but in spots, it sprang away exuberantly.

Frankie loved him like the brother she'd never had. She wouldn't throw herself in front of a bus for him, but she would do pretty much anything else he asked her. She wanted the house for him as much as she wanted it for all the other reasons.

Shifting from foot to foot, buttoning and unbuttoning his suit coat, he looked about to keel over with a heart attack.

"You okay?" she asked.

He looked down at her. "A little nervous. This is a big step for St. Paul's."

She patted him on the back. "Please don't barf."

He smiled weakly, greenly.

"Sorry I was late."

"I'm worried we won't get this. That we should have taken the house on Maplecrest." His voice came out unevenly.

"Maplecrest wasn't right," she said with absolute conviction. "Too small, too far away."

"The entire parish is behind this house, and I'm concerned that if we don't win the auction, we'll lose our momentum."

At his words, her heart sank.

She wasn't used to seeing him so pessimistic or worried. He was a guy who believed in God and miracles. Didn't that mean God had this all sewn up? St. Paul's had put three years into planning for the shelter, and now, the goal was within reach. She couldn't afford to let herself get distracted by her newly-reappeared mother.

"You look like you haven't slept in days," she said.

He jammed his hands in his pockets, clearly terribly discouraged. "Up late. I paid a hospital call on a sixteen-year-old trans girl who tried to take her life last night."

Her stomach took a dive. "Oh, no. What happened?"

"Bullying at school. Parents threatening to kick her out for being trans." He sighed deeply. "There's such need for a shelter. I believe it's part of St. Paul's mission." He looked at her with tired but trusting eyes. "A mission you helped shape, Frankie, and I'm immensely grateful for that, no matter what happens today."

Unable to find words, she stared at the toes of her boots.

He bowed his head, closed his eyes, and prayed silently.

She did likewise and felt her breathing slow and her pulse drop. Neither of them could do this; they needed God to pull it off.

As the auction progressed, she shifted her bidding paddle from one sweaty palm to the other. The auctioneer sold three properties in quick succession, each sale bringing the auction 61 East Avenue closer. Unlike TV auctioneers, this one spoke slowly and clearly and pointed at the bidders. That eased Frankie's anxiety a micron. At least she would understand him.

The auctioneer called out, "Now, we're ready to sell 61 East Avenue. Get your paddles ready if you want to bid."

"Ready?" Father Gabriel asked Frankie.

She forced a confident smile and nodded even though her stomach felt like she'd drunk paint thinner. A hot flash swept over her, like being on fire from the inside. She shed her jacket and slung it over her shoulder.

"You okay?" Father Gabriel looked down at her with concern.

"Just nerves." She couldn't really tell her gay, single, thirty-year-old priest about the effects of menopause.

Father Gabriel stepped forward.

Frankie's neck and shoulders tensed as she moved next to him. For a split second, no one else stepped up, and Frankie nearly jumped for joy. They were the only bidders!

Then, a debonair White guy strode across the hall, his posture tilted forward, wedging his way through the milling people as the prow of a boat cuts through the waves. It was as if he expected them to move out of his way. He came to stand by Frankie and Father Gabriel.

He was the kind of guy the Marriage Survivors Club referred to as an RWM: a Rich White Male.

Sixty-ish, with silver hair that bristled upwards, he had crinkles at the corners of his eyes and a slightly wrinkly neck. Aside from an age-appropriate softening around his middle, he was in pretty good shape. Hot, even. For a White guy.

His suit hung on his frame like a second skin, and he wore shiny expensive-looking shoes. Below his thoughtful forehead, his arresting, slate-gray eyes had a killer's stony gaze.

Frankie didn't get eye candy very often because she spent most of her time on job sites with her crew or at the big box stores picking up supplies. She'd bet that guy didn't smell like sawdust or Gorilla glue, either.

He smiled at her, his eyes sweeping her up and down the way a man checks out a much-younger babe. Goosebumps rose on her arms, and she felt a swell of warmth flood her body.

Where did that come from?

It had been ages since a man of any age had checked her out.

She was pleasantly surprised, then embarrassed, by the sizzle she felt. She was fifty-five and standing next to her priest!

But as Flicka always said, "We're menopausal, not corpses."

The hot White guy turned his attention to the auctioneer, and a sick feeling bloomed in Frankie's gut.

He was going to bid against them.

An un-Christian thought came to her: *Please, God, let lightning strike him dead!*

CHAPTER 5

Winners

My father raised me to be a barroom brawler
With steel-toed boots and brass knuckles
And a lightening response to insult,
contradiction or argument

Tossed so easily over your shoulder
The uppercut of your smile
Knocked me out of my skin
Kicked the breath out of me
Cracked the rib shielding my heart

One glance dropped me to the floor
Made me a passivist.
Who could or would
Fight such a smile as yours?

Sofia Barrow

. . .

Cam prepared to bid for 61 East Avenue. He expected the property to solve most, if not all, of his problems. Once he won the bid, he would go to Zoning, combine 61 with the other two adjacent lots, get his banker to sign off on the loan, and *voila!* The Essex condominium development would launch. He'd bought properties at auction dozens of times, but this time, there was more riding on the winning bid.

He would become solvent, and he could save Simpson and Sons, the company his father had started.

The auctioneer nodded at Cam and looked around the hall. "Anybody else?"

No one responded.

Perfect.

The only other bidders were the gorgeous Amazon standing with a guy who looked like a high school kid masquerading as a priest. Rookies. That would make nailing this easier.

He angled away so he couldn't see the Amazon. He couldn't afford to be distracted by a face like hers.

"All right then. Ready?" the auctioneer asked.

Cam gave a sharp nod, put on his gladiator face, set his legs slightly apart, and prepared for battle.

The auctioneer sang out, "Here we go! Seventy-five thousand is the opening bid."

The woman waved her paddle as if she were bringing a plane in at an airport gate. Clearly, this was her first rodeo. This would prove simple. Virgin bidders always lost courage when the going got tough.

Cam heard the priest murmur, "Easy," under his breath.

The priest was the one signing the check, then. Two lambs to the slaughter. Cam nodded to raise the bid.

They pingponged the bids for a while, he increasing it, but the Amazon matched him every time.

Muscles across the small of Cam's back twinged. He couldn't help but look at her now. She looked positively explosive with determination. She had balls; he'd give her that.

Bidding crept up in five-thousand-dollar increments. Like spectators at a tennis match, heads swiveled back and forth between the Amazon and Cam. As the price climbed, the Amazon matched Cam.

The price kept rising. Despite his experience, Cam's pulse sped up. He snuck a glance at the priest, who looked like he might pass out. He was the one who could put a stop to the Amazon, but she showed no signs of caving. In fact, with every bid, she seemed more determined, which only made her more beautiful.

Bidding was reaching the limit Cam had expected to pay for the property, but there was no way he could afford to let this slip through his fingers. If he did, the company his father built and left him went into the dumpster.

Amazon jumped the price by 10K.

He had to crush her.

Cam flicked his paddle. "One fifty," he said, jacking up the price by $20,000 in a single bid, way over what the property was worth to anyone except him.

The auctioneer's voice resounded in the room like repeated thunderclaps, each one causing a spasm in Cam's lower back.

Amazon shot Cam a glare. Fiercely, she rifled her arm into the air, holding the face of the paddle like a stop sign toward Cam.

Sweat trickled down Cam's spine as he matched her bid.

The priest groaned. "That's it, we've reached our limit."

Cam was about to breathe a sigh of relief when Amazon's arm shot up again.

Damn it!

The priest put a hand on her shoulder. "You have to stop!"

As though by reflex, she raised her paddle, but the priest yanked her arm back to her side. "Frankie, Frankie!"

So that was her name: Frankie. Her nakedly pain-filled face made Cam flinch. She seemed to have a lot at stake in this auction, but Cam did too.

The auctioneer pointed his gavel at Frankie. "Final call. Do you want to bid?"

Her head jerked forward in something of a nod, but it looked more like whiplash.

"No, no, we don't," the priest boomed out.

The auctioneer raised his eyebrows, and in an act of compassion, he didn't take Frankie's bid.

"Aaaall right, then! Soooold to the man in the nice suit!" The auctioneer smacked a wooden square with a hammer, and the sound shot through Cam like a bullet from a starting gun.

The small crowd erupted in applause, and he heard her mutter, "Lord, please let the property be a toxic waste dump!"

Cam didn't particularly believe in God or Higher Powers, but he did believe in winning. This was the only time he could remember taking no pleasure in doing so.

CHAPTER 6

The darker the night, the brighter the stars; the deeper the grief, the closer is God!

Fyodor Dostoevsky

Frankie felt she had let Father Gabriel, the Marriage Survivors Club, and the whole church down. After the auction, burning with humiliation, she stopped at the house to pick up her Goldendoodle, Beasley. Mercifully, her dad was out. She drove out to Calf's Pasture beach, where she could have time to herself.

She and Beasley wandered down to the end of the wooden pier, which jutted out into the Long Island Sound. Before her, an endless ocean roiled beneath an ominous cement-grey sky. Gusts tore at her braids, made her eyes water, and snatched at her clothes. At the end of the dock, the wind beat harder, but she didn't pull her jacket tight, taking the needling as a kind of punishment.

She sat on a bench and stroked Beasley's head. "At least you still love me."

He wagged his tail and stared up at her as if waiting to hear more.

Everyone would be sympathetic when news of her failure spread through the church, but she didn't want sympathy. Figuring out a way forward was the only thing that offered a shred of hope. But right now, she was out of ideas.

She looked into Beasley's almost-human amber eyes. "The Marriage Survivors Club fundraising gala is in a few weeks, but people won't buy tickets if there isn't a house to raise funds for."

He tilted his head in what she interpreted as understanding.

A gull landed on the pier rail and Beasley set to barking. She let go of his leash, and he chased the gull off.

"So much for you being a good listener," she called after him.

Neither prayer nor the Marriage Survivors quasi-Episcopalian ritual had helped pull off this harebrained scheme. Her plans hadn't panned out. Her dream was a dud.

Beasley returned to her side.

"I started this, so it's my responsibility to keep this dream alive for St. Paul's, but I'm out of ideas. You have any ideas?"

He smiled up at her.

"I thought so," she said. "All you ever think about are treats and ear scritches."

Far off to her right was the Sheffield Island Lighthouse, and she remembered another dream that never came true. Doralee had promised her a ferry ride out to the island. Frankie still remembered trying to wake her mother, passed out on the sofa, an empty bottle in her hand. She had covered Doralee with her doll's blanket. "You promised, you promised," Frankie said, shaking her. But that had been just one of many broken promises.

Today, Doralee, then the house, had slipped through her grasp. Maybe losing the house was the Universe telling her to stay in her own lane; that she was asking too much, expecting too much, that she wasn't deserving; that she wasn't destined to have the house or her mother.

Frankie took Beasley's leash and headed for the beach walkway, Beasley trotting faithfully along at her side. "I have about a million questions to ask. I suppose I could call Aunt Evelyn's and ask if Doralee's there."

Another dog walker passed her and, hearing her talking to Beasley, gave her a wide berth.

Why? There wasn't any answer good enough for that.

Where? It would hurt to hear that Doralee had lived and loved other people, not Frankie.

Why now? Doralee had looked like a skeleton. If she was sick, Frankie didn't want to be stuck caring for the mother who hadn't cared for her child. It certainly wasn't like Frankie had any responsibility to do so.

When? If Frankie found some tenuous connection to Doralee, what would it feel like when she left again, which she was certain to do?

Who? Who was Doralee Farris Carter? Did Frankie want to know what part of her came from her alcoholic mother?

Her phone pinged with a text. A message from Dad:

Dinner on stove. Come on home.

Home.

Doralee had never provided Frankie with a safe, loving home. Frankie was certain that 61 East Avenue was meant to be for kids who needed a home. She just had to find a way to make it happen. "C'mon, Beasley. Time to go home to all those guys we love."

CHAPTER 7

Home is where the heart (and the wine) is.

Frankie dragged herself through the front door of her house and sank onto the bench in the entryway. Her legs jiggled from the adrenaline rush of the auction, and her nerves were like overheated electrical wires that had melted their coating. Even her teeth felt tired.

Food. Wine. Bed. In that order.

The juicy, salty aroma of pot roast with potatoes, carrots, and celery greeted her.

Her dad, Vic Carter, had run his own construction company, mentored dozens of young Black and Hispanic men, raised a daughter all on his own, and somewhere along the line, he had still learned to cook.

She smacked her forehead with her palm. When she'd run after her mother, she had forgotten all the dinner fixings, which meant Dad had gone and gotten them himself. He must have walked to the store because God forbid he ask someone to drive him there. The angry, green gremlin of guilt ran around her insides shaking its fists at her.

"Right on time. Dinner's almost ready," her dad said.

At seventy-eight, Vic Carter was a man of few words, but his cooking said it all.

"Thanks for making my favorite meal."

"Thought a little celebration might be in order."

She turned away before he could see her wince.

He was a dark-skinned Black man with a bald spot on the crown of his head, a bum knee, and the patience of a saint. They shared the same broad shoulders, sturdy legs, and kinky hair, and as she got older, love handles. He had taught her to calculate profit and loss, to estimate how long a job would take, to save money without sacrificing quality, to figure material and labor costs, and to deal with demanding customers.

Failing to correctly calculate the purchase of 61 East Avenue meant she'd failed to use a lick of what he'd taught her. She dreaded seeing his disappointment.

"Coming," she called back. "Sorry I didn't get the groceries. Got tied up."

"I walked over. It was nice."

He crossed the kitchen with an uneven gait.

"Yeah, and now your bad knee will bother you for the next week. You should have asked one of the Marriage Survivors to drive you over."

How was it that her every little failure snowballed, picking up bigger consequences as they rolled downhill?

"I'll be fine," he said. Then, "Jordan call you for a ride?"

"No, he probably got a lift."

Jordan was her eldest and her dad's main source of worry.

Her youngest son, Javier, sat on the sofa in the living room, his head bent over a notepad drawing another of his intricately detailed pictures of a luxurious mansion. The lamp cast warm light over his face, still chubby with baby fat. Beasley flopped on the floor next to Javier and rested his nose on Javi's knee.

Javier didn't even look up when she sat down next to him. Used to be, when he was little, she would come in the front door, and he'd rush to her and throw his doughy arms with their dimpled elbows around her knees. He'd look up at her and say "I wub you," and her heart would melt.

She had adopted him when he was two. He had been traumatized, was barely walking, and was unable to say a word in Spanish or English. Frightened when a door slammed or someone raised their voice, it had taken a long time to gain his trust. His mother had overdosed six months before Frankie got him, and he'd been left in the care of an addict claiming to be his father. She shuddered to think what his life might have been like if she hadn't gotten him. Or what her life might have been like if he hadn't saved her.

Her arms ached to gather him to her chest and kiss the salty, sticky folds of his neck, but he hated being touched. And itchy clothes. And gooey food. And having his food touch each other on his plate. And being rushed. And transitions. And the list went on. That's the way it was with autistic kids, each one unique, complicated, and impenetrable.

She knew how to do electrical wiring, plumbing, frame a room, hang drywall, build a luxury kitchen, lay wood flooring, marble tiles, and install windows, but raising him was like trying to read Braille by listening to the dots. She never seemed to be able to love him the right way, and it wasn't his fault. She just hadn't figured it out yet. If she could speak doggie, she'd ask Beasley because he seemed to have broken the code.

"Hi, Javier," she said.

No answer. Not even a grunt. She noted that his socks were stiff from their third day of wearing. Even from a distance, his feet smelled like a mushroom farm.

"How was your day, lovey?"

"Rmpf."

"Sounds like you had fun," she said.

On days like this, when life had moved backward, and dreams fizzled, she wanted to gather her boys into her arms and feel like everything she needed was right there. She wanted to feel like loving her boys would make everything okay.

If only.

She hadn't married, but it had never occurred to her not to have a family. She just went about it differently than most women did. She wanted children to love, to give a home to, to make them feel safe, loved, and wanted.

"Six o'clock. Time to eat," she said.

Javier jumped up like a jack-in-the-box.

They took their seats at the dining room table, and Beasley lay down next to Javi's chair, hoping that something might fall on the floor. Before he sat, Javier pulled and pushed his chair in and out three times, like always. The front door opened and slammed, followed by the annoying thud of a basketball bouncing on the hardwood floor.

"No basketball in the house!" Frankie and her dad hollered in unison.

Jordan ambled into the kitchen, his high-top haircut grazing the top of the doorframe.

Adopted also at age two, Jordan had grown into a rangy six-six, with size fifteen feet, a killer half-court jump shot, and an appetite that threatened to bankrupt Frankie. His milk-chocolaty skin was smooth except for a smudge of hair on his chin. His hands were big enough to encircle the basketball, and his smile practically made girls' eyes roll back in their heads. He lived, ate, and slept basketball for now, but he wanted to go into engineering.

And, of course, because he was seventeen, he knew everything.

Her dad glanced at the clock over the stove. "Where were you? You're fifteen minutes late."

"I walked home." Jordan pulled his hoodie off over his head. He bent and scratched Beasley's head.

"You *what*?" her dad said.

Frankie knew he was going to launch into his lecture about being a young black target.

"Grandpa, Trey had to leave practice early, so I just walked home." Jordan shrugged. "No big deal. Not like we live in LA or something."

He shot his hoodie like a three-pointer down the cellar stairs for a wash.

Dad put his palms flat on the table and jutted his chin. "Listen, I don't know how many times I've told you. You are bigger than most grown men, young and Black. It is *dark* out. You *have* to be afraid of walking home. You *have* to be afraid of the police. You understand?" His voice was hard as flint striking stone.

Frankie was too weary to breathe, but love and fear for her son kicked in. "If you are going to be even five minutes late, you call or text," she said smoothly, letting her dad take the role of hard ass. "Next time, call for a ride if it's dark."

Jordan huffed a noisy sigh and didn't meet his beloved grandfather's eyes as he mumbled, "Sorry."

Jordan glanced at Frankie. His eyes, hard with adolescent anger, softened.

Her dad said, "We have to know where you are at all times. You think being big and young makes you invincible. Let me tell you, it doesn't."

"Sorry!" Jordan said, this time contrite.

He pulled out his chair, which was barely big enough for

him. He scooted his chair up, his voluminous chest and shoulders looming over the table. "I'm starving."

"Let's pray and eat." Her dad bowed his head and folded his hands. "Make us thankful for what we are about to receive and keep us mindful of those who have less and give us courage and faith to make your kingdom come into being here on earth. Amen."

It was pretty much the same prayer every meal, but it contained everything that was important to him about his faith and precisely what Frankie wanted to pass on to her sons. Having her dad help with the boys was a godsend, but he was also a much better cook than she was. Dad was just the kind of man she'd like to marry. Problem was, in all the years of dating, she'd never found such a guy.

Javier served himself, meticulously arranging his single round potato onto one-quarter of his plate, his roast on another quarter, exactly three green beans on another quarter, and his carrots on the last quarter. He took care the food didn't touch; otherwise, he would melt down and not eat anything.

"Mom, I need my other jersey for tomorrow." Jordan stuffed a golf ball-sized piece of meat in his mouth. Through his chewing, he said, "Oh, yeah, and I need a ride to Ahmed's after school tomorrow."

No *please* or *can you*. Just the assumption she would take care of his needs, which was what most mothers did without even thinking about it.

"Okay." Frankie mentally added yet one more thing to her seemingly endless to-do list.

"I need my blue shirt for tomorrow because it's Tuesday," Javier said.

Frankie said, "I already did laundry before I left for work this morning and didn't see it in the laundry. Did you put it in?"

"I need my blue shirt for Tuesday," Javier repeated flatly.

Dad said, "Then you should have put it in the laundry."

"I need my blue shirt for Tuesday," Javier said.

"You can wear my blue shirt, okay?" Jordan said with obvious annoyance.

"I need *my* blue shirt. Yours isn't the same." Javier began swinging his feet under the table, jerking his chair.

"Eat your green beans, Jordan," Frankie said.

Her bone-tired longing for a quiet, family dinner was no match for the scratchiness of her boys. At least no one had asked about the auction.

With a growl, Jordan said, "I hate green beans." He pinched a green bean between his fingers, tipped his head back, and dangled the single green bean down into the maw of his mouth. He made exaggerated chewing motions, wrinkling his nose like he'd been forced to swallow cyanide.

Javi said, "What about my blue shirt?"

"Enough about the shirt, man!" Jordan said.

The fact that Jordan and Javier weren't biologically related didn't keep them from squabbling like brothers.

She felt herself sinking like a stone under the weight of her family's expectations. She tried to be a good mother, but if this was what it took, she might end up on the *Terrible Mommy* list right after Joan Crawford. She hoped she hadn't put so many expectations on her own mother.

Javier said, "I need—"

Frankie raised her palm. "Stop, okay? Just stop. I'll get it done tonight. I just want to have a nice, quiet family dinner and go to bed. No more demands, no more arguments."

"I need my blue shirt tomorrow."

"I need forty bucks for the field trip on Wednesday," Jordan said.

Oh, for fuck sake! Frankie tried to keep herself from unraveling. "Okay, remind me after dinner."

"Did you remember to send in my permission slip for the field trip?" Jordan asked.

She had forgotten. "It's somewhere under the paperwork on my desk."

Jordan's mouth fell open. "It was supposed to be in today!" He banged his baseball-glove-sized hand on the table, and the flatware jingled. "You forgot? Now I won't be able to go."

She held up her hand. "I got it. Right after dinner."

"I need my blue shirt for Tuesday," Javier said.

Jordan said, "Didn't you hear her!? She told you she'd wash it tonight."

Javier said, "Don't forget, tomorrow's blue shirt day."

It was like being pecked to death by a thousand requests.

"Javier, your mom said she would do it," her dad said, raising his eyebrows at Javier.

Jordan held out his plate. "Could I have another slice of roast?"

Ever hopeful, Beasley set his head on Jordan's lap.

"*May I* and *Please*," her dad prompted.

"May I and please," Jordan repeated in exasperation, his default emotion.

Frankie jabbed the meat fork into the roast and savagely hacked off a slice.

"Mom, it's dead already. You don't have to kill it," Jordan said.

She slapped the meat onto Jordan's plate.

Javier said, "Why are you being all crabby?"

She set her knife and fork down and exhaled. She felt tired enough that if she didn't concentrate, she might tumble sideways to the floor in exhaustion. "I'm not crabby." Actually, she sounded like the Wicked Witch.

"Um, you do seem a little testy," her dad said.

It was too humiliating to admit her failure as a daughter, a leader, a contractor, a parishioner, and a friend. They were all silent, looking at her, waiting. She kept her eyes fixed on her plate, not wanting to see her dad's disappointment. All she wanted was to go to bed, pull the covers over her head, and sleep until it all went away.

"We ... I lost the house at the auction."

"Oh, man, that's a bummer." Jordan stabbed the last half-pound of roast and slid it onto his plate, dribbling juice on the tablecloth. "Mom, it's just a house. Another one will come along."

"Oh, I'm sorry. What happened?" her dad asked.

After she recounted how the RWM had outbid her by paying way more for the house than it was worth, her body and soul felt as though she'd been beaten with a two-by-four. They were all quiet for a minute, their knives and forks clinking softly on their plates.

She forked a piece of roast into her mouth and chewed. "The roast is super-tender and juicy, Dad. Best ever."

Her dad said, "I don't know why you want that house after all that happened there with her."

The bite of roast tasted like dried horse meat. Frankie ground her molars, trying to masticate it into something she could swallow, but the more she chewed, the tougher and more tasteless it became. She put her fork down.

Long ago, Frankie promised herself that she would never lie to her dad about even the smallest thing. They owed it to one another, she figured. She folded her napkin and placed it next to her plate. "I saw her today."

All these years, on the rare occasion they spoke of her, they only ever referred to Doralee as *her* or *she*, as if her name, like Voldemort's, was not to be spoken. Her dad's face stiffened into a mask, but she knew him well enough to recognize he was trying to cover up his shock.

Slowly, carefully, he laid his fork down on his plate, took a sip of water, and straightened his knife. "You must be mistaken. I thought she was dead. Why would she come back here after all these years?"

"Been wondering the same thing myself." Frankie drew a slow breath and exhaled. "Thought maybe I'd ask her."

A vein on his temple pulsed. They locked eyes.

Hunched over his plate in mid-chew, Jordan froze, his eyes darting between Frankie to his grandfather.

"Who are you guys talking about?" Javier asked.

"Javi, dude, eat your dinner, okay? I'll let you play with my Nintendo after dinner if you stop asking questions." With his fork, Jordan gestured at a piece of meat on Javier's plate. "You don't want that last bite of roast, do you?"

Javi pushed his plate toward Jordan, and the roast disappeared into Jordan's bottomless gullet.

"I'm sure it was her," Frankie said.

Her dad's eyes flared. Pain chewed through the steady calm of his gentle face. Roughly, he shoved his chair back from the table.

"Guess I'll get Javi's blue Tuesday shirt in the wash." And he stumped off down the cellar stairs.

As close as they were, she never wanted to bring up the subject of Doralee because Frankie had seen him react like this before, a turning away, a valley opening between them, the way his attention receded, sadness carved on his face for days. Hurting him was the last thing she wanted, but Doralee was back now, and she wasn't some fantasy Frankie had concocted.

For the first time, Frankie wanted to know Doralee more than she wanted to keep the peace with her father.

CHAPTER 8

*Do not dwell in the past, do not dream of the future,
concentrate the mind on the present moment.*

Buddha

When all her men had retreated to their respective man caves, Frankie rooted around in the back of her closet and pulled out the shoebox containing the last bits she had of Doralee. Growing up, Frankie convinced herself that she didn't need her mother, but the way she felt whenever she opened the box made her out to be a liar.

She took out the matching bracelet—the earrings of which now lay uselessly buried—in a hole at 61 East Avenue. The earrings and bracelet were the first gift her father had ever given her mother. Frankie clipped on the tarnished sterling-silver bracelet. The cool links settled against the bones of her wrist. As a child, she liked to turn the bracelet around on her mother's pale wrist and listen to the links make a clinking noise. Her mother would say, "Someday, this will be yours," and Frankie always assumed that would be when she grew up and got married. That wasn't the way it had worked out. She kept the bracelet in the box with the idea of giving it back to her mother when she returned.

Maybe the wait was over.

She set aside the yellowed, wrinkled ferry schedule to Sheffield Island and pulled out a photo of her and her mother. Doralee held Frankie's hand in her right and clutched her pocketbook in her left. They stood on the porch in matching straw bonnets and Easter dresses her mother had spent hours sewing. Frankie had stood on a chair while her mother pinned up the hem. That dress made Frankie feel like a beautiful, treasured princess. They'd gone to church, then home to chase about for plastic eggs and a special dinner.

If only they could have had more of those sweet days.

The next photo was her favorite: Doralee sitting on a bench at the Calf's Pasture beach, staring into the camera, her directness a mask in and of itself. She stared off into the distance as if imagining a destination to run to. The wind blew her curly blond hair around her head, giving her the look of a sea nymph floating in the water. Frankie had thought of Doralee as floating somewhere, waiting to find her way back to shore, to her daughter.

What had she done to make her mother leave? Had she been too difficult? Too stubborn?

Too Black?

A lump balled up in Frankie's throat, and the backs of her eyes burned. She returned the photos to the box and closed the lid.

By unspoken mutual agreement, she and her dad had ignored the unanswered questions about Doralee. Even talking about her was taboo. He had never remarried, and Frankie came to understand that he still loved Doralee. His pain, along with her own, made Frankie furious with Doralee. She was tough, but her dad had a soft caramel center, though he pretended he didn't.

Much as Frankie wished to spare him tearing the Band-Aid off the past, she didn't want today to be the last time she saw Doralee. In construction, when craftspeople couldn't get something to work, be it plumbing, electrical, or wood, the joke was "hit it with a hammer" and, if that didn't work, "hit it with a bigger hammer."

Finding Doralee, navigating her father, explaining things to her boys and her friends would require that she hit it with a very big hammer.

CHAPTER 9

Let us Build a House, Hymn No. 301

Let us build a house
where hands will reach
beyond the wood and stone
to heal and strengthen, serve, and teach,
and live the Word they've known.

Marty Haugen

Frankie found her dad in his workshop attached to the back of the garage. The space smelled of machine oil, glue, and sawdust. There was an accumulation of leftover wood, odd lengths of copper pipe, PVC plumbing supplies, a table saw, a wet vac, and all sorts of power tools he'd taught Frankie to use.

Her dad perched on a metal stool in front of his battered workbench mending a chair that Javier, in a meltdown, had kicked and broken.

She leaned against the workbench and crossed one ankle over the other. Unable to look at the pain carved in his face, she stared at the floor as she explained how Doralee had given her the slip at Stew's. "I'm positive it was her. I saw her drive off with Evelyn."

He listened, squeezing a bottle of furniture glue, and carefully laid a thin bead along the rung. He placed the two broken pieces together, and while he held the rung in place, she screwed the clamps on to stabilize the pieces until the glue set.

They did this without a word about what to do next. Sometimes, Frankie found it embarrassing to be close enough to her dad that they did things without speaking. She didn't imagine she would ever experience this unspoken synchrony with anyone except a partner.

The realization that she might never have someone special in her life besides her dad and boys left her feeling lonely in a new way.

With a rag, he scrubbed a bit of dried glue from his palm. "Can't imagine why she's shown up here after all these years."

His eyes fixed on the silver bracelet dangling from her wrist. He stared for a minute, then returned his focus to the glue on his hand.

"Aren't you even a little curious about what she's been up to? Because I am. I figure she owes us a few answers after all these years."

He scrubbed unnecessarily hard at a spot of glue that had dripped onto the workbench. "Try to collect on that debt."

"C'mon, what could it hurt to talk to her?"

"Are you serious?" He faced her, his eyes avid and hot as a soldering iron. "Frankie, you have more than enough on your plate. You have an autistic son, the shelter house fell through, now you have to figure out what to do about that, you have a business to run, and you won't hardly let anybody help you do anything. She's another disappointment and a chore you do not need."

"What makes you think she would be a disappointment?"

He snorted, peering at the chair rung with an excess of concentration. "She's a *drunk*. She left because she was a drunk. She stayed away because she was a drunk. Once a drunk, always a drunk. Isn't that disappointment enough?"

She chose her words carefully. "I feel like maybe ... with her coming back I have a second chance, you know?"

"At what?"

"Get some answers as to why she left when she did." She shrugged. "Get to know her a little bit."

What she really wanted and was too embarrassed to say was that she wanted to practice being a daughter because it might make her a better mother. Not that Doralee had ever been a good example of a mother, but Frankie thought it might help her get into Javier's complicated head, to get past the kick-in-the-gut of Jordan's intolerance of her.

She understood that, for him to grow up, Jordan needed to be intolerant of her, but that didn't mean she had to like it.

He rolled his eyes. "Do not count on that. She's. A. Drunk."

"You mean she's an alcoholic. It's a disease. You know how it works: they can't quit, they don't think like other people do, and their minds are thirsty for booze all the time."

It had been a long time since she'd been to Al-Anon, but her brain still knew all this. Her heart wasn't getting the message.

He looked at her skeptically. "You know, when you were little, I knew she was sneaking, drinking behind my back, no matter how many times she said she wasn't. She was a great cook, but she ruined so many pans, leaving them on the stove, stuff charred black on the bottom because she'd forget she was cooking. I was afraid she'd burn the house down! She'd drive to the store for a quart of milk for you and come back with a quart of Stoli instead. I have a hard time believing she's changed any." He turned back to his work, but a muscle along his cheekbone twitched.

"Maybe she's sober now," she said, hopefully, even though she doubted it.

"Really? What'd she look like?"

Frankie didn't want to rat Doralee out. She wanted to say something to make him want to see his wife as much as she wanted to see her mother. But she would not lie to him.

"She was ... old-looking. Broken down." Like a drunk.

He tested the other rungs and spindles for tightness and muttered, "'Course she's old. She's probably spent her life drinkin' rotgut."

"I was thinking I'd call Evelyn. Ask her what's the story."

"Evelyn!" He hurled the rag onto a pile of other dirty rags. His ever-steady hands shook with rage. "Evelyn's useless. When your mother left, I called her, tried to get her to act like an aunt to you. She couldn't be bothered."

He twisted off his stool, and it crashed to the floor with a jangling clatter. He stomped to a corner and picked up a wooden side table he had promised to repair for Carolina. Something about the bend of his back, the uncharacteristic fury, made her suspect he wasn't telling her everything.

She picked up and righted the stool. His agitation was like that of a man gripping a high-voltage wire, unable to let go.

He brought the side table back to the workbench and set it down hard. He rattled his stool around, the metal feet banging on the cement floor until he got it where he wanted it.

"Would you mind if I, you know, maybe I tried to see her?" she asked. Not that she knew what she would say.

"Why should I mind?" he said with scathing disbelief.

"Feels like I'm being disloyal to you."

"Nothing disloyal about it. You don't need her, Frankie. I'm just trying to protect you."

"Maybe she'd like to see you."

His grizzled jaw worked. "I would not like to see her. All you need to know is she chose vodka instead of us, and that's all there is to it."

"Do you know why she ... why she left us when she did? Any reason in particular?"

"Who the hell knows?" He rarely, if ever, swore, and the word was shocking as glass shattering on the floor. "She did whatever she wanted without thinking about anybody else. You try and see her; she'll just ask you for money for booze. Promise you."

"Was she an alcoholic when you married her?"

He scooted his stool into another position. "Why are you asking all these questions?" he asked, his irritability inching up. "It's been ages. Why you even think of her as your mother anymore?"

Frankie jammed her fists into her pockets to keep herself from grabbing a hammer and wailing away on the workbench. "Because all these years, you and I never talked about her, and now, I'd like to know some things."

"If I answer your questions, you agree not to go looking for her?" His nostrils flared, and his eyes were round and glaring like those of an enraged horse.

"That's not fair!" she said, resenting that she had waited all this time to see her mother, and now he wanted to cut her off.

"Don't have to be fair. I am trying to protect you, girl."

She bristled. "I'm fifty-five, Vic. I don't need protecting. I can make my own decisions like you taught me to do."

He shrunk on his stool, probably caught by the fact she had called him Vic, the way she signaled he'd gone too far.

"I taught you too good." He chuffed a small, bitter laugh, but his mouth cocked in a half smile.

She smiled at his backing down. "So was she always an alcoholic?"

He rubbed the stubble on his chin with the back of his hand. "Probably, but she hid it. I knew she liked to drink, but it was way worse than I knew. Back then, you know, we thought alcoholism was a weakness. I couldn't understand why she didn't just quit."

His voice was raw with emotion, and she wished she could spare him, but it was better to finally talk about the jagged past that had shaped their lives.

"She was a hard worker like you, but there was always something dogging her she couldn't even tell me about. I never knew anything about her background or how she grew up. When I asked her, she just brushed me off. Always said her people were dead. Only person she ever talked about was Evelyn, how close they were, how they took care of each other growing up."

Frankie sensed it cost him a great deal to tell her that he hadn't been fully aware of Doralee's drinking. There might be other, more poisonous things about Doralee which Frankie didn't want to know.

"You have any guess why she didn't talk about her past?"

He shook his head. "My advice? Forget you saw her. Wait to see if she contacts you."

"She might not."

"That'd be good."

With her fingernail, she scratched in a crevice in the top of the workbench. "After she left, did she ever try to come back?"

He took too long screwing the lid back on the glue bottle and setting it on the shelf. The way his cheeks lifted in a half-grimace gave her the answer: never.

Javier opened the door to the workshop. He wore his green Monday night pajamas. "Grandpa, Mom, I need my blue Tuesday shirt for tomorrow. Don't forget to put it in the dryer."

"Save yourself the heartache. She'll only turn her back on you again." Her dad rose from his stool and gave it a disgusted shove back under the workbench. "Coming, Javi." Her dad limped stiffly back into the house, leaving his bitterness smoking in the air.

What surprised Frankie most was how hungry she felt to know Doralee. She'd hammered that need down with: "you left me, you bitch," "who the hell needs you," or a thousand other angry phrases she had memorized and comforted herself with.

Frankie wanted a chance to love her mother, for that love to matter. She wanted to give her mother a chance to love her again. To be and act like a real mom. To forgive her mom. For her mom to finally be proud of her.

Frankie understood that the hurt of being left never left you.

Except for her boys and her dad, she decided long ago never to give anyone the power to break her heart. But if she wanted to see her mother, that little philosophy was irrelevant because this was going to hurt. A lot.

CHAPTER 10

Some people come in your life as blessings.
Some come in your life as lessons.

Mother Teresa

Frankie dodged out of her workmen's way while, at the far end of the kitchen, Olivia was beating back Marina Laszlo's unreasonable demands.

The custom-made white cabinets were in, their gleaming doors yet to be hung, and the hulking six-burner-two-warming-drawer Aga stove had arrived at the appliance store, awaiting installation. Two chandeliers that were to hang over the white quartz-topped island sat in boxes in the garage. Everything was top-of-the-line and over the top. The rest of the house was equally ostentatious, but if the client could afford it, the client got what they wanted.

"But my mother, she is coming more sooner than I think," Marina was saying in her Hungarian-inflected English. "It is soooo important to me for it to be finish when she come." She clasped her hands under her chin. "I want her totally love it! She will be so much proud for me."

"I understand," Olivia said with the patience and tone of a preschool teacher. "But we're already working at full speed. We can't work any faster unless we all grow more hands."

Marina tipped her head forward and fixed her attention on Frankie. "Your guys can go faster, no? Work through lunch and maybe after dinner? Harder to get kitchen done more fast?"

"Hold up," Olivia said, with a palm raised in Marina's direction. "If you want this finished sooner, it will cost you approximately half again what your contract says. For starters, you had four change orders that cost an extra three weeks."

Frankie always felt like if she worked just a little harder, shaved a nickel here or there, she and her crew would be good enough, but tiny titanium Olivia had no trouble demanding what they were worth and then some.

Frankie touched her forefinger to her lips to keep from smiling at the outrageous sum. She could practically redo her own kitchen with the new balance.

Marina gasped and put her hand to her chest as if struck by a heart attack. "But no! It's too much to get finish sooner."

Frankie had to hand it to her; Marina was good, but Olivia was better.

Olivia suggested vaguely that they had another job to start and would have to get back to this one. Marina caved and wrote a check for 50% more than they'd contracted for. Frankie practically jumped for joy.

As they returned to Olivia's car, Frankie said, "I love how you handle these whining clients. They think they can wring the last drop of blood out of us on their jobs."

"I don't mind it. I hate when people try to take advantage,"

Olivia said, sounding like she was chewing through a cast iron radiator, which, if pissed off, she could do.

Ariel, Olivia's daughter who had Down syndrome, sat in the car listening to music through a set of poufy, pink headphones. She waved and smiled her radiant smile that always made Frankie happy.

Olivia pointed her keys at the car doors, and they unlocked.

"You holding her prisoner?" Frankie asked.

"You know I always lock her in. That way, if someone tries to get into the car, the alarm will go off. I'm just protective, is all." Olivia tossed her purse into the back seat.

"How come you're afraid of killer bees, spiders, floods, earthquakes, falling meteors, drowning, rabid dogs, tropical diseases, tornadoes, and hurricanes, but you can face down someone like Marina without blinking an eye," Frankie asked.

"Because I know you're worth it. We're worth it."

"I know, I know. I keep trying to remind myself of that. Why's Marina making such a big deal out of impressing her mom? I mean, look at her. She's gorgeous, has a rich husband, money to burn, and she still wants her mother to be proud of her," Frankie said. "How much is enough?"

Of all the Marriage Survivors, Olivia was the only one who knew the dirty details of Frankie's childhood. She often reminded Frankie that she had missed a crucial relationship, even if Frankie didn't want to admit it. She encouraged Frankie, told her she was a good mom, and that being left never went away.

Frankie said, "If that's what it takes to make a mother proud, I don't have a prayer." She leaned against the car, riveted to the spot by Olivia's emotional X-Ray, and crossed her legs at the ankles. "I saw Doralee at Stew Leonard's. She's in town."

Olivia's mouth rounded in a surprised *O*. "Are you serious? What did she say?"

"She gave me the slip when I tried to talk to her."

"She did?" Olivia's face reflected the sympathy and understanding Frankie loved her for.

Frankie tried to sound breezy. "Yeah, disappeared between the sweet potatoes and the lettuce."

"You're sure it was her?"

"Oh, yeah." Frankie flipped her braids back over her shoulder and nodded. "She looked right at me, and I saw her eyes. They're just like mine." The bright sun made Frankie's eyes water, and she scrubbed at her face with the sleeve of her jacket. "Then, she took off. Moved fast for an old lady and drove away in my Aunt Evelyn's car."

Olivia laid a hand on Frankie's forearm. "Oh, Frankie, I'm so sorry. You must feel really hurt that she wouldn't even talk to you."

Frankie shrugged. "Oh, you know, I'm okay."

Olivia *tsked*. "No bullshit for any."

Frankie toed a piece of gravel. "It's been a long time. I don't even know why it matters to me."

"It matters because she abandoned you," Olivia said tenderly.

Olivia was the most emotionally intuitive of all the Marriage Survivors. Usually, Frankie didn't like anyone poking into the places she wished to keep private, but she trusted Olivia's insights and found them relentlessly enlightening.

Olivia said, "You didn't get to have the mother you deserved. Now you deserve to have her see that despite her shitty example, you're happy, well-adjusted, a good mom, you own your own business, that you're spearheading buying the shelter, that you're going to the church where you were raised in. She should acknowledge how successful you are."

Olivia leaned toward Frankie for emphasis, "But don't hold your breath. You might not get the recognition you deserve."

Frankie squirmed a bit. "Why do I even care what she thinks?"

"Because she's your mother. You have to find her; talk to her."

Frankie rolled her shoulders around in her jacket, trying to shift the weight she felt. "I wish I didn't want a relationship with her. I'm fifty-five, for crying out loud. I should just get over myself."

Olivia rolled her eyes. "It doesn't work that way." She poked Frankie in the shoulder with a finger. "Go find your mother. You'll get some closure if nothing else."

Frankie mock-scowled at her best pal. "I hate it when you're right."

"One for all and no bullshit for any!" Olivia crowed. "That's the price of being a member of the Marriage Survivors Club."

CHAPTER 11

The most difficult thing is the decision to act, the rest is merely tenacity.

Amelia Earhart

Cam hit the speed dial for his banker, Edina Gorski, at People's Bank. People's was based in Connecticut and had financed Simpson and Sons projects since his dad started building way back when. He used to say that People's Bank was the next best thing to a rich uncle.

"Edina, yesterday I bought the property we've been discussing. We should break ground in a couple months."

"You work fast," she said, shuffling papers in the background. "Do you have all the approvals and everything?"

He paused. The question surprised him. She never asked about the other end of the business. She just got the loan documents ready, he went in, signed them, she deposited the check in his business account, and off he went.

"I set up the LLC two months ago. Since I have both the properties in the rear, the zoning approval will be a slam dunk."

"On East Avenue, right?"

He wasn't used to the hedging tone in her voice. "I don't expect there to be any issues. The East Avenue property looks like a crack house, and the adjoining properties behind aren't much better. This will give me the frontage access from East Avenue, which is all I needed to make the project work. I've been sitting on those other two lots for three years. I'm glad to finally cash in on them."

In fact, due to current economic conditions, the lots were now worth less than what he'd paid for them. He'd borrowed against them and was currently underwater on the lots. And he had to get zoning approval to combine the three lots to build the condos. A pleasant meeting that would include the mayor, where he'd show his design drawings for the development, and would put any concerns of the Norwalk Zoning Board to rest.

Edina said, "Okay, call me when you get the approvals, and we'll draw up the documents."

His blood pressure rocketed up, and he thought his head would blow off. He kept his voice friendly, charming. "I have to wait until then? Usually, we pull the trigger on the loan when I've bought the properties. I just have a few loose ends to tie up. You know I'm good for it. Simpson and Sons condos always sell before they're built, and these won't be any different."

But to finish up those few details, he needed a cash infusion. He had to pay the architect his last installment so he could get the plumbing schematics. There was some site work to complete, the application for approval, and legal fees. To buy the East Avenue property, he borrowed against his condo, valued at over a million. He couldn't milk that cash cow forever. He absolutely needed to get this project financed and finished.

Cam spun his chair back and forth. "Getting the loan

approved at this point in the process hasn't been a problem in the past."

"Things are different now. Since the Wellington-Flint banking scandal, we must have everything in place before we do anything."

He heard her pen tapping on her desk. She was nervous.

"And I pulled a recent credit report on you and see you borrowed against your condo."

He squeezed his eyes shut and thumped a fist on the arm of his chair. "Okay, I'll get back to you soon."

He broke the connection, picked up a bean bag he kept on his desk for just such a purpose, and hurled it as hard as possible at the closed office door.

CHAPTER 12

I didn't fail the test, I just found 100 ways to do it wrong.

Benjamin Franklin

Frankie, Carolina, Olivia, and Flicka sat around their usual table at La Paella, sipping sangria and nibbling cheese. Bianca was in the bar, her eyeballs glued to the baseball game on the TV.

The restaurant was down the street from Olivia's design shop. It was a classy, white-tablecloth place with warm golden lighting, soothing Spanish guitar music, paintings of whirling Spanish Flamenco dancers, and the best food in Norwalk. Best of all, Jaime Lopez, the owner, didn't mind if the Marriage Survivors Club got a little loud—their usual volume—at their twice-a-month Thursday night debauches.

On tonight's agenda was a discussion of the progress on the upcoming fundraiser for the shelter, a gala dinner dance. Frankie wasn't eager to discuss the topic because she had lost the auction, and she was certain that would impact the enthusiasm of the parish.

"It wasn't until our wedding night that he asked me to spank him! Before that, I thought he was a nice, proper English gentleman." Carolina shuddered.

She and Flicka were discussing Al Kolinsky, Flicka's third ex-husband, who also happened to be Carolina's first and only ex-husband.

Flicka laughed raucously and said, "Those dreadful English prep schools can pervert even the dullest man."

Frankie found it oddly funny that Flicka, who wore sexy, slightly trampy-campy clothes, and Carolina, who favored a modest wardrobe, had married the same man. That said something about Al Kolinsky's taste in more than just his sexual peccadilloes.

Olivia said, "I believe that was definitely divine intervention. If you two hadn't both divorced Al, his last girlfriend wouldn't have strangled him during sex, and you never would have met at his funeral at St. Paul's, and we would never have formed the Club."

Frankie raised her glass. "The Lord works in mysterious ways." Another Marriage Survivors Club catchphrase that took in all the weird, wonderfulness of unexpected, strangely delivered blessings.

Bianca bopped in from the bar and plopped into a chair. She pumped a fist in the air. "Yes! Red Sox up by two in the middle of the fifth, and the Orioles pulled their pitcher."

Wind gusted through the front door, and Hélène blew in. She brushed back her black and white hair, which fluttered around her fine-boned face. "Hi, sorry I'm late. Tell me what I've missed."

Olivia poured Hélène a glass of sangria while Bianca gave

Hélène all the scores for the baseball, basketball, and hockey games, none of which she cared about.

Flicka *tinged* her knife against her wine glass. "Okay, now that we're all here, I hate to be a Debbie Downer, but ticket sales have tanked since word got out that we didn't get the house. People aren't willing to part with their cold, hard cash if we don't have a house."

Even though she had already briefed everyone in an email, heat still rushed to Frankie's face. She kept her eyes fixed on the white tablecloth in front of her.

"I'm really sorry. I should have done more research and figured out who owned those two rear lots. With the shape it's in, I couldn't imagine anyone else would want it. I-I'm sorry."

Flicka leaned down the table and pointed her dinner knife at Frankie. "Hey, nobody blames you, Frankie."

Nobody had to; she blamed herself.

Ever pragmatic, Bianca said, "Blaming yourself is crap and a waste of good mental energy. What's important is, what are we going to do now that this guy bought the house?"

Even if Frankie had had time to consider a different plan, she wouldn't have. Olivia was right: she did want Doralee to be proud of her, to know she was going to turn 61 East Avenue into a shelter.

"I'm going to try to get it back," Frankie said, clutching her fork in one hand and her knife in the other.

"And how do you propose to do that?" Hélène asked.

"I haven't figured that out yet."

Flicka gave Frankie a benevolent look. "Maybe it's time you moved on. There are plenty of other houses in Norwalk. I drove by the Maplecrest house the other day, and it's still got a for sale sign out front. We could contact the broker, see what they say."

"I don't want the Maplecrest house. It wasn't right then, and it's still not right. 61 East Avenue is perfect for the shelter and right across from St. Paul's. When we've fixed it up, it'll be welcoming, warm, and filled with love. I'm not giving up yet."

Hélène raised her glass. "One for all and no bullshit for any. I think you're a little stuck in the bullshit, Frankie."

Frankie frowned. She wasn't a quitter. She was a woman who got shit done. She had to figure something out.

Jaime came out of the kitchen and delivered the *tapas* to their table himself. Tonight, there was grilled octopus Galician style, chickpeas with goat cheese in tomato sauce, oxtail, and mushroom croquettes, a board of cheeses, olives, and fig spread, and crisp, warm rolls. They took a moment to pass the plates around and serve themselves.

"We know you want 61 East Avenue, and you think it's best," Flicka said. "But at some point, we have to move on and target another property if we're going to keep the congregation and the other stakeholders interested. Right now, our first priority is to sell tickets for the gala."

As she'd cycled through her husbands and before she'd moved to Norwalk, Flicka had been a Manhattan Society dame, helping to raise money for hospitals, ballet companies, and the opera. Judging from her rich husbands and excellent divorce settlements, she could charm the wallet out of any man's pants.

With rising desperation, Frankie looked at Bianca. "You're the legal shark. Can't you think of something? Can we find some reason he can't tear the house down or can't buy it?"

"I'm a divorce attorney." Bianca shrugged. "I don't do real estate law. The house and the land under it are his. I assume he can do what he wants with it."

"Could we buy all three lots?" Hélène asked.

"Only if Flicka got married and divorced again, then donated all the proceeds of her settlement," Bianca said.

They all laughed, but Frankie couldn't join in the laughter.

"What if you went and asked him if he'll sell it back to us at a small profit?" Olivia asked. "Maybe if you tell him what it means to us, he'll consider it."

It wasn't likely, but it was their best option, and Frankie couldn't think of anything else. "I'll go see him tomorrow."

"Want one of us to go with you?" Flicka said to Frankie.

"No, this is my fight. I'll go see him alone."

Because if she failed—again—she would rather do that alone, too.

CHAPTER 13

Let us Build a House, Hymn No. 301

Here the outcast and the stranger
bear the image of God's face;
let us bring an end to fear and danger
All are welcome, all are welcome
All are welcome in this place.

Marty Haugen

Monday morning, outside Simpson and Sons offices, Frankie sat in her van, working up her nerve and calming down her stomach. She'd done her face, put on lipstick, worn her skinniest jeans and a bright blue sweater that made her face not look quite so exhausted, and her black leather jacket. Instead of her work boots, she had on knee-high black leather boots. She was trying for a professional look instead of a contractor with a screwdriver stuck in her back pocket.

She checked in the rearview mirror for lipstick on her teeth and practiced a smile.

Prepare to be humiliated.

Then, to buck herself up, she bared her teeth and growled at herself.

Short of sleeping with—or bumping off—Cam Simpson, she would do about anything to get him to sell 61 East Avenue back to them. He'd been in business a long time and would not be a pushover.

Frankie had heard of Simpson and Sons before, but she'd never come across the company in her work. Before coming, Frankie had googled him. Simpson played in the big leagues: Greenwich, Darien, New Canaan, and Westport, where they built high-end luxury condos. She guessed that was what he intended at 61 East Avenue. Simpson and Sons had weathered the booms and busts of the real estate market for sixty years, and that took some doing. Hoping to hear him described as a cross between Hannibal Lecter and Dracula, she called a few sub-contractors she knew, asking for some background on the company.

She found out that in the last two years, Simpson had started paying his contractors at sixty days instead of his usual thirty, and then payment dragged out to ninety, and in one case, a subcontractor had slapped a lien on a building to get paid. Contractors didn't do that often because it was expensive, time-consuming, and got them a bad rap.

All that meant Cam Simpson was cash-strapped, which she hoped and prayed might make him more amenable to selling the house back to them. After all, he'd overpaid, and he still had two lots to build condos on.

Inside the office building, Frankie let herself into the Simpson and Son's offices. She found herself in a reception room with two ratty upholstered chairs, a shriveled-up palm tree, and a stack of half-dozen cardboard file boxes collapsing in a corner. Unopened mail slithered off one side of a metal desk which looked like it had been pulled from a dumpster.

It wasn't very Christian to feel gleeful over her opponent's financial misfortune, but she promised herself she'd light a votive candle at church.

"Hello?" she called out.

Cam Simpson, the RWM himself, opened the door. Something hot bloomed under her skin, and her insides went melty.

His offices were crap, but he was not. He was in shirtsleeves and a stunning blue silk paisley tie. His tanned face gave him the look of a man who spent hours lounging on his yacht next to a much younger, bikini-clad babe. Lines around his gray eyes made him look tense, but when he saw her, he smiled broadly.

"Mr. Simpson, Frankie Carter, I own Women's Work Construction and Renovation." She offered her hand.

Looking at Cam Simpson certainly made her feel ten years younger. She'd dated White guys before, but she'd never felt her brain caramelize in the heat of someone's gaze.

"Yes, I remember you from the auction. Call me Cam. Sorry if you've been waiting; I, uh, gave my assistant the day off. I heard the door, but I was on the phone."

His explanation didn't convince her, but she plunged right in. "Sorry for not calling ahead, but I was in the area and thought maybe we could chat." She forced a confident smile.

His return smile dazzled.

Cam stepped back and invited her into his office. It smelled like stale coffee, Chinese take-out, and newly sharpened pencils. The single, dirty window gave the light in the room a greasy quality. A mahogany desk the size of a conference table dominated the room. Aside from one framed photo with Cam on one knee beside a bunch of kids in basketball uniforms and a skim of dust, the shelves lining the wall were bare. There were no personal items anywhere, no photos of family, grandkids, no trophies or awards, no pictures of charity events with famous golfers, no trinkets or society gewgaws. Nothing that screamed "see how successful and well-connected I am!"

Her glee turned to pity for him because the place was rather forlorn and dispirited.

Behind his desk hung a life-sized painting of a man who looked like a more arrogant, grumpier, plumper, older version of Cam; the Simpson of which Cam was the son. Like father, like son? With his close-set, glaring eyes and Bassett hound face, the old man looked like a holy terror. She felt his eyes practically willing her to turn around and run back to her van.

"Have a seat." He motioned for her to sit. He sat in a worn black leather desk chair that could have doubled as a throne and then leaned forward. "What can I do for you?" For a second, something in his face flickered, a light, or a shift of expression in his eyes, as though a twinkle had been there, then a door slammed shut.

She felt his eyes on her, watching intently, and her mind zzzz'd with static for a minute. To concentrate, she stared at his hands, folded in front of him on the desk. He had elegant hands with pale, neat nails, smooth skinned. The men she worked with had callused hands with split nails, the white nicks of scars and scrapes, and knuckles that looked like they scrubbed them nightly with 50-grit sandpaper.

He wore no wedding ring.

Why was she noticing that?

She glanced up at his eyes and felt the same flicker she'd felt at the auction: the invigoration of being dunked in cold water. She had come, intending to reason with him, appeal to his better nature—if he had one—but prepared to despise his rapacious RWM-ness. But his eyes positively flat-lined her menopausal brain.

He said, "Did you want to discuss something?"

Frankie tugged on the belt of her coat. She couldn't think when he looked at her like that. She blurted out, "I'd like to ask you to sell 61 East Avenue to St. Paul's Church across the street."

One eyebrow cocked. His lips spread in an indulgent smile that she wanted to wipe off.

"Why?"

"We want to open a homeless shelter for LGBTQ youth." Frankie didn't want to give him a chance to object or herself to falter but forged ahead. "We've planned, saved, gotten a loan, held fundraisers." She scooted to the edge of her seat. "We've worked on this for three years. No one else was interested in that house because it was so rundown. We thought it was in the bag until you showed up."

He didn't wait a nanosecond before replying. "That's a nice story, Ms. Carter, but I own the two adjoining lots in the rear. I need 61 for my project, the Essex Condominiums." He picked up a Waterman pen and tapped it on the desk. "Now, if you want to buy all three properties, that's a different story."

Her hopes jumped at the tiny window of possibility. He was more reasonable than she expected.

"How much are you looking for?"

"Three million. That will pay for the lots and what I would have made on the condos."

His words were like the shot of a nail gun to the jugular. She couldn't speak for a moment and coughed into her fist. "St. Paul's doesn't have anything like that kind of money," she squeaked. "You can imagine what a shoestring budget our church runs on."

"That's what I need to do a deal. And why a home for LGBTQ kids anyway?" he asked. "Why not include adults too?"

"There's a huge need for a shelter for queer young people. Some of them get kicked out of their homes when they come out. Adults can get jobs and generally have access to more social safety nets than young people." She ticked off her fingers. "Gender-non-conforming youth are at great risk of abuse, getting killed, working as sex workers, getting HIV, using drugs, alcohol, and dropping out of school." The more she talked about it, the more excited she got and hoped he would get on board. "The suicide rate for these kids is more than four times the rest of the population. Nobody is doing what we want to do. And it's not just St. Paul's. We're working with other churches, non-profit organizations, and the Triangle Community Center—the local LGBTQ center—to provide a wrap-around support system. We want to provide or coordinate tutoring, mentoring, medical care, and mental health services, all of which keep kids in school so they can graduate and become productive, tax-paying citizens."

As she spoke, the lines of tension around his eyes softened, and she hoped she had moved him in some way.

He swiveled his chair halfway around, and his gaze flicked up for a split second to the painting of his father hanging behind him, then back to her. "I can see you're passionate about this. Why?"

She paused to settle her excitement. Business negotiations didn't usually veer into the realm of the personal. That was the last place she wanted to go, but something about him tempted her to tell him. "I know not everybody believes in religion, and not to sound all churchy, but this shelter is God's love in practice. At St. Paul's, we believe being a Christian means accepting everybody just as they are. We believe everyone is worthy of love. That everyone deserves a family and a home. We want to create a warm, loving, accepting environment for kids who have nowhere else to turn."

His expression shifted; now he looked a bit skeptical. He probably thought she was some cracked religious fanatic. "Why this exact house? It's in such bad shape the only thing to do is tear it down. Plenty of houses in Norwalk would work for your purposes."

But Frankie was certain that *this* house could save the lives of young people. "61 East Avenue, because of its size and proximity to St. Paul's, will let us offer intensive, onsite support to the residents." Frankie's hands carved the air, and her passion, as he called it, surged the banks of her common sense. "We don't want these kids to be shunted off down some dark alley. They shouldn't be made to feel ashamed." She wet her lips and saw his eyes follow her tongue. A moment of confusion spread through her.

He turned his chair but kept his eyes on her. "I don't want the house. I want the lot under the house. I've been waiting two years for 61 to come up for sale." He leaned back and patted a rhythm on the arms with his lovely hands. "Tell you what," he said. "It's a worthy cause. I'll be happy to make a substantial donation"—he raised a finger—"when you find another property."

She felt deflated but forced her smile to remain in place. "That's generous of you, but we don't want another property."

He looked vexed. "I've heard of your company, Women's Work, so I know you've been in construction long enough to know building and development necessitate flexibility. You'll simply have to find another location in Norwalk or another town. I'm sorry, but 61 is not for sale."

It might not be for sale, but that didn't mean she was giving up.

CHAPTER 14

Hope itself is like a star—not to be seen in the sunshine of prosperity, and only to be discovered in the night of adversity.

Charles Haddon Spurgeon

Frankie bit into her biscotto, but this evening, the ordinarily delicious cookie tasted like sawdust. She put it back on her plate.

"I'll take the rest of that biscotto if you don't want it," Bianca said, and Frankie handed it over.

The Marriage Survivors Club members were sitting around Bianca's kitchen table while her mom scurried around, clucking in Italian, pouring wine, and making sure they had enough of her homemade biscotti. They were concocting ways to sell the remaining tickets and raise more money at the gala. Fundraising was a never-ending cycle of planning and partying.

"So how did your meeting with Cam Simpson go?" Flicka asked.

Frankie gave her a thumbs down. "Asked for three million if we want to buy it."

"Ouch," Flicka deadpanned.

"I still say we should bump him off," Bianca said in her *Godfather* voice.

"What good would that do? He still owns the property," Olivia said.

The front door opened, and Hélène glided in. "Hi, everybody. Where's the wine?" Hélène sat next to Bianca, who handed her a glass.

Carolina had been quieter than usual. "What if we invited Mr. Simpson to the gala?"

"Wait, what did I miss?" Hélène said.

"Tell ya' later," Bianca said out of the side of her mouth.

"What good would that do?" Frankie asked. "He's already against us."

"Not necessarily; he just doesn't know us," Carolina said. "It would give us a chance to show him who we are. To convince him that we're right and he's wrong. He might be inspired to"— she shrugged—"give us the property."

Frankie had given up on getting Cam to sell them the house, but she was half considering the option of bumping him off. "Cam Simpson would have to be smacked in the head by all the angels in heaven to give us the property or even change his mind," Frankie said wryly.

"I think inviting him is a good idea." Flicka fluttered her fake eyelashes.

"She said invite him to the dance, not offer him a blow job," Bianca quipped.

Having quickly caught up on the conversation, Hélène joined in. "Let's do it. He might say yes."

Carolina, an optimist who believed in actual miracles, embodied the heart and soul of the Marriage Survivors Club.

She kept her spiritual compass even when everyone else's mind was on money. "Once he sees what's in our hearts, how could he turn us down?"

"Ask him, Frankie," Flicka said.

"Me? Why me?" Frankie said. "He already turned me down––and it didn't end on the best note." She added glumly, "Not to mention that I'm hardly batting 1000 on this project."

"Oh, Frankie," Olivia murmured and bumped her shoulder against Frankie's.

The prospect of asking Cam to attend the dance elated and terrified Frankie. But how was spending an evening with a hot silver fox, who was her opponent, supposed to work? The man gave her heat stroke whenever she looked at him.

"You're the one leading the project, you're the one who went to see him, you're the one who knows him, you're the one who's insisting on that house and no other," Flicka said.

Bianca raised a finger. "I second that emotion. We're not ready for a pinch-hitter yet."

"We're not asking you to go out with Jack the Ripper," Hélène said.

Frankie said, "C'mon, guys. It's not like a date or anything. The guy probably has a girlfriend he'd want to bring."

Bianca spoke around another cookie, the crumbs tumbling down her round chin. "How do you know?"

"Designer suits, Italian shoes," Frankie said.

Bianca said, "Maybe he's divorced."

"What's he look like?" Flicka asked. "Does he still have hair?"

Frankie squeezed her eyes shut, pretending to recall the face she couldn't forget.

He looked like canned heat. Like caviar. Like money. Like an RWM. Like he'd never agree to come to the dance.

"Yeah, he's got hair, and yes, he's good looking. Shockingly good-looking, actually. So if I ask him and he says yes, then what? It's not like he'll bring the deed to the gala in the pocket of his tux."

Flicka emptied the last of the wine into her glass. "Then we twist his arm with charm. People have a much harder time saying *no* when they're face to face with the people they're up against."

Bianca's mom appeared with another bottle of wine and set it on the kitchen table.

"Why don't you want to ask him?" Hélène asked Frankie.

Frankie scrambled for ideas. "What if the gala is a dud? What if only a few people come?"

"I think more people will come if they know he's coming," Olivia said. "Give them a chance to say their piece."

Frankie had to agree with Olivia, though she wasn't going to say so. "What if he says he'll come? Then what do I do?"

"Then you blow him," Flicka quipped wickedly, and this time even Frankie had to laugh.

"Since when are you a chicken?" Olivia asked, narrowing her eyes at Frankie. "You never avoid a fight, and if you can't find one, you pick one."

"Do not!" Frankie exclaimed.

They were quiet a moment as Frankie fought tears. "The truth is I'll feel terrible if he turns me down. I'm so ..." She swallowed hard. "So bummed by the house slipping through my fingers and by his refusal to even consider selling us the house." Frankie looked meaningfully at Olivia. "I don't think I can take another rejection."

"I hear you," Olivia said.

Frankie knew Olivia understood she was referring not only to Cam Simpson but also to Doralee.

Carolina said, "How can we make the invitation irresistible?"

"Frankie's pretty irresistible," Hélène said and laughed.

Frankie rolled her eyes and moaned, "Guys, c'mon, I already

had no effect on him. Flicka, you try. You clearly have a way with men."

"Yeah, ask her four husbands," Bianca said.

"This is Frankie's gig. We're just the enforcers." Flicka looked up and down the table. "Okay, here's the way this is going to roll. Frankie's going to ask him to the dance. We spread the word that the owner of 61 East Avenue is coming and that we're going to show him what kind of people we are. We'll sacrifice a fatted calf or whatever, so maybe he'll sell or donate the property to us. If he doesn't, then at least he'll feel like a shit."

Bianca brushed a crumb off the table into her palm and popped it into her mouth. "And if he doesn't come to the dance?"

"We'll send him a dead fish," Flicka pronounced in all seriousness.

Thrilled with the idea, Bianca gave a thumbs up.

Hélène asked, "And if he still doesn't donate or sell the house to St. Paul's?"

"Then Frankie agrees to move on to another house," Flicka said, pointing her biscotto at Frankie.

Frankie held up her two thumbs. "These thumbscrews are kiiiilling me."

"We need to get a house," Olivia said, draping her skinny little arm over Frankie's shoulder.

Of course, they were right. And it was an angle that might get them the house. At the least, she could lay eyes on Cam Simpson again.

"Oh, you guys ..." Frankie groaned. "All right, I'll ask him."

And when he refused, she would have to go back and tell them she'd failed. Again.

CHAPTER 15

All kids need is a little help, a little hope, and somebody who believes in them.

Magic Johnson

Frankie pulled into a parking spot. Her jaw ached from grinding her teeth as she listened to Javier's resistance the entire way to the Carver Center.

He said, "Why can't we just go to the aquarium? I like that. Nobody bothers me there."

"They won't bother you here, either. It'll be fun. I promise we'll go another time."

Javier groaned and leaned his head against the window. "I don't want to go to some program for autistic kids. You always say it's for kids with learning differences and social challenges, but I know it's for kids with autism."

"It's only an hour of basketball. You don't even have to talk to the other kids. I know how anxious you get in new social situations, but your therapist wants you to try new things. I'm only trying to help you because I love you."

Problem was, she wasn't sure he even knew what her love felt like.

The Carver Center was in an up-and-coming neighborhood of South Norwalk, but their programs brought in kids from all over town. There was a soup kitchen, food pantry, free after-school tutoring, a nurse two days a week, and various programs for low-income kids and kids with special needs.

"I'm not anxious," he ground out. "Basketball's Jordan's thing, not mine. Take me home. I'm gonna hate playing basketball with a bunch of autistic kids." He stomped his foot on the floorboard and bucked in his seat. "Why do I have to go to some stupid social thing? I already have friends."

That was the problem, he didn't have friends, but she didn't want to bring that up as it would hurt him. He was never invited to birthday parties, get-togethers, or sleepovers, and as he got older, he seemed to accept the rejection. Frankie's heart broke to see him stay home alone and draw. Like most things that didn't cooperate, she hit it with a bigger hammer.

She leaned against the door and looked at him. "You might make new friends. You might have things in common with these kids. Besides, it might be fun, and you need the exercise."

"I don't need exercise. I won't have fun, and I don't want to hang out with a bunch of autistic kids."

It was easier to bust up cement with a spoon than convince Javier to do something he didn't want to do. She sighed and paused to keep herself from yelling at him to get out of the fucking van and get inside. Why didn't he just accept that she knew better than he did, that it was like brushing his teeth, which he also hated doing.

She hated resorting to bribery, but sometimes, it was the only choice she had.

"Okay, if you go in and stay the whole time, you can get McDonald's French fries afterward."

He looked at her, his face a shade less red. "Large?"

"Large," she said on an exhausted sigh.

He unbuckled his seatbelt. "Okay."

She grabbed the poster for the gala on the off chance there might be someplace to hang it up.

The hallways smelled of lemon cleaning fluid, fried food, and mushroomy feet. In the gym, two men were sparring with a couple kids on the basketball court. Their shouts, squeaking shoes, and the pounding of the basketball echoed through the vast space.

"I recognize that big guy, Mom. Who is he?" Javier asked, pointing out had a football-player-sized chest and weight-lifter legs.

"Uh, Andy something or other. I've seen him occasionally at St. Paul's."

"Who's that other old White guy?"

She started when she saw the buzz of silvery hair, the angle of neck to shoulders, and the elegant hands dribbling the basket.

"That old White guy is Cam Simpson," she murmured, feeling warmth flow from her abdomen to her limbs.

"That's the guy what stole your house, ain't he?"

"Isn't he," she corrected. "He bought the house fair and square; he didn't steal it."

What was Cam Simpson doing slumming it in a community center? He certainly didn't strike her as the kind of guy to help at a program for autistic kids. Then she remembered the single photo on the shelf in his office. It had been taken here with kids from this program.

Maybe he wasn't only a rapacious RWM developer.

She and Javier watched the two men jazz around with the

kids. There was a kid about Javier's age, with pants too tight around his plump belly, and a kid whose upper and lower body seemed to move in opposite directions. The boys screamed with laughter and jumped around as Andy and Cam blocked one another, letting the boys get a clear shot at the basket.

Cam tried doing Harlem Globetrotter-type moves, which inevitably ended up with the ball being stolen by the opposing "team," which delighted them no end. But the way his feet danced across the beat-up floorboards suggested he was more adept than he was letting on. His laugh, as exultant and unrestrained as the boys', was infectious, and she found herself smiling. It was becoming harder and harder to dislike the man.

Cam wore gym shorts, beat-up Chuck's, and a much-washed tee shirt with the Simpson and Son's logo. When he jumped to make a basket, his muscular calves flexed, his shirt sleeves rose to show the bulge of a bicep, and the softening around his belly gave a little jiggle. He was a different shape than he was in his expensive designer suits. Sexier but softer, too.

But the most significant difference was in his face. That day in his office, his face had been intense and unyielding, but now, his smile was open and mischievous, and his eyes had—she resented admitting it—a twinkle. He didn't even look like the Cam Simpson Frankie considered her personal ogre.

If Cam laughed like that and took time to work with autistic kids, maybe he had a nicer side she hadn't seen. A nicer side that might make him say *yes* if she asked him and his date to the gala.

She looked at Javier out of the corner of her eye. "What'dya think? Maybe playing a little b-ball will be fun."

"I told you it's Jordan's game." His eyebrows lowered into a scowl.

"You see Jordan anywhere? This is for you, not him."

No response.

The ball bounced next to Frankie. She picked it up and

tossed it back to Cam. His eyes widened, and when he smiled, he was handsome.

For a White guy.

Something inside of her flipped, drawing her to him in a way she'd forgotten her menopausal body was capable of.

Cam tossed the ball to his teammate and sauntered over to them. He stuck his hand out to Javier, his voice quietly coaxing. "Hey, I'm Cam Simpson, the coach here."

Javier didn't meet Cam's eyes, but Frankie was grateful that at least he put out his hand for a limp handshake. Because Javi missed social cues, she had to nudge him now and then to teach him what others picked up by osmosis, so she prompted Javi. "What's your name?"

"I'm Javier Carter," he mumbled.

"Great to meet you. Thanks for coming," Cam said. "We're going to have a good time today. Some basketball, maybe a little dodgeball, some snacks. You like snacks?"

"Yes," Javier said, with no enthusiasm at all.

Cam leaned closer and said in a low, conspiratorial voice, "The kind of snacks your mom probably doesn't buy."

The beginning of a smile appeared on Javier's face, and at last, he raised his eyes to meet Cam's.

Cam grinned and twitched an eyebrow at Javier, whose smile broadened.

Frankie's heart swelled with gratitude that Cam could tweak a smile out of her recalcitrant, complicated son. That took a special kind of talent.

"You nervous?" Cam asked Javier.

Javier shrugged his shoulders and toed one sneaker on top of the other.

Cam nodded. "You know, everybody's nervous when they do something the first time. When you get used to me"—he looked pointedly at Frankie—"you'll see I'm not such a bad guy."

His directness, combined with his easy, direct way with Javier, made Frankie wonder if he had a special needs or autistic child of his own. Not many people made an effort to understand and relate to kids like Javi.

People often made the mistake of thinking autistic people were dumb, violent, or worse. They were perceived as rude when really, they were blind to social responses and had to memorize them. People with autism, like everyone else, were doing the best they knew how. This was precisely why she wanted the house: so kids could be themselves without fear of being judged.

She felt a flush of guilt. She had let her drive to acquire the house get in the way of seeing Cam for the whole person he was, the way people looked at Javier and saw only a weird kid. She had judged Cam based on a single factor: the house at 61 East Avenue. *Funny how life hits you with a left hook and makes you realize when you're being an asshole.*

Cam offered his hand to her. "And I believe we know one another."

She took his pale, elegant, smooth-skinned hand. Their eyes met, and she felt the heat of his hand all the way up her arm and across her collarbones. His handshake was lingering, and she didn't withdraw her own hand.

"We do know each other. What are you doing here?"

"I've been sponsoring a group here for a couple years." He turned to Javier. "So ready to meet the other guys?"

Javier shook his head and kept his eyes glued to the floor.

"We have Ring Dings for snacks," Cam said.

Javier looked up. "Those chocolate things with white icing in the middle?"

"Yup. But, if you want one, you have to work off the calories first."

"Okaaaay." Javier launched himself off the wall.

After a brief introduction, Javier shuffled after Andy.

As she watched her son wade into the mix, she wondered what would happen if Javier had a meltdown or if something else happened to make him feel he'd failed? What if he hit another kid, or another kid hit him?

As if reading her mind, Cam said, "Don't worry. Andy and I can handle him. We've been doing this a while."

She blew out a breath. "I kind of had to drag him here. New experiences are difficult for him, and he's pretty socially awkward and sometimes blurts out stuff he shouldn't say."

Two more boys and a girl drifted in and joined the game. Cam waved at the kids.

"Sounds like the other autistic kids here." He took a step closer to her. "Tell me more about Javier. We want to make sure we support him socially as much as possible. We started this because we knew autistic kids have a difficult time connecting, and we wanted to make it fun and easy. Help them be successful in a social setting."

She was surprised. "You talk the talk. How do you know so much about autism?"

"When I started, all I did was write a check, but I decided to get more involved. I didn't know anything, but kids and autism interested me. I guess because it's so far out of my wheelhouse. I read everything I could, watched a lot of videos, attended a few conferences." He shrugged his shoulders. "I'm no expert, but I want to be hands-on. To help."

When had the super-confident developer turned into a humble, helpful man? The kind of man her dad was. The kind of man she admired.

She became aware of how close Cam was standing to her. He smelled of spicy cologne and, not unpleasantly, of sweat. The space between them filled with molecules slamming into one another, eating up all the oxygen and making little sparks. His eyes met hers, and she felt as though she was gazing through an August heat haze rising from melting asphalt. He didn't look away. Her breath caught in her throat. Her knees went mushy. The air between them was dense, and her thoughts frayed. What was it about Cam that induced this effect? Maybe the fact that he looked at her as though he was hungry.

A ball bounced off the wall beside them, and Frankie felt herself land back on her feet.

Cam noticed the poster in her hand. "Whatcha got there?"

She gave him the paper. "Poster. Do you think I could pin it up on that bulletin board?" She nodded to a pock-marked bulletin board already crowded with posters for a dozen other community events.

"St. Paul's fundraising gala dinner dance," he read.

Only her utter, selfless devotion to the Marriage Survivors Club and her sheer stupidity could have induced her to agree to invite him. A pulse beat at the base of Frankie's throat. It was now or never.

"Want to come?" She was embarrassed by how her voice faded and went up at the end.

He laughed again. "So you can drag me into a dark corner and bludgeon me with a hymnal?"

She laughed. "No, I promise, no bludgeoning. I'd like to invite you and ... Mrs. Simpson or, you know, a date to be our guests."

He looked at her, and she couldn't bear to stare straight into his eyes, so she glanced away.

He said, "There is no Mrs. Simpson or nobody else for that matter."

She shifted from one foot to the other and felt surprise register on her face. He had the power to make unchristian thoughts pop into her head, but this one was different: *how nice that he had no one to bring.*

His smile widened, and he knelt, retied his sneaker as if to spare her embarrassment, and then stood. "Is there a Mr. Carter who might object to me dancing with his wife at said gala?"

It had been eons since she had flirted, but the weight in her lower abdomen told her they were definitely flirting.

"My dad won't mind," she said, smiling. "And neither will anybody else."

"Good," he said, his eyes brighter than before.

"If I go, will I have to spend the evening being importuned by a bunch of Bible-wielding church members? Scolded, pestered, threatened with going to hell, prayed over?"

Her face grew hot. "To be honest, I'm inviting you to come because we think if you understand who we are at St. Paul's, you might reconsider selling us the house."

His face hardened, and the air between them went from tropical to arctic.

He held up a hand to stop her. "Look, I don't want to get into a pissing match. I'm building on the property. Period. Like I mentioned when you dropped by my office, when the project reaches completion, I'll be happy to contribute to the church for your shelter."

He was nice if they weren't talking about the house.

"I promise no one will give you a hard time, and I promise not to bring it up."

He stared at her in a way that no one had stared at her in ages. It made her feel flustered and out of sorts, but in a pleasant way. He shifted on his feet, and she sensed him giving in. She felt a lift of triumph that they might have a second chance to bring him around to St. Paul's way of thinking.

"All right. But it'll take a lot more than prayer and wine to change my mind about the house."

"There won't be much praying at this event. It's at the Norwalk Inn. Silent auction, dinner, drinks, and dancing."

"Seriously? At a church function? That's a strange combination." He shook his head, but his smile was warm and unguarded again. "All right. You talked me into it. I'll wear my dancing shoes."

Of course, he could still cancel or not show up. Or worse, he would come, and the sizzle between them might be real.

CHAPTER 16

*The Lord is close to the brokenhearted and saves those who are
crushed in spirit.*

Psalms 34:18

Through the peephole of Evie's door, Doralee saw Francine on
the front stoop, knocking, her face beautiful and desperate.

"Who is that?" Evie asked.

"Francine."

"Let her in."

Doralee said, "I won't."

She knew who her daughter was. Remembered her sweet,
smiling little face, the way her tough little legs pumped as she
rode her tricycle up and down the drive. Or maybe she just
imagined that. These days, her mind played tricks, went to sleep
when she was awake.

"Dori, just let her in for a minute," Evie said. "Please, it's
not—"

Doralee shook her head. "No, you promised."

Keeping herself as still as possible, Doralee plastered her back against the front wall of Evie's living room. She wanted to hug Francine, talk to her, and tell her she loved her. Seeing her was everything Doralee wanted but couldn't have.

At least not without a stiff drink.

Francine always was a stubborn kid, but the only way Doralee could protect her was not to let herself get within an inch of Francine. Otherwise, she might never let go. All Doralee wanted was to spare Francine any more pain. God knew she'd already given the girl enough.

Evie opened the door. "Hello, Francine."

Doralee's heart drummed in her chest.

"How long will she be here?" Francine was saying. "Can I call her?"

"She's not here," Evie lied, shifting from one foot to the other.

Francine's voice was like water on Doralee's thirsty soul. She felt the nourishment of her words all the way to her bones.

Sounding angry, Francine said, "But I saw her at the grocery. I saw you drive away with her. I know she's in Norwalk. She must be here."

Doralee raked her broken nails up the flaky, red rash on her forearm. Her bloated stomach looked like she was smuggling a watermelon under her shirt. The doctors had told her that it had something to do with her drinking, but she couldn't remember what, and really, she didn't give a damn one way or the other. Her entire body itched as though mosquitos were stinging her from the inside. She had lost some teeth. Her chicken legs barely held her up, and she walked with a cane. Francine would be disgusted.

"Aunt Evelyn, please, can I call her? Can you give me her cell phone number?" Francine insisted, sounding desperate. "Can I give you my number and have her call me?"

"Take your foot out of the door, Francine." Evie sounded almost ready to give in. She looked back at Doralee, hiding, looking for permission to let Francine in.

Doralee squeezed her eyes shut and shook her head.

Trying to insist, Evie jutted her chin at Doralee.

She shook her head again.

Evie sighed and turned back to Francine.

"When will she be back?" Francine said.

"Francine, I'm sorry. Maybe another time when she ... comes up to visit." Evie blew her nose in a tissue.

"Why are you doing this?" Francine asked. "Can you tell me why?"

"It's just the way things have to be, Frankie," Evie said, a catch in her voice. "I wish it didn't have to be so."

Doralee squeezed her eyes shut, concentrating hard because her mind wandered around like a stray dog. She didn't want Francine to know that she'd fallen into the bottom of a bottle and done things her own mother had done. Things she promised herself she would never do.

But for a drink, she would do those things all over again right now.

Evie shut the front door, and the sunshine got swallowed up.

"She's gone," Evie said, her face bent up into a scowl. "I hate treating her like that. It's cruel. I've done that to her, for you, for more than forty years. You need to make things right."

Doralee eased away from the wall. Unable to resist, she lifted the corner of the curtain on the front window just enough to see Francine's retreating back. "Not cruel in the long run. Best make a clean break. She don't need me anyhow."

"I expect she'll come back, and I don't want to be a part of this anymore." Evie stomped into the kitchen.

Doralee traced Francine's figure on the window with a single finger as she walked to her car. Doralee's arms ached and throbbed as though something had been ripped from her embrace.

As if she knew Doralee was watching, Francine stopped, turned around, and looked directly at the window.

Doralee let the curtain drop and stepped back. Panting a few painful breaths, she pressed a fist into her stomach until she could stand the pain in her right upper belly.

Evie stood in the kitchen doorway. "You okay? Shall we go to the ER?"

Doralee bit the inside of her lip, fighting the hot poker of pain stabbing her belly. "The deal with me comin' up here was no doctors. You promised. You gotta keep your word."

"Damn it, Dori! You prepared to die without ever speaking to your daughter again? You going to let her go just like that?" Evie flung her arm out. "Never tell her you love her? Not tell her you're sorry? Never tell her why you left?"

"You think she'll believe I ever loved her, let alone love her now? You got it all backward. I love her enough to *not* see her. I don't want her remembering me like this dried-up old skeleton. She's sure enough hated me since I left her." Doralee banged her cane on the floor. "I'm not going to hurt that girl no more. I love her enough to spare her, and in my opinion, that's pretty good lovin'."

Seeing her daughter through the curtains, hearing her voice, had to be enough. Francine didn't deserve to be hurt anymore, and Doralee didn't deserve to see Francine again. It was the one penance Doralee could do.

"Don't you miss her?" Evie whispered, her eyes damp with tears.

Evie never cried. Never, not in all the years they'd been sisters, not in all the nights they'd spent sleeping in the church door, not all the times they were hungry, and their mother was blacked out, not when they shoved the bureau against their bedroom door.

Doralee faced her sister. "I done missed her every day of my life."

It doesn't take a lot to let go of your children; it takes everything.

CHAPTER 17

Jesus said, Suffer the little children, and forbid them not, to come unto me: for of such is the kingdom of heaven.

Matthew 19:14

The Wednesday six p.m. Celtic Eucharist in the Chancel had just ended. Ordinarily, the intimate Mass always left Frankie with a deep, comforting peace, as though she were floating in a pool of grace. She loved this Mass, but as the service went on this evening, she slipped into despondency. When the other congregants filed out, Frankie had dragged herself to this pew to pray for the strength to find a way to reach Doralee's heart.

Now, in the semi-darkness of St. Paul's sanctuary, Frankie sat in a pew next to the icon of the Black Virgin. Candle flames danced in the red votives, and tendrils of smoke trailed up from two sticks of incense. The icon Virgin sat on an easel, the circle of her golden halo gleaming in the light from the candles. Her blue eyes were partly closed, her chin down, her lips curved in an enigmatic Mona Lisa smile, as if she knew the secret to motherhood—having one and being one. Frankie wished the Virgin could give her a few hints.

When Father Gabriel strode down the aisle like a lifeguard coming to rescue her from a cold, dark, tossing sea.

"Good evening, Frankie. Would you like some company?" Father Gabriel asked, pausing for permission before joining her in the pew.

"I was waiting to talk to you, but ... I know you're busy."

He folded himself into the pew and, resting a knee on the pew, he angled his body to face her. "I'm never too busy to talk to my flock. All during the Eucharist, you looked upset. How can I help you?"

She bowed her head, hoping she didn't look as bad as she felt. She heard anguish crackle in her voice. "I want to apologize for my miscalculations about the shelter house."

"Why, whatever for?" He sounded bewildered and surprised.

She avoided looking at him. "I should have researched the other two lots and figured Cam Simpson might want 61. If I'd have estimated more, planned better ..." She swallowed. "We could have borrowed more for the purchase." Her voice dropped. "We might have gotten it."

He held up a hand. "Stop, Frankie. No one blames you. We're all in this together; that's what community is about."

He gazed at her through the shadowy light, and the bottomless compassion in his eyes touched her. "I'm not upset, and neither is anyone else."

"You're sure you're not?" she asked, relieved but not quite believing him.

"Don't give it another thought," he scoffed. "We'll find another house somewhere."

She picked at a smear of caulk on her jeans. "But see, I don't want another house. I want 61 East Avenue."

"Can I ask why?"

The sun was long gone, but from the outside, the passing car lights flickered across the stained-glass windows making the deep azures, ruby reds, golden yellows, glow. The rows of pews were empty, waiting like open arms. The stone pillars and floors gave off the dusty scent of cold stone. A singing silence filled the gothic arches. It was the safest, most peaceful, grace-filled place she knew.

It was only her and her priest. He would understand why she wanted 61 East Avenue. He might even have a deeper insight into her drive than she did.

She cleared her throat. "When I was a kid ... Bettina Catrambone from my second-grade class lived at 61 East Avenue. My mother worked there as a babysitter and housekeeper three days a week. She would meet Bettina and me at the bus stop, and we'd walk home together."

"So the house has fond memories for you?"

"You'd think so, right?" She felt shame claw at her, and she pushed the words out. "But not really. My mother was supposed to watch us, but she ... she would start drinking when we got to the house."

He waited, his silence an outstretched hand.

"I loved visiting that house. I felt so ..." She tipped her head back and gazed up at the high peak of the wooden ceiling. "Even if my mother was drinking, the house felt kind of magical. It had this massive stone fireplace and big rooms and a kitchen with lots of nooks and crannies and good smells. As a brown kid, I felt special to get to go to the house of the richest, prettiest girl in school. I felt—I can't think of the right word ...."

"Safe?"

The observation had flavor, an understanding, and rightness to it that had eluded her until now. "Yes, safe, even though my mom was drinking."

"Every little kid should have a special place that makes them feel like that. I take it the Catrambones didn't know she drank?"

"No. Drunks are good at hiding their drinking, and she was the best. Judge Catrambone and his wife were at work, and Bettina didn't suspect, so she never told her parents either."

"What was it like at your own home?"

Memories of her parents' shouting, her father's desperate pleading, and her mother's drunken rages brought the coppery taste of fear to her mouth. She gripped the edge of the pew beneath her to remind herself she was on solid ground.

"Dad would beg, and she would promise she wouldn't drink. So instead, she drank at the Catrambones'."

"Sounds like her drinking was pretty intense," he said without a hint of judgment.

"At home, she'd stash booze in my dollhouse or toy bin. Sometimes I'd come home from school and find her passed out in her vomit, and I'd clean her up."

Frankie bent and rested her forehead on the pew in front to let the grief she'd stirred up settle. She straightened. "When she screamed and carried on, I'd get scared, run to the garage, and hide behind the trash cans. To this day, if I smell a rotten tomato, I have a panic attack."

With his deep voice that always sounded like he was praying, he said, "You're as smart, determined, loving, and hardworking as anyone I've ever met. Now I can add resilient to that list."

She hadn't thought of herself in that way, but more like a bulldozer with alligator skin. He ordained her stubbornness with a saintly quality.

"My dad always said she chose booze over us. That she left so she could drink as much as she wanted. I haven't talked to her in forty-seven years, but now she's back in Norwalk."

His eyes grew round. "That must have been quite a surprise."

"That's putting it mildly." She sighed, feeling as though a bag of wet cement had dropped from her shoulders. "I'm angry at her, I guess. But I always wished I could have fixed whatever made her leave us. All my life, I wondered if I'd have been a different kid, smarter, happier, loved her more, maybe she wouldn't have left us."

"Oh, Frankie, it's never a child's fault when a parent leaves."

"In my head, I know that, but my heart still thinks that. She made me promise not to tell my dad that she was drinking there, but I'm sure he knew." Frankie paused to get control of her emotions. "I was eight when she eventually left. She left me at the Catrambones' house. I never saw her again."

He tilted his head to the side and said, "By insisting you not tell your dad she was drinking, she manipulated you into colluding against your father. She made her secret your responsibility. She flipped you to be on her team."

Frankie felt surprised by this. "I never thought of it that way."

"So, if I understand, you feel as though you have to pay for the sin of not being a good enough kid to make your alcoholic mother stay." He looked at her sideways. "Not that Episcopalians believe in sin." He bent forward and rested his elbows on his knees, letting his hands dangle. With a weary sigh, he said, "Humans are fragile and tender, incredibly subject to guilt and shame. Their self-flagellation breaks my heart." He made his hands into fists and shook them. "*Breaks it.* I'm not making light of your feelings, but sometimes, I wish I had some kind of icon or sacrament that would dispel such dark thoughts."

She gave a dry laugh. "Like what?"

"Oh, I don't know." He made a palms-up gesture. "A garlic-enrobed crucifix I could wave over a person, a spritz from a bottle of holy water, a holy fly swatter blessed by the archbishop. Something to drive off the evil of self-recrimination."

She could have been mistaken, and it could have been an

effect of shadow and candlelight, but she thought she saw heartbreak of immense depth cross his face. Something that didn't have to do with their conversation but something deeper about him.

What a shame that he had no one to love him for his ready smile, his wisdom, his height, his depth, his deep laugh, his compassion, his sense of humor, and his steel-blade mind.

He said, "Jesus didn't have a list of unforgivable sins that he waved around. He never told people to condemn or hate one another or themselves, but human nature seems intent on turning in on itself or others. They didn't teach us this in seminary, but I sort of think the real separation of man from God didn't happen in the Garden of Eden and isn't from sin. It's in not forgiving oneself."

This was why she loved him. This was why someone should be in love with him.

With a touch of chagrin, he said, "I could use a holy fly swatter myself now and then."

She laughed. "Guess my holy flyswatter is to give shelter and include people others reject. That's what I want to do with the house."

"You want to make something good out of something traumatic."

She hadn't thought of it in so many words, but his idea fit like a glove. "Yes."

"Frankie, you were a child. It's one of the basic fantasies of childhood that kids always think they're more powerful than they are. If they were stronger, they could have kept a parent from leaving, from hitting their other parent, from drinking, or doing a thousand other hurtful things."

His voice was filled with infinite compassion and wisdom. How was it he was not yet thirty and so wise?

He said, "If children could control what happened in families, every day would be Christmas, and ice cream would be a food group."

"You mean it's not?" she said with mock horror.

"No, but I have it on good authority that in heaven it will be," he said with the grin of a prankster.

Their shared laughter lightened the darkness.

"Father, you're so wise and good; why aren't you married to some lucky guy?"

He laughed. "I could ask you the same thing."

She sighed. "I suppose the answer is the same for both of us; the right guy hasn't come along yet."

His face grew sober, and he gazed at the stained-glass window of Jesus surrounded by innocent little children and fluffy white lambs with the words *Suffer the little children to come unto me* written below. "I'm sorry you were so hurt as a child," he murmured. He rested his hands on his knees, stared at the floor, and let the silence wrap around them for a while before speaking. "All these years, you've blamed yourself for her abandonment, but I'm sure she doesn't blame you for anything, and you certainly shouldn't blame yourself."

He was quiet for a few minutes, but she could hear his big brain ticking away.

"Maybe what you really want is to tell her you forgive her for leaving you. Are you blaming yourself instead of examining the ways in which you were hurt? I wonder if maybe you've built your self-image around the idea that you could take a punch instead of admitting how hurt you were."

He was even more brilliant than she gave him credit for.

She blew out a long breath. The idea of forgiving her mother upended her self-concept. She believed she could do whatever was necessary to be a good mom, friend, businesswoman, and parishioner. That if she worked hard enough, she could control everything.

He shifted in the pew.

She felt as though every molecule of his being was focused on her the way kids use eyeglasses to focus a beam of sunlight to set something on fire.

"Dealing with your mother now is the only thing that will make you whole. What she did was terrible and damaging and wrong. But you're still living with the trauma of that. Forgiving someone else means you have to first acknowledge that they hurt you. That you're still feeling pain. But forgiveness isn't one-and-done. It takes work."

She had bought into the illusion that invulnerability made her courageous and safer. The truth was that she was only staving off the more profound hurt of abandonment.

What was really going to require courage was to forgive the hurt done to her by her mother. That meant Frankie had to accept her as she was right now. She had to give up the fantasy of a mother-daughter relationship. And the real test was opening herself up to whatever God and Doralee had in store for her.

CHAPTER 18

The best way to not feel hopeless is to get up and do something. Don't wait for good things to happen to you. If you go out and make some good things happen, you will fill the world with hope, you will fill yourself with hope.

Barack Obama

Frankie drove by Evelyn's house for three days, hoping to catch another glimpse of her mother. Finally, sick of wasting time, she borrowed her dad's car, which didn't have her business logo plastered on the side. She parked at the end of Evelyn's street and waited for them to leave the house.

Scooched down in the seat, Frankie felt like a hitman waiting for her mark to appear. Inevitably, her mind wandered to the question of why her mother had never come back, visited, written, or even sent a birthday card? Why had she completely disappeared? And why was she back?

At 9:40 a.m. Evelyn and Doralee left the house, got in the car, and drove past.

Frankie's pulse jumped as she put the car in drive and followed them. They drove to Pinckney Park, a small park on an estuary of the Long Island Sound. Giant oak trees shaded two swing sets, a jungle gym, and a pair of slides. A couple little kids, squealing with joy, chased each other around a white gazebo. It was an odd place for two old ladies until Frankie realized this was a place her mother used to take her when she was small.

The memory snapped into focus: Doralee pushing her on the swings, Frankie kicking her legs high in the air, the wind fluffing her hair, the sun hot on her face and legs. She and Doralee watching sailboats on the water drift by like dreams.

They had taken a basket with sandwiches and a box of strawberries which they ate sitting on a blanket spread out beneath a tree. After lunch, Frankie had fallen asleep with her head on her mother's lap. She could almost taste the tart sweetness of the cold lemonade they had brought. It had been a happy day, a sober day.

Frankie felt the sharp loss of those days like an actual physical pain in her side.

Maybe Doralee had come to relive that day. Did those memories feel as weighty to her as they did for Frankie?

Evelyn opened Doralee's door. Even with her cane and with enormous effort, Doralee staggered unsteadily.

Frankie noted the similarities between Evelyn and Doralee Farris: the slope of their shoulders, the way they held their elbows slightly away from their bodies, the curve of their heads, and the way they turned their feet out at a slight angle. Aside from Evelyn, Frankie knew nothing of her mother's family, her background, or where she'd grown up or lived. Was there something in the sisters' lives that would explain more of Frankie to herself?

The pea gravel crunched under Frankie's boots as she crossed the parking lot to where Doralee and Evelyn stood.

Careful not to appear threatening, Frankie softly said, "Hello."

Evelyn froze and looked at Frankie, then Doralee.

Frankie thought Evelyn might chase her off, but she nodded and took a few steps away.

Doralee turned slowly and blinked her sleepy-turtle eyes at Frankie. Her brows racked up.

A gyre of excitement expanded inside Frankie and spread through her chest, down her arms and legs, to the tips of her fingers and the soles of her feet. An emotion that Frankie didn't have a name for writhed and bit at her insides like a hungry animal.

Want. That's what the feeling was: want. It didn't mean Frankie wasn't angry or hurt, but her anger was wax compared to the smelting furnace of her want.

To get what she wanted, she would have to open her heart to Doralee. She wanted to know where her mother had gone, to tell her about herself. She wanted to give Doralee a chance to be a mother. Not a fairytale mom, but a good enough mom. She wasn't there yet, but Frankie_wanted to forgive her. And she could, too, if she only tried hard enough.

Frankie advanced slowly until she stood in front of Doralee. She had a mildly confused half-smile on her cracked lips. Her eyes registered fear. There might not be another chance if Frankie scared Doralee off. There would be time to ask questions later. Now was the time to approach her cautiously.

"Hello, Francine," Doralee said in a dry, scratchy voice.

Her mother was the only one who had ever called her Francine.

"I've ... I've missed you. Can we just ... maybe just talk for a minute?"

"Oh, I'm not—I don't know. I'm not too sure about that," she said, flicking her gaze toward Evelyn as if looking for permission.

Doralee's skin was sallow, and her cheeks laced with bright spider veins and deep wrinkles. The whites of her sunken eyes were no longer white. That was from drinking, but they might clear up if Frankie got Doralee someplace to dry out.

"It's okay, Dori," Evelyn said, surprising Frankie. "Go have a chat. I'll just wait here."

Frankie gestured to the gazebo across the lawn. "Would you like to sit down?" She tugged at the front of her jacket. "I'd like to get to know you a little."

There was a kind of surrender in Doralee's eyes when she nodded, and Frankie restrained the urge to let out a whoop.

Leaning heavily on her cane, Doralee shuffled to the gazebo, her breath coming in short wheezes. Her shoulder blades poked out the back of her ratty navy raincoat, and she clutched the crumpled black purse under an arm.

Frankie was tempted to take her elbow and steady her, but it seemed too presumptuous. As she walked behind her, praying Doralee would not fall, Frankie felt a sort of jerking backward to when she was a child and led Doralee to bed so she could sleep it off.

Frankie's heart ached, and she felt an overwhelming responsibility wash over her. In her mind, she heard her child's voice say, "You can do this."

After a treacherous journey across the grass, with a grunt of effort, Doralee dropped onto a seat in the gazebo.

She gazed long and hard at Frankie. "You look beautiful. All grown up. Pretty," she said in an almost-shy way.

Frankie sat, trying to remember what she'd worked out to say, but the words had turned to dry stones in her mouth. Instead, she clenched her hands into one big fist to keep herself from reaching out to touch Doralee. She watched Doralee's face for a reaction, but there was only the flat, expressionless gaze as though the muscles of her face no longer worked.

"Thanks," Frankie finally managed to say.

"How you doin'?" Doralee asked, her gaze drifting over Frankie's shoulder.

Frankie said, "I ... I wanted to say *hi* when I saw you at Stew Leonard's, but you ran off."

"You saw me?" Doralee said, confusion on her face. "When?"

Frankie kept her voice neutral, non-accusatory. "At Stew Leonard's? You looked at me."

Doralee ducked her chin like a cornered bird drawing its wings shut over its head.

Frankie rushed to reassure her. "I only wanted to ask how you've been. See what you've been up to."

That was obvious: she'd been drinking.

Doralee drew back, increasing the distance between the two of them. Resting on the top of her cane, her hands shook. Her head bobbed as though she was keeping time to music only she could hear. Her stomach protruded abnormally, and her chest rose and fell in laborious breaths.

A lump of dread plummeted to the bottom of Frankie's stomach. Perhaps Doralee was sick with something incurable, and because Evelyn was a nurse, she had returned to Norwalk for treatment.

Frankie risked prying. "You have a bad tremor in your hands. Are you sick?"

"Oh, you know." Doralee waved a hand, the fingers twisted by arthritis, the nails yellowed and chipped. "When you get to be my age, stuff goes wrong. Just live with it, you know." She gave a dry, unconvincing chuckle which broke into a cough.

Frankie reminded herself not to leap to conclusions or push too hard. A house was built one nail at a time. Doralee could have a few good years, and perhaps they could spend some of those years together. Not wanting to startle her, slowly, slowly, Frankie reached over and laid her strong, callused hand atop Doralee's gnarled knuckles. "Nice you came back. Are you staying in Norwalk for a while?"

"Yes, I ... I suppose so. I'm not really ... not sure." Doralee shifted her gaze, looking anywhere but at Frankie.

Frankie fixed her eyes on the worn wooden floor. "I wonder if we could maybe, you know, spend some time together, I mean, me and you. Get to know one another. Have you meet my sons."

Doralee gathered her raincoat around her and shook her head. "Oh, Francine, I don't think that's such a good idea."

Cold shot through Frankie, and she felt she would shatter like ice cracking if she moved.

Doralee shifted her skeletal frame. "It's been a long, long time. I'm not such good company."

"Just a cup of coffee now and then. I don't want, you know ..." Frankie stoppered up her want.

"Francine, you've done fine with just Vic. You don't need me around, reminding you I left."

Doralee betrayed no trace of regret. Maybe these gauze-thin words were all Doralee had to offer, and Frankie had to settle for that. Maybe there wasn't any more. Maybe an apology would never be forthcoming.

That didn't mean Frankie didn't have to try to forgive her anyway.

"I'd like to hear about your life," Frankie said, hoping for anything that would help them connect.

"Nothing come to mind." Doralee shrugged and stared out across the water of the Sound.

"Really, a short visit is all." Frankie hated to sound so needy. Neediness only opened you for more heartache. But then, how much more heartache was there to be had from someone who'd walked away? And wasn't admitting to heartache the point of forgiveness?

Doralee rubbed her hands back and forth on the top of her cane.

Frankie, used to hitting everything with a hammer, pushing to get her own way, waited silently, patiently, the way she'd seen Father Gabriel do. It was killing her.

"All right, but I don't want to be no bother," Doralee finally said.

Frankie felt as though she'd been swung high up into the air, an endless blue vista filled with sun and light spreading out beneath her. There was clear, sharp, fresh air and a sky cloudless all the way to the horizon. Warmth rushed to her face and spread through her from head to foot.

Doralee coughed a dry, wracking cough, the force bending her double over her cane.

Frightened at the intensity, Frankie asked, "Do you need some water?"

Evelyn came over and handed Doralee a cough drop. "We should be going now, Dori."

Frankie felt a dropping sensation pitch her downward. "Do you have a cellphone? Can I get your number?"

Doralee blinked. "I do ... but I don't ..." She turned to Evelyn. "What's the number?"

Evelyn took out her phone and shared the contact with Frankie. It was so easy. Why hadn't Evelyn done it ages ago?

The dream of her mother, the fantasies in her head, the mix of blame, rage, and regret, longing, and yearning were familiar to Frankie. But she had no idea what spending face-to-face time with the stranger, her mother, would be like. A relationship, or whatever form knowing one another might take, wasn't something Frankie could plan or measure with a tape measure or laser level.

Whatever shape this relationship took, it would probably not respond well to *hitting it with a hammer*. It would be like walking into a buzzsaw and hoping to come out the other side with all her fingers.

And her heart.

CHAPTER 19

Your first obligation as a parent is not to bring chaos into your kids' lives.

Anonymous

Doralee fought for breath, picking her way over the gravel back to Evelyn's car. Doralee's body shook, and her mouth felt like a desert. If it wasn't already pickled, she would have given her left kidney for a bottle. Her insides felt as though they were being weighed down by bricks.

"What'd she say?" Evie said.

"Wants to see me, if you can believe that."

"'Course, I can believe it. You're her mother. I've been saying all along you need to see her."

Doralee snorted. What she had done to that girl was unforgivable. *Unforgivable.* Even if she apologized and asked Francine to forgive, it didn't mean she would. It was too much to ask of anyone. "That's not what I need. What I need is a drink. A fifth of vodka, to be exact. Let's swing by the liquor store before we get home. I got money."

"You know I'm not going to do that." Evelyn shut the car door and went around to the driver's side.

There had to be some way to get something to drink. Evelyn had long ago quit keeping liquor in the house when Doralee visited. She used to bring something with her and hide it in the garage, outside under a bush, under the deck, or sneak out to the liquor store when Evie was at work. This time, breathing was too hard, and her legs too uncooperative to walk to the liquor store.

Evelyn put the key in the ignition and glanced at her, worry pinching up her forehead. "We'll go to the doctor tomorrow."

"The hell we will." Doralee gasped. "You try that, and I'm"— she gasped again—"catching the next bus back to Lafayette." Not that she knew where the bus station was or could even get there, but damn it, a promise was a promise, and she and Evie always kept their promises.

Evelyn sighed. "They can help, Dorie. I'm sure there's—"

Doralee cut her off with an air karate chop. "Forget it! I done lived long enough. Done enough damage in this world." She paused to suck in a breath. "I'm ready to go. When I called you, you promised no doctors."

"Yeah, but I thought I could get you to change your mind once I could look you in the eye."

"I'd change my mind for a bottle," Doralee suggested affably.

"The hell you will."

Doralee remembered their mother and how the men would bring a bottle, sometimes two, and disappear behind her bedroom door for an hour. How their mother cried when she drank. How hunger carved out their bellies. She hadn't wanted to put Frankie through that, and she hadn't. If she could be proud of one thing, it was that.

They rode in silence for a few minutes, and her breath settled into a high, short rhythm.

"You going to tell her?" Evelyn asked.

"You asked me that the last time, and my answer's the same. No, and why should I?"

At the stoplight, things looked familiar but distant. Where were they again? What town?

"You could be honest for once, you know."

"Don't be so self-righteous," Doralee snapped. "You don't know what it was like to leave everybody you loved behind. If I tell her, she'll think she has save me or something. She'll think it's her job to make me happy, and I don't want to put that on her."

The only way to deal with leaving Francine and Vic was to forget, and what better way to forget than to drink. A lot. Buckets full.

She wanted to remember when Francine was little, but these days, her mind was a jumble of miscellaneous junk: which soup kitchen was open on Wednesdays. Was today Wednesday? Where she'd hidden an extra pair of shoes. Why was she in the back of the police car? When it rained, which bleachers at the high school football stadium stayed the driest underneath? What year was it? Which friend shared a bottle, and who didn't.

She really wanted to forget how she'd hurt Francine, but that thought seemed to stick to her like flypaper.

"It was a stupid decision to leave," Evelyn said with her usual high-and-mighty disgust. "Just plain stupid."

Neat little houses glided by. The kind Doralee might have lived in if she had been able to quit drinking and stayed with Vic. But right now, if she could make it to the liquor store, she would.

"No, it wasn't stupid." Doralee leaned her elbow on the door and put her knuckles to her mouth, feeling the hard white bones against her rotten teeth. "What was stupid was comin' back up here. I should have just stayed in Lafayette, then I wouldn't never have run into Francine again. I wouldn't be a burden to you."

Evie sniffled.

Doralee hated when Evie cried, and she was doing a lot of that on this visit.

"I'm glad you came up. It's just that I don't want you to be alone when ..." Evelyn choked back a sob.

Doralee patted her arm. "Now, don't go getting all soggy on me, Evie. You done more than anybody could or shoulda done for me for my whole life. It'll be okay." She said that to ease Evie's worries, but she didn't think dying was going to be okay. If it was anything like trying to get sober, it would be sheer hell. She wasn't about to admit to Evie how scared she was because Evie would use it as an excuse to haul her to the doctors. Instead, Doralee kept up her careless attitude. "But I really could use a drink."

"Forget it."

She banged the door with her fist. "What's the damn difference? I'm dying anyway. Not like it's going to change things; make it go faster or slower."

At least she wouldn't be dying under the bleachers at Lafayette High School, mid-hurricane.

CHAPTER 20

And let us not grow weary of doing good, for in due season we will reap, if we do not give up.

Galatians 6:9

It took forty-seven years and three phone calls to arrange to see Doralee, enough time that Frankie thought she should have been nonchalant about it. Frankie's stomach was a sloshing crater as she rang the bell to Evelyn's house. She wanted to make a good impression because this first real meeting felt kind of like a first date with her mother. Weird word, *mother*. It didn't really fit what Doralee was to Frankie, but Frankie couldn't think of a better word.

"Hi, I'm here to pick up Doralee," Frankie said.

"You could call her *Mom*," Evelyn suggested. "Might make her feel, you know, more cared for."

Frankie stiffened her smile. "I barely know her, but when the time's right, I'll get around to it." She jerked the front of her jacket closed. "She ready?"

"Almost. You'll have to be patient because she's slow. She'll be out in a minute."

Evelyn let the screen door close.

That was it. Frankie wouldn't be sent packing like some door-to-door salesman, so she pulled open the screen door again. "Can you tell me something?"

Evelyn raised her eyebrows.

"Why do you hate me?" Frankie thought the only way to deal with hateful people was to be civil but honest. Evelyn had scared her when she was a kid, but Frankie wasn't about to let her get away with trying to intimidate her anymore.

Evelyn looked taken aback. She spoke with less edge. "I don't hate you. I'm just protecting my sister. She doesn't need you accusing her or blaming her."

"You're making a big assumption that I'll blame her. Not to mention that no matter what happens today, nothing I do will have the least impact on her."

Evelyn's face softened, and she glanced back inside the house. "Yes, I suppose that's right. She's sober now, so I just don't want her upset, is all. "

"Neither do I. I guess I'll wait in the van until she's ready."

Frankie supposed it wouldn't kill her to be patient for a few more minutes. She kept the engine running. But the longer she waited—five, ten, then twenty minutes—the tension in her shoulders ratcheted tighter, and her doubts boiled over. Maybe Doralee had changed her mind about seeing her today. Or any other day. That thought sat on Frankie's chest. This had probably been a stupid idea to begin with.

She took out her cell phone and called Olivia, who always had some insight into the way people thought and acted.

"Hey," Olivia said when she answered. "How's it going?"

Frankie told her how long she had been waiting. "Maybe I should just give up."

"Since when are you one to do that?"

"Never."

"Right. What do you have planned?"

"I'm taking her to Marina's. That's pretty neutral, and she'll see what I do. The house will blow her away."

"I know it means a lot to you for your mother to feel proud of you."

Frankie swallowed hard, wanting this meeting not to mean as much to her as it did. "It feels like meeting a stranger."

Gently, Olivia said, "You are strangers. Long as you keep your expectations low, you'll be fine. Remember what you want to get out of it, but more than that, what she's able to give."

"A lot and probably not very much," Frankie said.

"It's like you bought a lottery ticket. Could be you win a two-dollar scratch-off or the jackpot. Probably going to be somewhere in the middle or low end. I know you have a million questions but hold off on the heaviest until later. You don't want to put her on the defensive, or she might not see you again. Tell her about the boys, your work. Easy stuff like that."

Frankie said, "You mean I can't say, what the hell were you thinking when you abandoned me?"

Olivia chuckled, a sympathetic sound that made Frankie feel understood. "It's going to be fine. Just think two-dollar scratch-off, and you'll be okay."

"Thanks."

Doralee came tottering down the steps, poking the sidewalk with her cane. Enormous, dark sunglasses hid most of her face, and her white hair skittered up from her head like a volcano. She carried her same black purse and the shapeless, navy overcoat. Her oddly bloated stomach had to be a symptom of some illness. The sunlight emphasized the smoked-Gouda-cheese color of her skin. The purple spider veins raged across her cheeks and nose as if they had been clawed into her face.

Something tumbled in Frankie. A thought rang in her mind as brightly as a hammer striking a steel I-beam: Doralee had cirrhosis. Maybe she was even dying from it. Frankie felt a breathless desolation as though all the air had been squeezed out of her chest.

How could she have been so blind? What should have been clear before crystalized: Doralee might not have much time left. Frankie would never have the emotional connection she craved. Then it occurred to Frankie that Doralee had nothing to give. She was, essentially, an empty booze bottle.

Frankie remembered that Father Gabriel said in moments of hardship and difficulty, try to find the grace in the world to help you get through.

Grace. This moment was grace. She had been given something most people don't get: a second chance. It was God's grace that she had found her mother again; this was a second chance to be her daughter again. And it was going to hurt like hell, but whoever said God made living easy?

Frankie swallowed her grief and stepped out of the van to help her mother.

Doralee waved her cane at Frankie. "Naw, naw. I got it. I got it," she said through wheezing breaths.

Frankie backed off, feeling chastened. She opened the van door and set a step stool on the ground since the van sat high. She took Doralee's arm to help her up and was startled to feel how fleshless the knob of her elbow was.

Two-dollar scratch-off.

Once underway, Frankie kept her eyes on the road, unable to look at the yellow wrinkles ringing Doralee's neck.

"What're we gonna do?" Doralee asked.

Frankie's inner alarm clanged. She glanced over at Doralee. They had spoken this morning, and already Doralee had forgotten. From her reading and research about alcoholics, Frankie knew they could have cognitive problems, but this was unnerving.

She kept her voice light. "I'm a contractor, and I do high-end kitchens and baths. My client wants me to come every day to check on the progress my crew is making. I thought maybe we'd go over, and I'll show you around. It's a good example of my work."

It wasn't the best mother-daughter experience, but it was something Frankie knew she was good at. Afterward, they could get lunch or coffee. Keep it easy. Undemanding.

"Sounds good." Doralee stared out the window, nodding.

They rode in silence while Frankie searched her mind for a neutral line of conversation. "What's your house like in Lafayette?"

"Oh, you know. I don't have an exact address. Move around a lot."

Oh God, she had been homeless. Frankie swallowed her shock. "I see. Do you ... still have family there?" *Do you have another family?*

"No."

Years of questions waited to spill out, so Frankie intentionally took a wrong turn to stretch time out. "How did you ... you know, spend your time there?"

"Oh, little a this, little a that." Doralee coughed. A dry, gravelly sound.

"So why did you choose to go to Lafayette?" *When you left Dad and me?*

"S'where me an' Evie grew up. Where our mother's buried."

A five-dollar scratch-off. "Oh, I didn't know that."

"Yup. Grew up on the outskirts of town on Bartlett Street. Dirt road. No running water, no indoor plumbing. A shack, really."

Frankie didn't know if it was appropriate to say *how awful*, or if Doralee was proud of having survived such a childhood. "How old were you when your mother died."

"Sixteen. Evie was fourteen."

A ragged heaviness struck Frankie in the chest. "Oh, I'm sorry. That must have been devastating for you. You were only a kid."

But then she had been eight, half as old when Doralee left her.

"We managed," Doralee said without regret or self-pity. "You know, them bastards come to visit my mother, they tried botherin' me and Evie, but I wouldn't let 'em. I fought 'em off. I fought 'em for Evie. Kept 'em off her."

Frankie ground her teeth. It sickened her to imagine what her mother had gone through. No wonder she drank. But Doralee's mind wandered, so were those memories real? Frankie hoped not.

They rode in silence for a bit until Doralee asked, "Vic still livin'?"

Frankie held her breath a moment. "Yes."

"He remarried?"

"No, we live together. He had a triple bypass about fifteen years ago, and he's got a bum knee." Frankie wanted to add he's still in love with you, but she didn't.

"You married?"

"No, Dad's my measuring tape, and I've never found anybody within a foot of him. I do have two adopted boys, though."

"Really? I have grandbabies? Why didn't you say so," Doralee said excitedly.

Finally, safe ground.

Frankie had told her before, and again, she felt a sense of foreboding. "Jordan is seventeen. He's a junior. Plays center on the Norwalk High basketball team. He's six-foot-six." Frankie chuffed a laugh. "Last time I checked."

"So tall! My, my, my."

"And Javier is thirteen. He's ..." How to explain autism to a woman who had spent a significant part of her life drunk? "He's in seventh grade. He's a little ... quirky."

"Ain't we all," Doralee said with a scratchy chuckle, and the tension Frankie felt up the back of her spine eased.

"It would be nice for you to meet them."

Dead silence.

After a bit, Frankie said, "Maybe you can come to church with us on Sunday. I still go to St. Paul's. Remember when we used to go when I was little?"

"St. Paul's. Now there's a blast from the past." Doralee stumped her cane once on the floor of the van. "Ask me Sunday, and I'll see how I feel."

Hope popped up in Frankie. Maybe it wasn't too late to build new memories to replace the ones branded into Frankie's brain.

Doralee said, "How old were your boys when you adopted them?"

The question was a tiny pearl. "Jordan came home to me fifteen years ago. He was two." Frankie was doing everything she could to keep a casual tone. "Now I can hardly keep him in clothes. Javier also came home at two."

"Nice you saved them kids."

Frankie had heard that phrase so often she was ready with her stock reply, which of all the things she knew to be true, this was the truest. "They saved me. They've made my life full and rich. I don't know what I'd do without them."

Clearly, Doralee had never felt about Frankie the way she felt about her boys. They had saved Frankie, but she'd been unable to save Doralee. Whatever they had left would be time stolen from that devil, vodka, but Frankie would do whatever was necessary to get as much time with Doralee as possible.

CHAPTER 21

From Rock Me to Sleep

Backward, turn backward, O Time, in your flight,
Make me a child again just for tonight!
Mother, come back from the echoless shore,
Take me again to your heart as of yore;
Kiss from my forehead the furrows of care,
Smooth the few silver threads out of my hair;
Over my slumbers your loving watch keep;
Rock me to sleep, mother, — rock me to sleep!

Elizabeth Akers Allen

At Marina's, Frankie introduced Doralee to her crew. They all praised Frankie, which embarrassed her. The kitchen wasn't nearly done, but it was impressive because it was the size of a bus terminal.

Doralee had left her sunglasses on, so Frankie couldn't read her eyes. She longed to see an expression of surprise, admiration, and pride. Just some recognition that Frankie could do this.

Nothing.

Was Doralee's blank expression the result of long-term alcoholism? If her brain, her liver, and probably her kidneys, were damaged, what must it be like inside Doralee's head?

Marina appeared, glowing with sweat from a workout in the in-home gym Frankie and her crew had also installed.

"Oh, you are Frankie's mother," Marina said in a sing-song voice which made her seem almost likable.

"Yes, I am, and you have a beautiful house," Doralee said.

Marina said, "Let me show. Frankie builded my bathroom, my workout room, the bar in the living room, and now my kitchen. Can you walk up my stairs?"

"That'd be nice, and I can manage the stairs." Doralee removed her oversized sunglasses and stuffed them in her purse.

Marina's eyes flared. Frankie read the shock on her face when she saw how yellow the whites of Doralee's eyes were.

She pointed with the head of her cane. "Lead the way."

Marina led Doralee past the opulent living room towards the stairs.

Frankie puttered around, pretending to work, until Marina and Doralee returned.

Doralee said, "You done a beautiful job on that bathroom, Francine. So big!"

Frankie was pleased. "Well, Olivia did all the design work. Me and the guys," she gestured to her crew working around them. "We just put it in."

Olivia was right. Even as old as Frankie was, it did feel good to hear Doralee's praise, so why was she playing it down?

Marina put her hands on her hips. "Now, this window."

She launched into a barrage of questions about whether a window, which had already been framed in, should be moved three inches to the left if it was big enough for a good view of the rolling, golf-course-green rear lawn.

Doralee perched on a nearby chair for a bit, then said, "Oh, I left my purse in the living room. You two keep on talking, and I'll be right back. I can manage."

"I can get it," Frankie said.

"No, no, you're busy," Doralee snapped. "I *told* you I can manage."

Doralee stumped off, leaving Frankie feeling a slap of shame.

Frankie finished convincing Marina that the window was perfect, and they made their farewells.

As they made their way back to the car, Doralee's black purse, slung over her shoulder, seemed to unbalance her, but Frankie wasn't about to offer help and get a scolding in return. Doralee climbed back in the van and dropped her purse with a heavy clunk to the floor.

Frankie pulled out of the drive. "Would you like some lunch?"

"No, I'm tired. I want to go home."

Frankie hid her disappointment. "Maybe tomorrow or another day?"

"Maybe. Let's see." Doralee squinted. "Where are we? I don't recognize this part of Lafayette."

Frankie slowed the van to a crawl. "This is Norwalk. Where you used to live."

"I did? When?" Doralee said belligerently.

It was like watching an injured bird flutter and hop, struggling to take flight again.

"Oh, never mind. It doesn't matter."

Frankie took the longest route home, tried to hit every light, drove the speed limit, and stayed behind a bus. She started out with an easy question. "Did you come back up to spend more time with Evelyn?"

"Ain't much time left 'cause we're both old. So, yes, I guess you could say that."

Doralee's words made Frankie's stomach hollow out. "Are you sick?"

"No, just old," she said without emotion.

Even Frankie knew that was a lie. "I'm glad you came along today. Marina's a tough customer, but the job is turning out beautifully, and she keeps adding things for us to do."

Frankie pulled into Evelyn's driveway and shut off the ignition.

Doralee finally smiled, sending Frankie's heart into the stratosphere. "Thank you for showing me. I used to know a man did good work like that. His name was Vic Carter. He was a nice man. Not like them men used to come and visit my mother."

Frankie stared at Doralee for a long time before she could speak. "Can I take you out for coffee next week?"

Doralee paused, her hand on the door. "Well, okay. But I don't want to be any trouble."

"No, no trouble at all."

"Don't want you getting' your hopes up or anything."

"What do you mean?"

"I got to go back to Lafayette soon. That's where I ..." Doralee trailed off, and Frankie saw in her eyes that she had lost the thread of what she meant to say.

The beginning of the trip had been like a root canal but was ending with the two of them making a teeny bit of connection. Frankie had to find a way to help her, to hurry things along between them because Doralee's mind seemed to slip like a bad clutch. Frankie jumped out of the van, rushed to Doralee's side, and put the step stool down for her. To Frankie's surprise and pleasure, Doralee let Frankie help her out of the van.

"Shall I take you to the door?" Frankie asked.

"Oh, naw, I'm fine."

She watched to ensure Doralee made it up the stairs okay.

When she reached the door, she turned to wave.

Frankie waved back. She couldn't stop grinning, but when she went to close the door, Doralee's purse was on the floor of the passenger seat. Frankie picked it up, and it was oddly heavy. How had Doralee been able to carry it out to the car?

Frankie picked it up to take to Doralee. "Wait, you forgot your—"

Something heavy fell out of the bag and shattered on the pavement. Shards of glass glittered in the sunlight. Liquid splashed Frankie's pants and boots, and a puddle spread at her feet. The stink of vodka, a scent she knew so well, stung Frankie's nostrils. Her throat constricted. She looked for a place to hide like she had when she was a child, and Doralee was drinking the *stinky stuff*.

A two-liter bottle of Polskaya vodka had fallen out of Doralee's purse.

Frankie drove home, her hopes reduced to roadkill. Evelyn had said Doralee was sober, but obviously, she wasn't. That was as disappointing as the stolen bottle. Yet again, Doralee chose booze over her daughter, and it was like a dull spike to the heart. The one plus was that Doralee couldn't drink the vodka since the bottle had broken.

How could she have a relationship with Doralee if she'd risk Frankie's job, reputation, or the possibility one of her crew would be accused of theft.

She had stolen from Frankie's client! She could have just knocked back a snootful on the sly, but nooooo, Doralee had to steal a two-fucking-liter bottle.

Frankie remembered a day when she was little. Doralee, her ever-present tumbler of orange juice glued to her hand, had sent

Frankie outside to ride her tricycle in the driveway. She begged Doralee to come out and watch how fast she could ride, but she said she was too busy and shooed Frankie out.

She rode her tricycle up and down the drive until her trike tipped over. She scraped her knee, bumped her elbow, and ground dirt into her palms. She went inside, crying, but Doralee was too drunk to stand. Feeling desperately alone, Frankie had washed off the scrape and put on a Band-Aid all by herself.

Now, she felt that same loneliness all over again.

CHAPTER 22

You have wings.
Learn to use them and fly.

Rumi

After the basketball game, as per Jordan's express instructions, Frankie waited in the van until he finished showering. She was parked, head out, in the school lot beneath a circle of light from an overhead streetlamp. She watched the spectators, kids mostly, piling out of the gymnasium. They were loud and jostling, filled with confidence she had never possessed. Would she have had such bravado if Doralee had stayed? Only if Frankie had been able to help her stop drinking.

She caught sight of her son swimming through an adoring crowd, high-fiving and fist-bumping his teammates. His smile was as magical as his jump shot; effortless, confident, unwavering, all-encompassing. A gift. She sighed and pressed her palm to the window as if she could pat his cheek.

Lord, she missed that boy who had turned into a man. He'd been twelve the last time he had smiled at her like that. Then puberty hit, and he became an alien. People said teens turned back into humans in their twenties, but she didn't think her heart could wait that long for his smile.

Jordan climbed into the van and threw his gym bag behind his seat. He grunted something she assumed meant *hello*.

Frankie said, "Great game."

"Yeah." He stared out the side window and tapped his hand on his knee to some rhythm in his head.

She leaned over to give him a hug.

He slouched away from her. "Mom!"

His brush-off stung like a poison dart, but she let it slide, cranked the van over, and headed home. "You're passing more, and that's a good thing."

"Thanks." He settled back against the seat.

As they drove, she contemplated bringing up her mother. There was no point in putting it off. She unnecessarily adjusted the rearview mirror. "So I want to talk to you about something."

He practically jumped out of his seat. "My grades are fine! Coach said I can play next game! What's the problem?"

What was that phrase about kids not knowing that another world existed outside their own? She had been thinking about how best to present the idea that she wanted the boys to meet Doralee, but she hadn't come up with an elegant way to launch the topic. Jordan was loyal to his granddad and would probably take his side. At least in the car, Jordan had to listen, even if he didn't respond.

"That's not what I'm talking about. I wanted to talk about something going on with me."

"Oh, okay." He pulled out his phone and began to stick his in his earbuds.

She laid a hand on his arm. "Can you wait until after I talk to you?"

Even though his face was turned away, she could feel his eye roll.

"Okay, what?" He sighed with a level of annoyance only a teenager could generate.

"From our conversation the other night, you might have figured out that my mother has come back to Norwalk."

"Well, that's nice, I guess."

"I'd like you and Javier to meet her."

He was quiet. The temperature in the van felt as if it had dropped twenty degrees.

"I'm thinking about asking her over for dinner."

Without missing a beat, he said, "Better talk to Grandpa first."

"I didn't say I'd asked her. I said I was considering it."

Having her mother in her home felt right, even if it caused her dad grief. Holding on to his love for Doralee was how he'd dealt with her departure. Frankie had dealt with it by holding on to her loss and rage. Now, a new pathway had opened. Figuring out how to navigate between her kids and her mother was the latest in the tightrope walk of being a parent and being a child.

"I wanted to ... tell you a little about what she's like."

"I already know she left you and Grandpa when you were a little kid. She's a drunk, ain't she?"

"Isn't she," Frankie corrected. "And, yes, she's an alcoholic."

"Okay." He put his earbuds back in the case, signaling a willingness to talk.

"She's not healthy. When you meet her, you might not like her."

"I already don't like her," he said, shuffling his big feet against the floorboard of the van, trying to find room for his too-long legs.

"Why? You haven't even met her. You don't know a thing about her. Don't be judgmental."

"All I need to know is she left you. That's cold."

She could hardly argue with that.

Then he said, "So, like, why'd she leave you with Grandpa?"

Frankie thought she knew why, but what if she was wrong? She didn't want to put him off Doralee before he met her, but she wouldn't lie. "Because she was an alcoholic."

"And you still want to see her?"

"Yes. It's been a long time. I'd like to get to know her, and, like I said, I want her to meet you guys."

"You forgive her for leaving you?"

"I'm ... working on it, but I still want to get to know her."

He shrugged his sawhorse shoulders. "Why?"

"She's my mother. I'm going to ask her to church on Sunday."

"What?" He screwed up his face like an actor in a sitcom. "You want all our friends to see your al-co-hol-ic mother?"

"Well, I don't think she'll show up drunk." Doralee showing up drunk hadn't occurred to Frankie. Now that he'd suggested it, the possibility of disaster loomed. She shoved the worry aside. "Even if she does show up smashed, it's St. Paul's. They take everybody."

He shook his head with an air of dubiousness. "Okay, but you might be embarrassed."

"Maybe. But I'd like to try to include her in our family."

He shook his head. "Look, don't you think that's kinda dis-loyal to Grandpa? When he was the one who raised you?"

God truly gave you children to torture you.

"How come you want to hang out with some random woman who left you?" His voice rose with revulsion. "We're your family. Can't you just leave us out of it?"

"Because you and Javier are the best parts of me, and I want her to see that."

He ducked his chin and glanced away.

Her heart turned to mush. It pleased her to be able to move him with a declaration of her love.

"Do you even remember her from before she left?" he asked.

They stopped at a light, and she didn't have to think too hard. "Yes, I remember lots of things. One thing was she used to make the best seafood gumbo. She's from Louisiana, and she grew up making it, and I used to help her." It all came back to her, clear as though she were standing on the stool. "We'd put in andouille sausage, crawfish, oysters, chopped onions, diced tomatoes, and okra—"

"Okra? What's that?"

"A vegetable."

He made a gargling sound in his throat. "Sounds nasty."

"It was fun cooking with her. I felt soooo grown up."

"Didn't make you a good cook, though," he teased.

She laughed. "Yeah, too bad about that."

She pulled into the driveway and shut the engine off. Now that he was listening, she was desperate not to let him leap out of the van and flee to his bedroom. She turned in her seat to watch his beloved face and asked, "What's your most important memory from when you were a kid?"

He gawked at her. "Mooom, how embarrassing!"

"C'mon," she cajoled.

"Uhhh." He rolled his eyes again.

"C'mon. Just one."

He let out a long noisy sigh. "Okay, but then we're going in."

"Deal."

"How you used to get me up every morning at six to practice reading."

He gave her one of the rare smiles she craved. She would forever take comfort that teaching him to read was one thing she'd done right. If she could keep him safe until he reached manhood, he would turn out all right, despite her mothering.

"I was behind the other kids. The teachers were giving up on me." He shook his head. "But you would not give up. You just kept at me an' kept at me, an' kept at me. Used to drive me crazy! All I wanted to do was sleep."

This conversation was like winning the mom lottery. "I had to get you up when your brain wasn't worn out already."

"That's what you used to say." His voice was quiet and reverent, his words traversing the emotions kids wanted to avoid in front of their parents at all costs. "Lots of moms—maybe even my birth mom—might have given up on me, but you didn't." He paused, his Adam's apple bobbing. "You believed in me. Said all I needed was practice. I believed what you said. Now when something's hard, I just remember how hard you worked teaching me to read, and then I try harder, too."

She reached out to hug him again, and he leaned into her this time. Her heart felt full as the first day they'd put him in her arms. She loved him in a way that made her ache right down to her toes.

Doralee had missed those motherly feelings of joy and pride. Frankie wanted to give her a taste of what it felt like, and maybe, that emotional connection might save her.

If it wasn't already too late.

CHAPTER 23

To a father growing old, nothing is dearer than a daughter.

Euripedes

"So you see her?" Dad asked. He folded a clean kitchen hand towel and laid it aside.

Her. "She has a name, you know." She handed him a tea towel. "Yes."

He kept folding clothes.

The kitchen, still warm from the heat of the oven, smelled of lasagna and garlic bread and a touch of suspicion. Wordlessly, her dad pointed to a blue towel in the jumble of her clothes basket.

She dug it out and handed it to him to fold. "Did Javier do his reading?"

Her dad grunted an assent.

The air crackled with his unasked questions, and she wasn't sure which would be worse for him: telling him she had spoken to Doralee or not. He was doing a shitty job pretending not to care. She folded two more bath towels and let him stew.

She said, "I invited Doralee to church."

He froze, the pillowcase he held by the corners dangling in midair. "You what?"

His face looked like she had told him she had given birth to a Martian. "Church. You know, St. Paul's?"

"I know what you mean. I don't know why."

"You don't have to come." Suggesting he skip church made her feel guilty like she'd kicked him out. *St. Paul's takes everybody except you for this one Sunday.* He liked going, seeing all his old codger friends, eating stuff at coffee hour that she'd never let him eat at home.

"'Course, I won't come."

As if he'd catch the plague sitting in the same room with his wife—who wasn't technically his *ex*-wife—because, as far as Frankie knew, they'd never actually divorced. "Besides, I don't even know if she'll come."

He ransacked his clothes basket, letting a pair of underwear fall to the floor.

She bent to pick it up.

He said, "She won't come. But just so I know when not to come, when'd you invite her for?"

"This Sunday."

He made a big show of scrunching up his nose. "The kids sing this week and Jordan's crucifer. Did you think about how they'd feel before you invited her?"

"Yes, I did. I thought it would be nice for her to see Javier sing. See Jordan carry the cross."

He picked up a stack of kitchen towels and placed them in a drawer, smacking the drawer shut with the side of his foot.

Frankie wasn't the only one that had forgiving to do.

She understood if he was a little jealous; she had been his

cherished little girl, his flailing teenage daughter, his business partner. They argued about the boys and got on each other's nerves. They were sort of a couple. If she had a partner, she might be folding clothes at ten o'clock on a Thursday night with him instead of her father. The thought made her lonely and momentarily sorry that the only men in her life were her sons and her dad.

Since his heart attack, their roles had done a 180. She'd become more of the parent, keeping an eye on his cholesterol and blood pressure, ensuring he renewed his medications, and getting him to take care of his bum knee. Inviting Doralee to church was like switching allegiances late in the game. He had a right to be hurt.

She was flying blind on this: neither being a parent nor having older parents came with instructions.

"And what if she's drunk?" He made a growly noise in his throat. "What am I saying? She *will* be drunk."

"Evelyn's keeping her sober." It wasn't technically a lie to leave out the part about the stolen Stoli or that she had seen Doralee twice already.

He said, "If I couldn't keep her off the sauce, Evelyn can't."

The sound of the smashing bottle falling out of Doralee's purse rang in Frankie's ears.

"Okay, maybe she's still drinking," she conceded. "But maybe she's learned to manage it with Evelyn's help. Maybe she drinks less, maybe only at certain times."

With a snap, he flapped out Javier's pajama bottoms. He folded them so there wasn't a single wrinkle to rub against Javier's skin. He did the same with the shirt. "What do you expect from her?"

Since she had first met Doralee, Frankie had lowered her expectations from TV fantasy reunion to a notch above less-than-hostile: a two-dollar scratch-off. She figured she was giving herself lots of chances to love her mother and forgive her.

"What do you expect to happen?" he repeated.

"You and I are the only family the boys have. I want them to meet her. Meeting the boys might give her the boost she needs to go to AA."

If Doralee would just meet her boys and act for a few minutes like a grandmother, it would be easier to love her mother a tiny bit. To forgive her. But forgiving was a repeat exercise, and Frankie was having trouble with the warmup.

"Don't kid yourself. This isn't about them; this is about you."

She frowned and smacked a pair of socks into his clothes basket.

One of the downsides of living with him all these years was his uncanny ability to nail her ass to the wall when she was deluding herself. It was infuriating and made her feel ten years old again. A wire flashed across her brain that meant she was about to lose her temper.

"It's about all of us." She clipped her words.

"Not about me, it's not." He moved the socks to a different basket.

She moved them back.

He said, "I don't need nothing from her. Take her to church, and you best be ready to answer a lot of questions about your White mother."

"My best friends already know I'm bi-racial. I don't give a shit about the rest." He hated it when she cursed, so she'd thrown it in. A dart against his resistance.

"Don't mean they won't ask," he shot back. "And if she's drunk? What you gonna say then?"

"Look," she said, imitating Jordan's exasperated tone. "She might not even come. Raising me in church was about the one good thing she did for me. I thought she might like to go back and see it."

"And don't try bringing her here either," he snapped.

He still refused to use Doralee's name as though it would turn him into a block of salt. Maybe after Doralee attended church, Frankie could broach the subject of a family meal with him.

"That's why I choose St. Paul's. It's a neutral place."

She handed him a pair of Jordan's shorts to put in the basket with the boys' clothes. He refolded them and added them to the basket.

He laughed, and the hard grooves of his face softened. "I remember how she made us go and sit in the front row every Sunday. Dressed us up all Sunday pretty and kept her nose in the air, walking past all those old White biddies. I can't imagine what all those people thought, her bringing in her Black husband and little brown kid, parading down the aisle to the front row and sitting there."

"I remember, but I didn't notice the White-Black thing." She rested her hands on the edge of the basket. "She had balls. It's like she was the first one to make sure people who were different belonged at St. Paul's."

At this, his hands paused working, and finally, a moment of silent agreement passed between them.

She folded another of Jordan's tee shirts. "Things have changed. The boys can feel like they're surrounded by love, not like someone's going to firebomb the place."

"I'm done trying to protect you. You're determined to get disappointed, but it's those boys I'm talking about. You invite her, she'll find some way to hurt my boys."

His boys. Lord, he was a good man, a good father, and a good grandfather.

He hefted a half-full basket of clothes, and she watched his angry back as he stomped off down the hall toward the boys' bedrooms.

All her life, she had run from anything that might hurt her. She kept her circle of friends tight and backed away from men who might hurt her. This time with Doralee, she wasn't going to run away from the possibility of being hurt. Trying to love and forgive meant Frankie might get hurt, but she didn't think Doralee could cause any catastrophe Frankie couldn't manage.

She'd just hit it with a bigger hammer.

CHAPTER 24

To heal a wound, you must stop scratching it.

Paulo Coelho

At St. Paul's on Sunday morning, Frankie introduced Doralee to the Marriage Survivors Club. They were all gracious and kind, as she knew they would be, but Doralee's expression remained flat. Frankie had checked with Evelyn to make sure Doralee was sober. But that didn't guarantee a smooth ride.

They sat in the same pew they'd occupied when Frankie was a child and where she and her dad sat now. Doralee's hands trembled as she crushed her sad, black purse to her lap and glanced around nervously. Frankie had checked the weight of that purse to make sure Doralee wasn't smuggling a bottle.

A memory Frankie hadn't recalled for a long time shot into her brain. When Frankie was young, sometimes Doralee took her purse to the Angel Chapel for a few minutes and came back stinking of alcohol. Frankie realized that this was why, when her boys were little and got fussy, she chose, instead, to take them outside until they calmed down. It reminded her that Doralee had gone into the Chapel to drink.

She rolled her neck from side to side, trying to ease the tension. Everything had gone okay up until now, but at the procession for the Gospel, Doralee began to wriggle around. She scratched a rash on her arms and neck. Her cane banged against the pew. Her ratty raincoat made an annoying *zhu zhu zhu* sound with every movement. It was like sitting next to a caffeinated, sugared-up three-year-old.

"*Shhh*," Frankie hissed and put her finger to her lips.

Doralee didn't acknowledge her but flapped her leaflet at the incense blowing their way.

Zhu zhu zhu.

Without turning to look, Frankie took hold of Doralee's wrist, gently encircling it with her thumb and forefinger to still her. The slender boniness of Doralee's wrist shocked her as it registered that she was touching her mother's skin. Since their reunion, Frankie had only ever touched Doralee's elbow through her coat. Daughters probably touched their mothers all the time, hugging, kissing cheeks, walking arm in arm, rubbing a sore neck, putting a comforting arm around a shoulder. With Doralee, Frankie felt as though she was overstepping, manhandling a stranger. But Doralee looked up at Frankie and stopped her squirming.

Wat Crabtree lit into the hymn like his feet and fingers were on fire. At the sound of the organ, Doralee jumped and crooned, "Ooo!"

Because they had spent their lives apart, Frankie didn't know which of Doralee's reactions were happy or unhappy. At least she didn't make any more noise.

The organ was joyfully deafening, making the slate floor vibrate beneath Frankie's feet. She hoped Doralee would feel the love that suffused the air of St. Paul's. Frankie was trying hard, but all she felt was wary vigilance. Her love for Doralee was as precarious as a rotten porch step or crumbling bricks waiting to plunge Frankie into the abyss of smashed hope.

She closed her eyes and prayed to be more loving and compassionate. *God, it's too bad you can't beam me down an instant transformation.*

The sweet singing voices of the choristers flew to the rafters. Frankie teared up to see Javier singing his heart out. Doralee sang off-key, out of rhythm, and louder than anyone else in a voice ravaged by booze. She still remembered the hymns, and Frankie was silently pleased that they shared this moment of joy unburdened by the past.

They settled into their pew, and Carol Baxter, the church's most beloved kook, tottered in late. She sat exactly in front of Doralee.

As usual, Carol carried her dead, stuffed Lhasa Apso, Winnie. On her head was a St. Patrick's Day hat with a two-foot-long peacock feather that shivered whenever she moved her head.

Doralee leaned from side to side, trying to see around the hat. She looked at Frankie, pointed at Carol's hat, and sneered.

Please, please, please be nice.

Carol had the happy, harmless kind of crazy Frankie could deal with. If Doralee came to church regularly, the congregation would get used to her brand of alcoholic weirdness.

St. Paul's takes everybody.

Father Gabriel began the sermon. Like a shepherd speaking to his beloved lambs, his comforting wisdom floated across the congregation. Frankie tried hard to concentrate, but Carol kept nodding in agreement with Father Gabriel, making the feather tremble. In turn, that made Doralee chuckle and further distracted Frankie.

Out of the corner of her eye, before she could stop her, Frankie saw the hook of her mother's cane rise and knock Carol's hat from her head.

"Oh!" Carol squealed.

Gasps and guffaws rose in unison.

Father Gabriel glanced in Carol's direction, pausing a moment before continuing, but it didn't matter. No one was paying attention to him. Frankie felt the stares drilling into the back of her head. Blood rushed to her face, and she stifled a groan. She wanted to sink to the floor and crawl on her hands and knees down the side aisle and out the rear door.

Carol turned, and she was laughing instead of the fury Frankie expected.

"That hat is getting on my nerves," Doralee said, spewing her rotten-potato breath over everyone.

Carol stuck her tongue out.

Doralee reciprocated.

Carol twiddled her thumbs in her ears.

Doralee did the same before Frankie could grab her wrist again.

Someone laughed. Someone else muttered. From his seat in the Chancel at the front of the church, Javier stared at Doralee. Embarrassed horror was writ large on his face. Jordan, also in the Chancel, covered his mouth with his hands, mocking I-told-you-so laughter in his eyes.

Carol crossed her eyes.

Doralee thumbed her nose.

Frankie jacked out of her seat, took the sleeve of Doralee's wretched raincoat, and half-dragged her out of the pew to the Angel Chapel. Frankie felt pity for her swell across the congregation.

Yanking open the door, Frankie guided Doralee inside and

shut it behind them. "Can you cool it, please, just 'til the end of the service?"

"Where's my purse?" Doralee said in a wide-eyed, whiny panic. She scuffled around the cozy room, rooting through the wicker baskets of toys and books. "Where's my purse? Have to have my purse."

"It's out there." Frankie pointed to the sanctuary, her temper barely under control. "It's not going anywhere."

There was something pathetic about her jerky, frantic movements that trumped Frankie's irritated shame. Doralee couldn't act like a normal person because she wasn't normal. She had her own reality; St. Paul's and Frankie weren't part of it.

Inviting her mother to church had been a terrible idea, but she wanted Doralee to be part of her family, to feel included and loved. The only way to get answers from Doralee was to spend time with her, to move closer to her. But it was proving impossible. She made Frankie feel needy, weak, and helpless. Trying to have a relationship with Doralee was like trying to hammer water.

"Wait here. I'll get your stupid purse," Frankie spluttered. She returned to the sanctuary, avoided meeting anyone's gaze, and retrieved Doralee's battered purse from the pew. Frankie checked again for booze or pills, but there was only a cheap flip-phone, some foil wrappers, a tangle of yarn, and a package of tissues.

Frankie handed it to Doralee.

She clutched it to her chest. "Thank you, thank you. I got to have my purse. Got to have it."

Her relief at getting her purse back was like seeing a child with a beloved teddy bear safely returned. Instead of feeling loving, Frankie felt pity, a failing for which she wanted to kick herself.

Doralee looked around in confusion. "Why'd we come in here? Where are we?"

Frankie's stomach twisted into knots. Alcoholics forgot things, lost track of time, and had blackouts, but Doralee's symptoms seemed beyond that. Today's debacle only confirmed Frankie's suspicion that Doralee was extremely sick.

Trying to keep her panic at bay, Frankie focused on the brilliant colors of the stained-glass window. The morning was spoiled. Javier and Jordan's teenage scorn was likely at full throttle. They would refuse to meet Doralee now. Frankie should have listened to her dad when he warned her that things would go sideways at church.

"We're in here to give you a chance to calm down," Frankie said. "You were too noisy, and it seemed you needed a couple minutes to get yourself together."

Doralee narrowed her eyes and lifted her chin. She tucked her purse under her arm football-style. "If that's how you feel, I'd best go home."

She was an old, broken woman, shriveled and befuddled. Frankie struggled to get her heart to bend toward love, understanding, and forgiveness, but it was like trying to bend an I-beam with her bare hands.

"What? No, no, I didn't ... I didn't mean for you to go home. Let's just take a breather." Frankie motioned to the rocking chairs. "Let's sit a minute, okay? I know the boys are looking forward to meeting you at coffee hour afterward."

But it was too late. Doralee pulled out her cell phone, flipped it open, and pushed a button. "Come get me." Pause. "No. I'm *done*," she growled.

At least she remembered to call Evelyn.

"But the boys—" Frankie lifted one hand in a helpless gesture.

Frankie watched Doralee disappear through the swinging

doors, the sound of her stumping cane echoing through the church.

Frankie dropped into one of the rocking chairs and held her head in her hands. The entire congregation had witnessed the episode. She might as well have broadcast the whole catastrophe on fucking Facebook.

The door to the Angel Chapel swung open, and Katelin Riddle, carrying her two-month-old daughter, Sophie, stepped in. Frankie didn't raise her head but snuck a glance out of the corner of her eye.

Katelin took the other rocker, unbuttoned her blouse, and popped her breast into Sophie's mouth. "Ahhh," she sighed. "I thought my boobs were going to explode."

Frankie laughed. As Sophie nursed, she made tiny suckling noises and satisfied grunts. Katelin gazed down and traced Sophie's cheek with a single finger. Their shared tenderness made Frankie's heart hurt.

That had been her and Doralee once, in love with one another, the only way a mother and child can be. Dependent and frightfully intertwined, sharing the smells of infancy and childhood, living skin-to-skin, and the imperturbable intimacy of sleeping beside one another.

The idyll of infancy was part of the natural order of things. Frankie imagined that when her boys grew up, they would remain connected to her by an invisible, elastic membrane that stretched and contracted to allow love and space.

Between Doralee and Frankie, there seemed to be only an aching, empty space, no matter what she tried.

CHAPTER 25

From On Friendship

And a youth said, Speak to us of Friendship.
And he answered, saying:
Your friend is your needs answered.

Kahlil Gibran

Frankie planned to wait until the church emptied and she could sneak out, but the Marriage Survivors Club cornered her in the Angel Chapel.

"Well, that was a shit show," Bianca blurted, and Flicka elbowed her.

"She's right," Frankie admitted from her place in the rocking chair. "I guess I shouldn't have brought her."

"Your heart was in the right place," Olivia said.

"We all want people we care about to experience St. Paul's, but maybe it was too long for her to sit," Carolina offered.

"I wanted her to meet the boys," Frankie said.

Bianca said, "Don't worry about them. They're downstairs plowing through coffee hour goodies right now.""

Olivia gave Frankie a hug. "Are you all right?"

"Of course," Frankie said. "I can take a hit."

"Who do you think you are, Wonder Woman?" Bianca asked.

"You don't have to *take a hit*, as you say," Hélène said gently. "It's okay to feel hurt. Anyone would feel devastated if they went through that."

The sun shining through the stained-glass window threw a rainbow of light on the floor. Laughter and chatter echoed in the sanctuary as it emptied of people.

They were probably talking about Doralee.

Frankie searched for words to describe how she felt. "She's so ... different than what I hoped. I wanted to get to know her, but she's ..."

"An alcoholic," Flicka said with the certainty of firsthand experience.

Carolina said, "Church service might be overwhelming for her. Maybe there are other things you can do with her. Lunch or a manicure."

"A drive along Calf's Pasture Beach," Hélène suggested.

"Or watch a basketball game on TV," Bianca said, provoking laughter from the others.

When they'd stopped laughing, Hélène said, "Maybe you could take her over and show her the house. Describe what we want to do with it and how you've had a dream to do this."

"That's a great idea," Frankie said.

"You know we'll do whatever we can to help you," Carolina said. "A meal, a ride, anything. All you need to do is ask. And, of course, we'll pray for her, won't we?" She glanced at the others, who all nodded.

Carolina was surely a saint in civilian clothes.

"Some of my favorite memories of her are when she brought me to church here when I was a kid. It was stupid, but I guess I was trying to replicate those memories," Frankie confessed.

"I can understand how you might want to do that," Hélène said.

Flicka folded her arms and leaned her hip against the little altar with a statue of the Madonna and Child. "Mothers are never everything their kids need or want. There's no such thing as a good mother, just a good-enough mother. You're a mom; you should know that. Cut yourself some slack."

It brought tears to Frankie's eyes because that was the kindest, warmest, most un-Flicka-like thing she'd ever said.

"Says the woman who would eat her young," Bianca said.

This time, Olivia elbowed her.

CHAPTER 26

I know nothing with any certainty, but the sight of the stars makes me want to dream.

Vincent Van Gogh

Cam picked up his phone, looked at Frankie Carter's phone number, set it down, picked it up, and set it back on the seat beside him. He was parked in front of 61 East Avenue, sitting in his car, trying to imagine three stories of luxury condos with a sign marked *Sold Out*. But all he could see was Frankie's face crushed by the loss.

He could hear his father pontificating, "That's business. Someone wins, and someone loses."

In this case, Cam was sorry that Frankie Carter had lost. It would have been more satisfying to him if there had been some scenario in which they both could have won.

Cam needed this development. Simpson and Sons needed it. And his ex-wife needed her final alimony payout, which was already six months late. One call from her to her lawyer and Cam would be toast. The quicker he got the project underway, the better. All he was waiting on was his zoning approval, which he expected any day now. He just had to hang on until he got his letter, then the loan would get approved. The interest rate might be higher since he'd borrowed against his condo, but he could still save the company, if not his ass.

He considered offering her the contract to install the kitchens to soften the blow. He couldn't afford the financial loss, but maybe the church could buy one of the condo units before they went on the market. But he was pretty confident that would be beyond the church's budget.

Frankie had seemed so shy when she invited him to the fundraising gala disguised as an arm twisting. He would have turned them down flat if anyone besides her had invited him. He was actually looking forward to going with her, dancing with her, seeing her eyes light up with something besides fury. He'd dated lots of women, but never anyone with as much heart and passion disguised as hard-ass determination.

He picked up his phone and stared at her number again. "What the hell," he said aloud to himself. "Since when did you back away from a battle?"

He hit dial. Frankie answered on the third ring. In the background, he heard hammering, the whine of a saw.

"Hi, Frankie, Cam Simpson here."

"Well, hey."

Her velvety, sensuous voice made him press the phone closer to his ear as if he could pour the sound into himself.

"I, uh, I wanted to talk to you about the dance."

"You haven't changed your mind, have you?" she asked anxiously.

A door closed, and the racket of the job site quit.

"No, no. Were you hoping I would?"

He heard a smile in her voice when she said, "No, I was just afraid you had."

"Actually, I wondered if you would like me to pick you up?" he winced, prepared for a smackdown. It had been a while, but still, a guy never got used to that.

"Oh, that's a nice offer," she said. "But I have to get there early to help with any last-minute details."

"Are you sure?" He drummed his fingers on the steering wheel.

"Yes, thanks."

"I don't recall what time you said I should be there."

"Six-thirty should be fine."

"Great." He didn't want to hang up. "You'll be happy to know I can still fit into my tux." He experienced a little triumph at her laughter.

She said, "I'm glad you called though, because I, um, I wanted to ask you a favor."

He wanted to reassure her that she needn't be so tentative. "How can I help?"

"I wanted to stop at 61 and show someone the property."

She didn't mention who, and he hoped it wasn't some investor with deep pockets she planned to sic on him. He wanted to develop the property on his own, but a big buyout would be tempting. Except that would mean he might not see Frankie the Amazon again.

"No problem. I could meet you there and open it up if you'd like to see the inside," he suggested, hoping for an excuse to see her before the dance. He was also curious as to why she wanted to see the property. Maybe she had an attachment to the place beyond wanting it for the church.

"That's not necessary, but thanks."

Being disappointed was a bit silly. He wished he knew

exactly when she planned on dropping by so he could accidentally drop by at the same time.

"Okay, then," he said reluctantly. "I'll let you get back to work, and I'll see you at the dance."

He hadn't looked forward to anything so much in a very long time.

CHAPTER 27

Let us Build a House, Hymn No. 301

Let us build a house
where prophets speak
and words are strong and true,
where all God's children dare to seek
to dream God's reign anew.

Marty Haugen

Frankie's van jounced over the potholes in the driveway of 61 East Avenue. She parked at the end of the driveway so she and Doralee could see the entire front of the house.

A giant sign in big, red letters was planted in the front yard: DEMOLITION.

Frankie's heart dropped to her feet. The only way she might be able to stop the destruction was by dancing with the man who'd stolen her dream.

A feeling of impending doom shrouded the house as though she knew Cam was coming with the wrecking ball. There was a sense of resignation to the third-floor dormers, to the blind windows, to the weathered front door, to the hammocking front porch steps. Wind worried at the loose corner of a shutter. Trash whipped about the lawn. The big double front window, where Frankie had waited for Doralee, glared out at them.

An ancient lilac bush stood at the corner of the house, its branches twisted and contorted. When she was little, she and Doralee had cut blossoms from that bush and carried them home. Their fragrance had filled the entire house with heady sweetness.

Doralee leaned forward in her seat and scowled out the window at the house. "This place looks like a dump."

Frankie ignored the tightness at the back of her throat. She was trying hard to be loving and forgiving, but her heart was the size and hardness of a walnut.

"Don't you recognize the house?" Frankie asked.

Doralee pursed her cracked lips and shook her head.

Frankie was stunned that she didn't remember. They had gone here three days a week for a whole school year.

Frankie watched Doralee for signs of recollection, but her face, as always, was a blank expression. "This the old Catrambone house. It's where you used to work when I was little."

"I did?"

"Yes. Do you remember Bettina Catrambone?"

"Not really. What the hell we doin' here?" Doralee shivered and pulled her coat tighter around her.

She was like a small, yappy dog that might bite at the slightest provocation, and Frankie's bullshit meter wasn't cali-brated as to what might set her off. It was impossible to tell if she was afraid, confused, or flat-out lying.

A cold gust of wind slithered into the van through some

unseen crack. The spot where Frankie had broken her arm when she was a baby ached.

"It came up for sale at a foreclosure auction, and the church tried to buy it. I'm head of the committee to buy the house, but unfortunately, we got outbid."

"Good." Doralee spat the word out.

"Why do you say that?" Frankie turned her face away to hide her hurt. She thought Doralee would be proud of her for doing something important for St. Paul's.

"Looks like an ol' wreck to me. Why would anybody want this pile?"

Doralee's voice, like the rasp of a hacksaw on an iron pipe, set Frankie back. "The church wants to renovate it for an LGBTQ-plus youth shelter."

"Why?"

"To create a warm, safe place for kids who are different. I think it has a lot of life left in it."

"I don't remember it, but it must be important, or you wouldn't have brought me," Doralee mumbled.

Frankie had always felt that at one time, their past had been two pieces of rope, twined together, which later unwound. She hoped to somehow bind them together again. The disconnect between their memories yanked Frankie's mind into a knot. How could they have a future as mother and daughter if Doralee couldn't even remember what little past they shared?

Frankie tried again to jog Doralee's memory. "For a year or so, you worked for the Catrambones, babysitting, and house-keeping. After school, you would meet Bettina and me—we were second graders—at the bus stop and walk us home. We'd play together while you cleaned house, folded clothes, or got their dinner ready."

Doralee frowned, and Frankie saw her memory starting up like a cold engine.

"I guess I sorta remember. Little blond girl, wasn't she? Kinda whiney."

"That was Bettina." Frankie laughed, relieved. She didn't want to shove the past into Doralee's face like a serving of crow pie, but skirting the truth wouldn't make it easier for either of them. Best to get it out there and be prepared for the two-dollar scratch-off. "You drank while you worked there. They didn't know, but I did."

A wet, gritty silence filled the van, and Frankie was afraid she'd pushed too far, too hard.

"Oh, that. Thought you were going to say I burnt the place down or something." She laughed, making her attempt at a joke hurtful.

Hurt seared the front of Frankie's throat. A shower of sparks leaped in her brain. She was helpless against the words escaping from her mouth. "Don't you think drinking was a little irresponsible when you had two children in your care? Don't you think something terrible could have happened?"

Doralee waited a beat. "But it didn't. And you're fine."

The rest of her life, Frankie would never forget the lethality of her own words, the feeling of white rage racing along the path of her thoughts, fire headed for a keg of dynamite. She would remember the contorting of her face, the slapped shock on Doralee's face. And she would feel a mixture of guilt and shame, relief and outrage, every time she recalled it.

"I'm *not* fine! You left me there and never came back. You left me because you drank. Because you were an alcoholic. You *are* an alcoholic."

Doralee's face went slack, and her jaw dropped. Her lower lip trembled. She yanked the door handle making a *thwack-thwack-thwack*, metallic sound with each pull. The auto-lock feature—which kept Javier safe from jumping out at stoplights when he was mad—was engaged, and she couldn't get out.

"I"—*yank, yank, yank*—"I couldn't help it. I couldn't—nobody helped me." She grabbed her pathetic purse and held it against her chest like a shield.

Frankie grabbed the bag and felt for a bottle, but it was empty. She shoved it back at Doralee who clutched it to herself again.

Frankie's guilt switched on. When she was little, she had thought it was her fault that Doralee kept drinking. She thought that if she told her dad, the Catrambones, her teachers, her priest, anybody, maybe Doralee would have stopped. Now, Frankie knew that nothing she did as a child could have changed Doralee's trajectory over the edge.

"Nobody could help you," Frankie said, unable to look at Doralee. "People have to want to quit, but you never wanted to."

Doralee was quiet. Her hands moved in their rhythmic tremor, her head bobbing.

Frankie leaned forward and looped her arms over the steering wheel. She stared out at the last place she had seen Doralee when she was eight. An old loneliness dug fingers into her heart.

"You promised Dad that you wouldn't drink at home, but you drank here."

Doralee blinked as though Frankie's logic eluded her.

Frankie couldn't admit to Doralee how devastating it had been not to have a mother. How, sometimes, she still felt the effects of abandonment. Frankie couldn't look at Doralee. She listened to Doralee's labored breathing, waiting for some new revelation that might change the dark past into a sunny future. "Why did you leave when you did? I was just a little kid."

"Vic kicked me out."

Frankie's world toppled sideways in slow motion, twisting, creaking like a fifteen-story metal crane falling in a windstorm, the crashing of metal against pavement, a screeching, monumental collapse. Her dad's story was that Doralee left because she chose booze over them.

"I had it under control, but he kicked me out. I went to Lafayette, and I got sober. I told him I wanted to come back, but he said no. Everything I had to live for—you, Vic—was gone. I didn't have no more reason to quit."

Frankie could barely push the words out. "How long were you sober?"

"Oh, I don't remember. And as for my drinking here, I would never put you in danger. You know that, don't you?" Doralee said, her voice cloying and simpering.

Doralee was like an unpredictable stranger, and her attitude disgusted Frankie. The number of times Doralee had put her in danger was beyond counting.

"If Vic had given me one more chance, I could have stayed sober, but on my own ..." Doralee trailed off. "If I'da had you to live for, I coulda stayed off the sauce."

Inside, Frankie felt an unholy fire roaring against her dad. She loved him and had absorbed every ounce of his wisdom. He had raised her on his own, taught her not to lie, to drive, to brace a sagging floor joist, and how to raise safe, young black men.

And he had lied to her.

CHAPTER 28

Good fathers not only tell us how to live, they show us.

Mark Twain

In the kitchen, Frankie's dad and Javier were sitting at the kitchen table. Lying under the table, Beasley rested his wise head on Javier's foot. Javier bent over his book, pencil gripped in his stubby fingers, his tongue poking out of the corner of his mouth as he worked a math problem.

Dad stirred his coffee and squinted up at her. "What are you all het up about?"

Needing support, she leaned against the counter. "Dad, I need to talk to you."

Javier's head popped up. "We're not done yet."

"Please go to your room. I need to talk to Grandpa," she ordered.

"Can I play Xbox?" Javier asked.

"No, please go to your bedroom." She paced around the kitchen.

"But I want Xbox. I've done all my homework."

"Go. To. Your. Room."

Sensing the tension, Beasley rose and turned his condemning gaze on Frankie.

"But what about Xbox? Can I have it—"

"Now!"

Javier got up, pushed his chair in three times, and went to his room.

She stared at her dad. If Doralee had stayed, her relationship with her dad would have been entirely different. She might have married and moved out. He would never have taken her to the job sites, and she wouldn't have learned everything she did. She might have a different job. She had accepted so many things as inevitable, but his decision had shattered the possibilities.

He leaned his elbows on the kitchen table. "Say what you got to say."

She took a deep breath. "Doralee said you made her leave and told her never to come back."

"Huh!" he snorted, setting his coffee cup down with a *thunk*. "And you believed her?"

She waited, staring.

A muscle in his cheek twitched. "It's not that simple." He got up and rinsed his cup at the sink.

"So if that's not the story, what is?"

"That's old history. Why bring it up?" He turned to face her. One beefy hand rested on the counter, the other at his side, fingers flicking against his thumb like they did when he was nervous.

Those hands had taught her everything she knew. How to swing a hammer, to measure twice, cut once, to shim a window frame, to frame an addition, sheetrock, and tape walls, how to cost out a job, big or small, and not lose her shirt. He had lavished all his love on her, sparing nothing because he had no one else he wanted to love. It seemed disloyal and thankless to accuse him of lying. It wasn't as if Doralee was the most reliable source of information.

"You always said she left us because she was a drunk, but she said you made her leave. That she tried to come back when she was sober, but you wouldn't let her. Is that true?"

"Can't you leave it alone?" he said, his voice a pebbly growl.

"No, I can't. I want to know the truth."

The story of her mother abandoning her made her who she was, carved her edges, planed her surfaces, sanded away her self-confidence, and nailed her with doubts that she had been unworthy of love. Without that history, Frankie wasn't Frankie. But then, who was she?

"There is no one truth, Frankie. It's all true."

They locked angry gazes.

"Goddamn it!" He hit the counter with his fist. "I knew something like this would happen if she came back."

He slumped against the kitchen counter. "Yeeesss, it's true. I made her leave." He drew in a ragged breath. "I have to sit down for this one."

He trudged to the living room to his chair, his limping steps those of an old, old man. He eased into his Barcalounger, flipped up the footrest, and folded his hands over his paunch. She sat across from him on the sofa, grateful for the solidity of the hard floor beneath her feet since everything else in her life had suddenly become a tilt-a-whirl.

"She quit drinking when she was pregnant. She was so excited and happy after you were born." He smiled. "Those were our best years. But then she started up again when you were about two. She thought she was hiding it, but I knew." His eyes filled with misery. "I'd come home, you'd have a wet diaper, be hungry, screaming in your crib. The house would be a mess. She'd be passed out on the floor, drunk as a skunk."

He sounded like he was doing surgery on himself with a rusty hacksaw.

"There was never any food in the house because she was buying vodka with the grocery money. I begged her to go to AA." He bobbed his head from side to side as he recited. "She'd say she didn't have a problem, say she was going, say she could quit on her own, say she'd already quit, say she was drinking less, but it was all lies. I was stupid to believe her, but I didn't know what else to do. Nothing I did made a dent. I'd find bottles hidden around the house, and she always stank of booze, like it was her personal perfume, that vodka. It got worse and worse until she was hardly ever sober."

"But she might have gotten sober if you had given her another chance." Although she'd tried to keep it out, Frankie heard the accusation in her voice.

He gave her a sour look. "Do you have any idea how many chances I gave her? How many passes? How many times I scraped her off the kitchen floor?" He shook his head. "I don't doubt she tried to quit, but it had its hooks in her, and she couldn't quit. You know how you broke your arm when you were two and a half?"

"I fell down the stairs."

"Yeah, you fell down all right. But 'cause she'd been drinking and passed out. Best I could figure, you'd climbed up the stairs and then fell down. She hadn't even put you in the playpen!" He scrubbed his trembling chin with a beat-up, calloused hand.

Beasley ambled into the living room. He stared at her dad with his almost-human amber eyes and laid his head in his lap. He stroked the dog's head. A soft sob caught in his throat.

"Dad, it's okay, you don't have to—"

"No." He slapped the arm of the chair, and Beasley jumped. "You started this. Let's finish it once and for all. They had to operate and pin your arm to fix it. At the hospital, social services came sniffing around because they thought I did it." He glowered. "Black man's always first one to get accused. I took the rap. Told them she was away. That you climbed out of your crib when I put you down for a nap. I pretended I was a fool, like I didn't even know how to diaper you, and of course, they believed me. First, I was scared you might die in surgery." His voice was a hoarse, barely controlled whisper. "Then after, I was afraid social services would take you away from me." He squeezed his eyes shut, and a tear leaked down his cheek. "God, I thought I was going to lose you. I've never been so scared in my life."

Loving Doralee had torn him apart, jeopardized everything he cared about, cost him his dignity and nearly his daughter. He'd lived with this every day of his life, and yet, his love for Doralee had twisted him inside out.

"Didn't that scare her into sobering up?"

"For a while, then she'd start drinking again."

"Why did you finally tell her she had to leave?"

"'Cause of the day she let you and the Catrambone girl go home alone. Judge Catrambone was furious and rightly so. When I came to pick you up, he threatened to get me arrested."

"He did? How could he do that?"

"Because he was a judge, and I'm Black. That oughta be obvious. He was a powerful man, could get me thrown in jail on some trumped-up charge, and I'd never see you again." His voice broke, and it took him a minute to get himself under control. "He said I should have known not to let her alone with you girls. He was letting me off because his little girl liked to play with you." His jaw went rigid, and he spit the words like they were hot nails. "It was like he expected me to bow and scrape like some field nigger."

For him to say the n-word was like being smacked across the face with a frying pan. Once, when Jordan had used that word, her dad lifted him off his feet by his shirt front and shook him. "You never say that word again in my house!" Jordan never uttered it again.

Her throat ached with sorrow. "I'm sorry you had to go through that. How humiliating."

"Wasn't nothing new," he said, but his eyes glittered with tears. "She didn't come home 'til the next morning."

He was the kind of superhero no one ever wrote about; a man who defied the evil powers of the universe, leaped over life's challenges, and did anything he could for those he loved. He had been her rock all her life, and she'd never known about that humiliation or how broken his heart had always been. And he'd raised her as though she was a princess.

"I'd do it all over to protect you. Of course, she was fired. Catrambone said he was going to call the school so's they'd keep an eye on you, keep you safe." He pinched the bridge of his nose and paused a long minute.

She wanted to go to him and put her arm around his shoulder, but she felt betrayed in a way that upended her world. She had to find solid land again, find a way of believing.

"I'm sorry, Frankie. I knew I couldn't keep you safe, stay out of jail, and make a living. I had to do something. Next morning, after I dropped you off at school, she showed up at the job site. I didn't know where she'd been. She probably didn't, either. I bought her a one-way bus ticket, sent her back to Lafayette, and told her never to come back."

His thick eyebrows lowered, making his eyes even more bleak. "When you broke your arm, you were too little to talk, but now, at eight, you could. There was a chance you might accidentally tell someone about her drinking. The neighbors might tell, and I could lose you. I had to make a decision. It was her or you." He raised his eyes to her. "I chose you."

"Oh, Dad."

He seemed to have aged ten years in ten minutes. Raising a girl child alone was tough for any man, but for a dark-skinned Black man, raising a light-skinned little girl on his own deserved some kind of man prize, like a solid gold tire iron, a lifetime supply of beer, or eternal ESPN.

At this moment, she loved him with an intensity she thought she'd put away when she was a child. He had never betrayed his grief but made her feel safe, valued, and loved, doing everything he could to make up for the lack of a mother's love. He never showed an ounce of resentment about raising Frankie alone. His sacrifices, his pain, and his dedication to rearing her by himself humbled her. She hoped, one day, her own boys would feel the same supernova of the heart which happens when you realize how much you've been loved.

He wiped his face with the back of his hand. "I had to kick her out because I finally knew I'd already lost her. Maybe I never even had her. Maybe the vodka had her all along. At first, I thought she couldn't quit because she was weak or didn't love me enough, that she hadn't planned how hard it would be to marry a Black man and raise a Black daughter. Finally, I realized she was never going to kick it. The booze was stronger than our love for each other or her love for you."

His dark brown eyes were pools of sorrow, heartbreaking in their depth.

"It was too dangerous to have her around you. What if she was drunk and had a wreck with you in the car? I couldn't have lived with that, knowing I should have done something and didn't. I could live without her, but I couldn't live without you."

Frankie felt as though she'd been shaken. Everything inside

of her had fallen off the shelves, and she had to figure out how to reorganize the jumble that was herself. She pulled a tissue from a nearby box and swabbed at her face.

"What was it like when she was first gone? Were you … you know, relieved?"

"At first, I could hardly get up in the morning. Felt like I'd cut off my arm with a chainsaw." He shut his eyes for a few moments. "But it passed after a while because you needed me, and I needed you. You were all I had left of her. Kicking her out was the only way I knew to save you, to save us. I take no pride in saying it, but it was the right thing to do."

Frankie recalled the bottle of vodka falling from Doralee's purse, the shattering sound like an implosion in her mind. "She's still drinking."

He shook his head. "Can't believe it hasn't killed her yet."

"Why didn't you tell me you made her leave? Why did you let me think she abandoned us?"

He sounded as if he was wrenching every word from deep in his belly. "You had lost your mother. I lied to you because I didn't want you to hate me for kicking her out or hate her being a drunk." He threw up his hands, an expression of bewilderment on his face. "But what the hell did I know? I wasn't much more than a kid myself. I was doing the best I could."

"Oh, Dad," she said on a sigh.

"I didn't expect my love to make up for your losing your mother, and I didn't want to treat you like her replacement, either. But you were the last little bit I had of her. I couldn't lose your love, too." He gazed at her with the love only a father could bestow. "I'm sorry, Frankie. I really am. I never meant to hurt you or lie to you."

She nodded and then went to him, bent over, and hugged him. "You made the best decision you could."

It was what she hoped, for all her mistakes, shortcomings,

and bad decisions, what her boys would say to her one day. It was as though a book she had read over and over suddenly had a new ending. One full of possibilities for a new chapter. Doralee wasn't innocent, but she hadn't simply turned her back on Frankie and Dad. He had thrown Doralee out, but maybe Frankie could reel her back in.

CHAPTER 29

From: There was a Child Went Forth

The early lilacs became part of this child ...

Walt Whitman

Cam and Frankie stood on the lawn of 61 East Avenue beside the demolition sign. When he called her, he wasn't sure she would actually show up. She wore red work boots, a shirt with the name of her company, *Women's Work*, printed on it, jeans, and maroon lipstick that drew his eyes to her lips. A lot of women wouldn't look feminine in those clothes, but she looked every inch a woman with curves and swells all in the right places. She wouldn't have been sexier if she'd been in a designer dress.

"How's Javier?" he asked. "Is he coming back for basketball?"

Her eyes lit up.

The way to a woman's heart was through her kids.

She laughed. "Yes, he said he likes the snacks."

"Great. He seems like a good kid."

And Cam would get to see her again when she brought Javier back.

"He is, he is, but the autism makes him"—she blew a raspberry—"a challenge."

"I love watching the kids. Once they start playing with the ball and laughing, they just have fun."

"Thank you for doing it."

"I probably get more out of it than they do."

Her eyes tracked to the demolition sign. "It's really going to come down."

He wished he could say no, but he couldn't. "Yup. Did you get to show the house to the person you wanted to?"

He stepped closer. She smelled of something floral, light, and comforting.

"Yes," she said.

Before she turned away, he recognized the expression in her eyes. He'd seen it when he outbid her on the house: wounded but still fighting against a whitewater current.

He waited for her to say something, but she didn't. "I asked you to meet me here because I thought you might like to have a souvenir from the house. A piece of railing, the mantel, something you can keep. Something that would help you remember this house before it's demolished."

Her eyes were bright when she turned back to him.

"Thanks for asking," she said, her voice filled with longing. "What made you think of it?"

"I thought it might make it easier for you and the church to move on."

"That's a nice thought." She gave a sigh. The wistful look on her face softened the contours of her face. Made her even prettier. "But I'm not sure I'm ready to move on. I've been dreaming of her for a long, long time."

Her. She called the house *her*, which made him suspect Frankie had more interest in the house than as a shelter.

"I know. And I'm sorry." And he really was sorry. For the first time since he'd encountered Frankie at the auction, he had some sense of what losing the house was costing her.

"Nice of you to make the offer to give me a keepsake."

He said, "Trying to soften the blow."

She dug a toe into the dirt. "I appreciate that you thought of it."

He'd thought of it because he couldn't quit thinking of her. "Have you started looking for another house for the project yet?"

She shook her head, and her hundreds of tiny braids swayed from side to side. "Not yet. We just have to ... shift our mindset."

He assumed she meant her mindset. He jingled the keys in his pocket. "Want to go inside?"

She squinted up at the house. "Not today. I'd rather look around the outside."

He held out a hand. "Lead the way."

"I can go alone." Her eyes traveled up and down his figure. "You don't want to get burrs and ticks and stuff from walking through the weeds in your nice suit."

He was sorry he'd worn this suit, which he'd so carefully chosen this morning. Obviously, she wasn't impressed by a custom-made suit, and he wondered if impressing her was possible. "I'd like to keep you company."

After a minute, she nodded solemnly.

They waded through the knee-high weeds around the side of the house, and he nearly stumbled on a mound of dirt. He frowned, hoping someone hadn't dumped something toxic on his property. "Wonder what that is."

She chuckled. "Big groundhogs, maybe."

As they strolled, he caught her appraising the house in a yearning way.

"What do you see?" he asked.

Without missing a beat, she said, "Possibility. Hope. A home. A dream." She paused and turned to him. "But you see something different."

He understood the emotions she attached to the house. "I see the ground underneath. I see new homes. A future. Families. In a way, we see the same thing, just differently."

"Then how come you're happy, and I'm wrecked?"

"Sorry that circumstances aren't different."

Her smile was enigmatic when she said, "I'm hopeful that circumstances might still change."

They both laughed, and he was amazed at how her laugh gave him a jostling feeling in his chest. "Things won't change, but maybe we can reach a truce."

"I'm not ready for that yet," she said with a half-cocked smile.

"Tell me when you are."

She shielded her eyes from the sun and gazed at him questioningly.

"I was thinking, I don't have all my subs signed up yet. What if I hired Women's Work to do the kitchens in the condos?"

She winced.

Well, that wasn't the reaction he'd hoped for.

"We do high-end residential, and my crew's not big enough for a job this size. We'd hold you back." She tucked her palms into the back pockets of her jeans. "Besides ..." She sighed. "I'd only be reminded that I didn't get the house."

Before he could respond, she started around the house again, and he followed.

He was used to being able to give his ex-wife and girlfriends what they wanted with the flick of a credit card, but the one thing Frankie wanted, he couldn't give her.

When they reached the corner, she paused before an old, nearly leafless shrub with wrist-thick, leggy, lichen-spotted branches. The gnarled branches testified to the many winters, rainstorms, and harsh winds the shrub had withstood over the years. But on its smaller stems, green leaves were unfurling. With a nostalgic look in her eyes, she reached out and brushed the leaves as if the bush were an old friend. She knelt on the ground and pushed the weeds back from the base of the shrub.

"What are you looking for?" he asked.

"See these?" She pointed to some green sprouts about two feet high with the same glossy, oval leaves as the bush.

He braced his hands on his knees and looked closer. "What are those?"

"Lilac shoots." She stood and dusted off her palms. "I'll take some of those."

"Really? That's what you want?"

"Yes, I love lilacs. Have since I was a kid."

He was glad he'd finally found a way to reach past Frankie's hurt. He would have bought her a truckload of lilacs if he'd known this was the way to reach her. He couldn't understand why she had this effect on him, but he felt awake in Frankie Carter's presence. It was a sort of internal vibration he hadn't experienced since he was in his thirties. His divorce had left him bleeding emotionally and financially, and he hadn't dated since. Frankie made him feel hope and an eagerness to connect.

She, not the house, made him sense a whiff of possibility. The air grew still and hot. His eyes fixed on a spot at the base of her neck. He resisted the urge to stroke a single finger over the pulsing spot. "I'm looking forward to the dance."

"I'll just ..." She pointed to her van. "I'll get ... there's a ... need a shovel."

He watched her weave through the weeds, her hand open, palm skimming the tops. She returned with a much-used spade, dirt clinging to the end.

"I don't associate shovels with construction. You always carry one in your truck?"

She seemed flustered. "Oh, you know, sometimes you need to dig a hole for ... stuff."

He held his hand out. "Here, I can do it."

"I got it. You're wearing dress shoes."

He lifted one foot and looked at his stupid, expensive shoe. "It's no problem."

"No, really, I got it."

He laid a hand on the shovel handle and, with quiet insistence, said, "Please. Let me do this for you."

She blinked and let go of the shovel.

He plunged the shovel into the ground and levered up a couple of shoots.

She knelt and tenderly set aside each one.

After they had collected a half-dozen, she said, "That's good. I'll have no end of lilacs in a few years."

"Maybe I can come see your lilacs."

She smiled up at him. "Maybe so."

He carried the shovel back to the truck, and they returned with a tarp which they spread on the ground. They bundled the lilac shoots in the tarp and hauled them back to her van.

She closed the van's rear door and brushed her hands off on her pants. "Thanks."

He didn't want her to go yet. "I know it's not the house, but I hope it'll make you feel like you got something. If you want anything from inside, let me know."

She nodded and climbed into her truck, an Amazon who loved lilacs. He wondered if she might go out with him after the dance and after he didn't sell the church the house. Why should she? He was an old White guy with a bad prostate and crummy low back, and she was probably ten years his junior. Worse, he couldn't give her what she wanted. She'd always think of losing the house whenever she thought of him. Somehow, she'd rattled something loose in him; something he thought might just be his heart.

CHAPTER 30

I Believe

I believe in the sun,
Even when it's not shining.
I believe in love,
Even when no one's there.

I believe in God,
Even when God is silent.

Anonymous Jewish poem

After several phone calls, Frankie convinced Doralee to come to dinner. As Frankie set down Beasley's food dish, a terrible thought came to her: what if Doralee was afraid of dogs? Or allergic? Or what if she hated dogs?

She was excited for Doralee to finally meet her boys. What if she didn't like the boys? *Please, God, don't let Javier have a melt-*

down. She knew they wouldn't like her mother—she'd warned Jordan not to make any snarky comments—but everyone should be able to hold it together for one night. Everyone except her.

After the debacle at church, most people might have given up, but not Frankie. She was a woman who hit it with a bigger hammer. She got things done. She was not giving up.

Frankie looked around the kitchen and twisted her apron in her hands.

Doralee might hate the house. Maybe Frankie should have bought new curtains. Maybe she should have cleaned the living room carpet. Too late. Instead, she rushed to the half-bath off the living room and cleaned the toilet. Again.

Back in the kitchen, she wiped down the table legs and chairs until she was satisfied that they were clean. The kitchen smelled more like cleaning fluid than the cauliflower-cheese soup.

She'd tried three outfits until she'd settled on loose pants and an African print top but then worried that Doralee would think Frankie was getting in her face with the top, so she changed it.

Her dad popped his head into the kitchen. "Smells good."

"I'd love it if you stayed and had dinner with us. She probably would too."

"Thanks, nope." He squinted. "Why'd you use our nice china?"

Hoping he'd change his mind, she'd set a place for him, and as she did, the memory of a disastrous dinner exploded in her mind.

Doralee had made boudin and rice. Frankie had set the table with this china. The two of them sat at the table, staring at their plates, the food growing cold because her dad was working late. Doralee sipped her glass of *orange juice*, saying she deserved a drink because he didn't appreciate her. Frankie could still hear the china shattering against the wall. She had hidden under her bed, listening to the shouting, pleading, and crying. Her dad had pulled her out from under the bed and tucked her under the covers.

This china was getting a new start tonight. No more hurled plates. Just a nice, friendly, mid-week family dinner. *That's not too much to ask, is it, God?*

She said, "This was your wedding china, and I thought she might remember it."

He snorted. "She'll wish she sold it for booze before she left." He waved a backward hand over his head as he clumped to the front door. "I'm going to DeLuca's to watch the game."

"Dad, will one evening kill you?" she pleaded.

He turned, his eyes softer, filled with love. The kind of love she hoped to feel toward Doralee tonight. *Make me a loving daughter, God.*

"What you're trying to do isn't going to work." He clapped his Red Sox hat on his head and adjusted it thoughtfully. "You're going to get hurt, the boys too. Don't know how, but she'll do it. Wish I could protect you all from her, but you have to find that out for yourself. I'll be back when it's over."

He closed the door, and she stared at the blank spot where he'd stood.

Frankie put his place setting back in the china cupboard and rearranged the plates and chairs for four. He might be right, but Frankie wanted a chance to include Doralee in their family.

Tonight didn't have to be perfect. She would settle for friendly. *Just friendly, okay, God?*

Frankie stirred the soup on the stove. Instead of winging it, she used an actual recipe. What if Doralee despised cauliflower-cheese soup? Or salad? She checked on the bread warming in the oven. Should she have bought gluten-free rolls? She forgot to check if Doralee had any food allergies.

She knew next to nothing about Doralee, but tonight, that would change.

Javier appeared in the kitchen door. "Did you make that horrible cheese soup?"

"It's not horrible."

"I hate cheese."

"I know." But she'd forgotten. "You can have a veggie burger."

He shuddered. "It's six. If we don't eat in five minutes, it will be too late to eat."

Her insides clenched. He was starting up already. She had been precise and asked Doralee to come a few minutes before six.

"You need to be a little flexible. The food will taste the same at six thirty as it does at six."

"You know I have to eat at six oh five, or I cannot eat."

Please, oh, please, oh please!

"Doralee's a little late. She'll be here soon. How about a glass of milk while you're waiting?" She took the milk from the fridge and poured him a fresh glass because he wouldn't drink it if it was room temperature.

He tested the milk, drank, and wiped his milk mustache with his sleeve. "Where's she going to sit?"

She pointed to Dad's chair.

"If she's sitting in Grandpa's seat, where's he going to sit?"

She scrubbed the kitchen sink again. "Grandpa decided to go to DeLuca's."

"He'll miss her. He was married to her, right?"

"Right. But he doesn't feel ... happy to see her."

"Do you? Feel happy, I mean?"

It was a loaded question with a dozen answers, all of them accurate. Frankie didn't exactly feel happy that Doralee was coming to dinner, as much as she felt hungry to know Doralee, to show off her boys. It was an opening, a chance.

She glanced at the clock again. "I'm happy she's coming to dinner."

"I'm going to ask her why she left you and Grandpa," he said.

She put a hand to her already throbbing temple. "Please just don't, Javi, okay? It's not the kind of question you ask someone."

He studied her with his soft brown eyes, and she could tell he was trying hard to figure out the right thing to say. "Okay, but I don't know why she left you because you are a great mom, and you were probably a great kid, too." Then he put his arms around her waist and leaned his head into the crook of her shoulder.

This hardly *ever* happened. Her heart shot fireworks, and angels sang. She laid her cheek on his mildly stinky head. His curls tickled the side of her neck as she petted his back. *This, this was mom heaven.*

Then he jerked away, leaving a little patch of warmth lingering under her chin. "Five minutes, then I have to eat." Javier disappeared into the living room, taking Frankie's heart with him.

Jordan's heavy tread descended the stairs. "Dinner ready? I'm starved."

"Didn't you eat a ham sandwich only an hour ago?"

"Well, yeah, but that was a whole hour ago, and now it's dinner, so I'm hungry again."

"We're waiting for Doralee."

"She gonna have another meltdown like at church?"

"I think tonight will be better." Her cheeks hurt from keeping the smile on her face. "She's your grandmother, so please be on your best behavior, okay?"

He crossed his tree-trunk arms and looked down at her. "I have enough family, and I sure don't need some alcoholic grandma."

She gave him a scornful stare. "She's the only one you've got.

One night, okay. Just—" She stirred the soup. "Let's all try to be loving and kind and … Christian."

He huffed a noisy sigh. "I'm going to stop going to church if every time something's freaky, you say we have to be Christian. What if I'm not feelin' the Christian vibe tonight?"

The tendons along the sides of her neck tightened. "Please go back upstairs and put on a shirt that isn't wrinkled and doesn't smell like a locker room."

She heard his elephantine footsteps tromping up the stairs.

The clock on the microwave said 6:45. It seemed to be running at double time. Her chest felt as if a belt was wrapped around it.

"Mom, I'm hungry! It's after six," Javier whined from the living room. Soon he would be too agitated to eat.

"Five minutes," she called back.

She stirred the soup, checked the bread in the oven again, and straightened the linen napkins she had bought especially. She poured ice water into the glasses, then thought Doralee wouldn't want ice water and changed it for regular tap water in her glass.

Jordan thundered down the stairs in a clean tee shirt. "Okay, so where is she?"

Frankie felt as if an increasing amount of current was running through some invisible third rail, and she didn't know how to avoid getting fried. "I … she's coming soon. I'm sure of it."

God, you're not listening! Frankie's assurance had shrunk to zero, but she wasn't going to admit it. She didn't want them to feel like they were the ones that had been stood up.

Javier came into the kitchen. "It's six minutes to seven. We have to eat." His fists were clenched, his lower jaw jutted forward, and his eyes were narrow slits; all warning signs of a screaming, shouting, cursing, chair-hurling fit.

Jordan looked at his little brother, then at her. His voice

carried a warning she was already sensing herself. "Mom, I think you better let him eat. I need to eat too. I got homework to finish, and I'm starving. Might even pass out from hunger."

Her heart crumpled. "Okay, let me feed you guys."

At least they could come down and say hello, and she would have more undivided time with Doralee. Frankie dished up soup and set it in front of Jordan and a nuked veggie burger for Javier. She slid it from the microwaveable plate onto the china plate and set it in front of Javier.

He frowned. "I don't like this plate. It's not my regular plate. This one has a shiny gold stripe around the edge."

"It's special. For Doralee," Frankie said.

"Well, she's not here. I want a regular plate."

Jordan said, "Javi! Cool it and just eat, man. Mom made a nice dinner, and she even made you your own burger. Chill and chow, dude."

Javier scowled at his brother but ate.

Amid her own apprehension, Frankie was grateful for Jordan's big brothering.

"There's more soup on the stove, Jordan." He was almost done with his first bowl. She hoped he'd leave some for her and Doralee.

"'Kay," he mumbled around the bread in his mouth.

She moved to the front living room and dialed Doralee's cell phone.

No answer.

Evelyn didn't answer either at home or on her cell phone.

Frankie had had no texts, calls, or messages. What if there had been an emergency? What if Doralee had gone to the hospital? Maybe she'd had a stroke or gotten drunk and was lying in a ditch somewhere. She went to the front window and scanned the street for Evelyn's car. She checked to make sure the porch light was on.

A little flame Frankie had been frantically fanning inside herself since seeing Doralee grew dim and snuffed out. A kind of desolation settled on her like sawdust.

The boys finished and put their dishes in the dishwasher. Jordan went up to his room to study. Javier took Beasley upstairs and put himself to bed.

Frankie sat at the table, staring at the salads wilting on the plates, the bread turning into a brick, and the soup congealing to the consistency of spackle.

You on vacation tonight, God?

At ten, the front door opened and closed. She didn't want to face her dad but couldn't rouse herself from her chair where she sat.

He took one look at her and opened his arms for her. "I'm sorry, Frankie, I'm sorry."

She got up and let him fold her in his arms as if she were eight years old all over again.

CHAPTER 31

Hope has two lovely daughters, anger and courage.
Saint Augustine

Doralee smiled, hugged her purse close to her hip, and tried to remember the name of the woman across from her. *Francine. My daughter. We are having brunch in a diner. Brunch is something people with money do.*

She couldn't remember when she'd last eaten in a restaurant. She was used to picking through the dumpsters out back.

"What's the name of this place?" Doralee asked, sucking in her breath with effort.

Francine tilted her head. "I told you. Penny's II."

"I remembered you told me; I was seeing if you remembered." Doralee laughed hard with conviction.

When she didn't know what was going on, Doralee had learned to cover up, to pretend. *Fake it 'til you ... how did the saying go?*

Somethings she couldn't remember at all, whole days,

months, places, people, then other things she wanted to forget popped up like a bad smell.

But the one thing she remembered: she'd left so she wouldn't hurt Francine, but now she would end up doing it anyway.

"It's a nice place. Real nice. Thank you for bringing me."

"Do you remember when we came here when I was a kid?" Francine poured milk into her coffee.

Doralee sorted through the jumble in her mind, looking for a time when that might have happened. "Sure," she said, unsure. "We came on Sunday mornings, and you liked pancakes."

"Saturday mornings, actually. I like waffles, but they're almost the same thing." Francine poked at the eggs on her plate. "I wish we had had more of those times."

Francine's pretty face looked like a funeral coming.

Doralee said, "Yes, I'm sorry we didn't have more of those times, too."

Francine smiled so tenderly that Doralee felt guilty for trying to keep her at a distance, but it was for her own good. Moms did things for the good of their children, even if their kids didn't know it. Even if it broke their mom's hearts.

"You were a sweet child. You liked ..." Doralee narrowed her eyes in concentration. "Church. You liked church and ... that man, your father." *What in the hell is his name?* "You liked him."

Doralee knew she'd said something right because Francine grinned.

With her fork, Francine pointed at Doralee's eggs. "Eat up; you need the calories."

Doralee patted her bulging belly, which grew every day, stretching her skin as tight as a drum, tilting her forward. "Not with this on me, I don't."

She had no appetite because the top right side of her stomach felt like it was on fire. A drink would dull the pain.

There was a line of bottles behind the cashier's counter, but Francine turned her down flat when she'd asked if she could have a Bloody Mary.

"I wondered if it slipped your mind about dinner the other night?" Francine pinned her with her eyes.

"What night? What dinner?" The smell of burnt toast and scorched coffee soured Doralee's stomach. She felt shadows stirring inside, climbing behind her eyes, pushing to get out.

"You were supposed ..." Francine bit her lip and started again. "I invited you to my house for dinner two nights ago. Did you maybe forget?"

Doralee roamed around in her brain, but there was no dinner invitation in there. "I don't remember you inviting me." She pulled herself up straighter, trying for dignified. "I certainly would have come if you did." Doralee recognized the hurt in Francine's eyes. Hurting Francine was the last thing Doralee wanted to do. Her daughter didn't deserve any more hurt.

Doralee would have remembered about dinner if Evelyn let her have one damned drink. Everything was easier with a snootful of vodka. Nothing hurt, not her stomach, not her heart. She could forget on purpose.

"You said Evelyn would drop you at my house for dinner. I missed you."

"I don't know about that. Maybe some other time."

"On Sunday, I was hoping you'd get to meet my boys after church, but you got upset and left."

"Sunday? What happened on Sunday?"

Thinking this hard made Doralee's teeth feel sharp and snaggly like she wanted to bite. Sometimes, the feeling came out of nowhere and grabbed her by the hair, making her say and do stuff she knew was mean, wrong even. Like now. But she couldn't stop herself. "Are you trying to make me feel bad or something? Like I'm crazy? You never invited me anywhere."

Francine sat back in her seat. "You don't have to get angry. I'm just trying to understand some things."

Doralee might get a little turned around sometimes, forget where she was, but she wasn't crazy. Besides, she had her purse to hold a bottle. Her purse was the one thing she'd had for years and years, through everything. If she had it, she was fine.

"Guess you forgot about Sunday," Francine said softly.

Doralee lifted her coffee to her lips, but the shaking made her slosh the coffee on the table. She set the cup down hard in the saucer and glared at Francine. "I'm seventy-eight. Old people forget stuff."

"I'm worried about you."

Why was Francine worried about her? "Oh, you don't got to worry about me," Doralee snapped. "I survived winters, hurricanes, half-starving, living in shelters, sleeping under bridges. I don't need looking after like I'm some doddering old fool."

"I didn't say you were a doddering fool. Just that I'm worried about you." Francine wiped up spilled coffee with her napkin. "Why does that make you upset?"

"Well, don't." Doralee clawed at the nasty rash on her arm, which had climbed up her neck, arms, and inside her legs. The itching kept her awake and made her crazy. It was like having a million stinging fire ants inside her skin.

Francine noticed Doralee scratching and pointed. "And that rash on your arm, have you had it a long time?"

Doralee looked out the window where a steady drizzle had turned everything to sloppy grey puddles. Under a polka dot umbrella, a woman with a coat on her dog sloshed past.

"Look at that funny little coat on that lady's dog," Doralee said. The woman and her dog disappeared into a cloud of fog.

Francine's features melted into a fearful expression. "There's no woman with a dog," she whispered.

"Yes, there was," Doralee bit off. "They just walked by too fast, and you missed seeing them."

Frankie turned her coffee cup around in the saucer, sipped, and set it down again.

"I could take you to my doctor," Francine said. "Dr. Goldpin is really nice, and I think you'd like her. She could give you something for that rash. Maybe see what's going on with your tummy. Check you out."

"Nah. I don't trust doctors. Give you medicine you don't need just to make money. Do experiments on you. Take out your kidneys and sell them on the Internet."

Francine's eyebrows flew up.

She probably didn't take to those kinds of ideas, but to Doralee they made perfect sense.

"I ... don't think she's that kind of doctor." Francine took her fancy, big phone out of her pocket. "I'm going to call and see when they have an opening, okay?"

Doralee pushed Frankie's hand with the phone down to the table. "Listen here: I'm old. I drank my whole life. Nothing no doctor can do now will help me. I am not going to no doctor. You're real nice, but you don't have to worry about me."

Francine looked like she'd seen someone get run over by a car. "They can ... maybe do something." She swallowed hard, tears mixing up in her eyes.

Doralee said, "I don't want to be why you get upset."

"At least she can give you cream for the rash. I know that forgetting is a sign of normal aging, but they might have something to help your memory."

"Only medicine I need is hundred-eighty proof. I'm perfect then." Doralee laughed, and a thousand knives stabbed up under her right ribcage.

Her thoughts went slip-sliding away, turned from doctors to dirt to dogs, from bacon to bedbugs to beatings. She pulled her black purse closer, kneaded the fabric, and picked at the peeling fake-patent leather with her broken fingernails. A bottle in the bag would have settled the clacking in her chest.

Francine said. "I can get you good medical care."

She was upset, but Doralee couldn't think what to say to un-upset her.

"I want us to have time to get to know one another better." Francine's words came out choked, and deep grooves carved into her beautiful face. "You know, have more times like this."

"Like this? With you nagging me to go to the doctor's, telling me I forget things? Why'd I want more of that?"

"Please, *please* don't get mad. I only want to help."

"Oh, hell." Doralee couldn't hold out against her daughter. "You sure are one determined woman."

Francine lifted her eyebrows in question.

"Lord, okay, okay." She reached across the table and patted Francine's hand. "You don't want me, Francine. You want the mother I should have been. I don't want to hurt you no more. No more."

CHAPTER 32

We are all full of weakness and errors; let us mutually pardon each other our follies.
Voltaire

Frankie dragged herself into the Chittim-Howell House at church. After her brunch with Doralee earlier in the day, the bruise on her heart still ached. Father Gabriel had failed to warn her that trying to forgive and love someone could be so exhausting and demoralizing.

Olivia, Flicka, Bianca, and Carolina were gathered around an oval conference table, wrapping baskets in cellophane and adding ribbons. Late, as usual, Hélène still hadn't arrived.

Frankie was astonished when she saw the dozens of silent auction items spread around the room. Gleaming silver and crystal stood next to delicate china. Gift certificates for local businesses and offers for vacation homes were displayed in plastic placards. Leather designer handbags stood next to bottles of expensive wines. Sports collectibles were arrayed on yet another table.

Bianca took one look at her and said, "You look like hell. What's going on?"

"The master of tact speaks," Flicka said acidly.

"Sorry." Bianca turtled her head between her shoulders.

Exhausted, Frankie dropped into a chair and let her head rest back against the wall. "I was humping sheetrock this afternoon because one of the guys was sick." She sneezed into her elbow. "I still have dust in my nose."

"Go home and rest," Carolina said. "We got this."

"Yeah, but you guys have all done more than your share. I want to help get the silent auction items ready."

"You don't have to try to do everything," Bianca said. "We can actually do it without you, you know."

Olivia tied a bow around a cellophane wrapper on a silver wine bucket. "No offense, but you're not the best at making stuff look lavish unless it involves marble and dentil crown molding." She smiled warmly.

Frankie laughed. "Look at all this awesome loot."

Flicka was sipping wine from a long-stemmed, cobalt blue wine glass.

"You didn't take that wine from the donations, did you?" Frankie asked her.

"There were three bottles." Flicka coyly lifted one eyebrow. "I'm testing to make sure they're still good." She pointed to a satin-lined box where the mate to the glass she was using nestled. "Try some?"

Frankie gave her the side eye.

Bianca lifted a baseball jersey signed by Dustin Pedroia to her nose and inhaled. "Bye, Dustin. I love you." With a melodramatic sniffle, she folded it and laid it in front of Carolina to wrap.

Frankie was touched by her friend's love. Bianca's heart had probably broken when she chose to part with the jersey. But any of the Marriage Survivors Club would make an equal sacrifice for the others if anyone of them ever needed it. "I can't believe how many people donated things," Frankie said, filled with humble amazement.

"Everybody loves you, and they believe in your dream and in the shelter," Carolina said.

Carolina's words embarrassed Frankie, reminding her how she had blown their trust. More importantly, this was her last shot to convince Cam to sell them back the house. After that, they would have to go back to the drawing board, re-estimate what a shelter would cost, raise more money, apply for another loan, and on and on. It might add years to the project.

It might be her last excuse to see Cam Simpson, and that gave her a pang of frustrated longing.

"We should make a lot of money. Ticket sales are finally picking up," Flicka said, swirling her wine in her glass. "For a while, I thought the only people going would be Father Gabriel and us."

"I wish I could invite Doralee to the gala," Frankie said.

All bustling movement stilled, and the atmosphere went prickly.

Bianca said, "After the show she put on Sunday morning, you want to bring her to the gala?"

Flicka give Bianca an eye roll.

Frankie was glad for the pause offered by Hélène flying in the door and tossing her orange coat on a chair.

"Hi, sorry I'm late!" Hélène sang out. "Tell me what to do."

Everyone studiously avoided making eye contact with Frankie. The air in the room felt electric with unspoken questions.

Hélène looked around at their somber faces. "Okay ... it

looks like my timing is off yet again. What's going on?" She took the chair next to Frankie.

"Frankie wants to bring her mother to the gala," Bianca said.

"Oooh," Hélène said, touching a hand to her white/black hair. "I—mmm—I see."

"She's never done anything fancy. I wish I could give her a special night."

Hélène said, "But she distressed you on Sunday morning."

"Distressed is a pretty good way to put it," Frankie said.

Flicka tried to pour another glass, but the bottle was empty. "If she put on a good ol' show like she did Sunday morning, what do you think everybody will think after all the work you've put into this? You think they'll still trust you and be willing to cough up all the money you're asking them to."

"Flicka," Carolina admonished.

Flicka could be funny or bitchy when she drank a lot, but it only magnified why Frankie loved her. Flicka had the balls to say what the others didn't, and it wasn't always pretty.

Gently, Hélène said, "This evening is important. You've worked hard and deserve to have a good time, too."

"You're all right, of course," Frankie conceded. "It was just a thought."

"How are things going with the two of you?" Olivia asked as she set aside a basket nearly as big as she was.

Frankie said, "She agreed to let me take her to the doctor."

Hélène said, "That's great news."

"I hope they can give her some medication to help her mental and emotional state," Frankie said.

Bianca said, "My Uncle Giovanni was an alky. He was pretty crazy at the end." She hurried to add, "Not that I'm suggesting your mother is crazy or anything."

"What do you mean he was crazy?" Frankie asked.

"Not knowing where he was, confusion, couldn't remember

anything, running around without his pants, wacky mood swings." Bianca said, "But look, it's probably not like that for every alcoholic."

The similarities made a cold pit open in Frankie's stomach. How could she have a relationship with someone who didn't remember who she was? What would losing her mother all over again feel like?

Flicka broke in. "Give up the wish of bringing your mom to the dance. You're Cam Simpson's date." She poked her finger at Frankie. "This house is your baby, and you're the one who has to convince him to sell the house to us. That'd be hard to do if you're babysitting your mom."

Cam Simpson, who turned her brain to mush and made her feel fluttery. She had to entertain and introduce him around. It would be hard enough to do without having to keep an eye on her mother.

"I'm well aware that everybody's counting on me," Frankie said. "This is a big night, and I just wanted to make her happy, share it with her."

"Bad idea," Flicka said as she stalked over to the window, her rigid back to all of them as she stared out into the darkness.

She had done most of the heavy lifting in terms of organization, and she was used to getting her own way. That's why she was a princess, and Frankie was a general contractor.

Hélène said, "We don't mean to make this hard for you, Frankie. I think we all understand why you want to do this." She sighed and brushed her palms down over her skirt. "But not even you can do everything at once."

Olivia rested a hand on Frankie's shoulder.

Frankie laid her hand atop Olivia's tiny hand.

"You don't have to justify it to us," Olivia said. "It's a perfectly good reason, but we just wonder if it's good for the church or her, but most of all, good for you."

Flicka said, "We get you want to make her proud. Show her you still love her after she treated you like shit. Believe me, I get it."

Something about her delivery felt like Flicka was digging a needle out of her own flesh.

Flicka turned to face Frankie. "But you can't make anyone happy, Frankie, least of all, an alcoholic. This is our last shot with Cam Simpson."

"I know that!"

Flicka went on. "You're the one who wants that exact house, so you're the one who must do everything—except blow the guy—to get it. We're 100 percent behind you, whatever you decide to do, except bringing your mom to the dance."

"Not to mention, there will be a lot of liquor around to drink. Alcoholics aren't supposed to be around liquor, are they?" Carolina asked no one in particular.

Flicka gave a husky laugh and held up the empty wine bottle. "Can't keep me off the bottle; I'm not even an alcoholic."

"Says who?" Bianca snatched the empty bottle away.

Hélène tilted her head. "You know how I hate to agree with Flicka, but you don't want her to ruin what's taken you years to pull together."

Frankie nodded. They were right, but she still felt dejected that her mom was going to miss the most important thing—besides adopting her boys—Frankie had ever done.

Flicka said, "Look at us. We're here because we love you. We're here to help, to take some weight off your shoulders." She bent down and looked Frankie in the eye. "You're not stuck with the family you were born with. You can choose."

Olivia said, "This is one night that needs a focused effort. Maybe you can take her shopping."

"Maybe buy her a nice dress or some pretty jewelry," Carolina said.

Frankie bent forward and rested her forehead in her hands. She felt her bones creak. The muscles in her low back screamed, and her feet felt as though she'd been walking barefoot over gravel.

"I feel like I have to choose between the house and Cam and Doralee. I just found her again, and I want to do everything I can to make her life better."

Carolina said in her serene voice, "There's a human limit to what you can do."

Hélène stroked Frankie's back, and her voice had a humming quality. "You're not just physically exhausted; you're emotionally exhausted too. Who wouldn't be if their mother showed up out of the blue?"

Frankie sat back. "I guess you're right. Cam Simpson and the dance are my priorities."

"You always try to do everything for everyone," Olivia said. "You act like you have to do everything alone, that no one can help you. We're here for you. Let this one slide. We suggested before that you do something else with her. If you're busy and need a hand, we can help with errands or the kids."

Everyone nodded.

The Marriage Survivors Club was a collective conscience with extra brains, more hearts, and deeper understanding than any one of them had. Frankie was grateful and couldn't imagine what her life might be like without them. She loved them. She wanted them to be wrong, but they weren't.

Hélène stood, took Frankie's arms, pulled her to standing, and hugged her. "Go home. We will finish. You've already done enough." She steered Frankie to the door, opened it, and gave her a gentle push. "We love you, okay?"

"Me too," Frankie said.

CHAPTER 33

From Jabberwocky

'Twas brillig, and the slithy toves
Did gyre and gimble in the wabe

Lewis Carroll

To Frankie, Doralee said, "I need a drink before we go in. I can't go in without a drink." Even with her purse clamped in her arms, fear noosed her neck.

"Why?"

"Makes me settled, you know? We could get a drink, then see the doctor. Just a little one, okay?"

Francine gave her a side glance and didn't answer.

"Shit, you're a hard ass," Doralee muttered as she thumped her cane on the elevator floor.

"Thank you."

"What's your name again?"

The pretty woman with dark eyes, light brown skin, and pretty braids all over her head said, "Frank—Francine. I'm your daughter."

"Yes, I remember now." But she didn't.

Things had been getting worse. Everything faded in and out. Her hands were shaking more, and the spot on her upper lright side hurt all the time. A drink would fix her up, though.

They stepped into the elevator. Doralee was certain that someone was spying on them from the overhead lights. She hugged her purse tighter and backed into the corner. "Look out," she whispered to the woman with her. *Francine. That's her name. Don't forget, now.*

In the waiting room, Doralee said, "What's all that racket coming from the bathroom?"

Francine looked at her and glanced at the closed bathroom door. "What?"

Doralee pointed, whispering so the spies wouldn't hear. "In there, can't you hear? Like whispering and sounds like people screaming and shouting something awful. I need a drink."

Francine gave her a hug. "It's okay. You can trust me. Nobody's going to hurt you while I'm here."

A nurse took them into an exam room, where they sat in nice chairs. All the equipment and cabinets were new and shiny. The room smelled clean, not like the clinic in that other town—Lafayette—she thought, where all the addicts, drunks, and poor folks like her went. That place smelled like piss and puke.

Doralee rooted around in her purse. "Where's my bottle? I need a drink."

"You're not supposed to drink," Francine said.

"Says who?"

"Your sister, Evelyn."

"She's a hard ass, too."

"Lucky for you," Francine said.

A woman with a pink polka-dot umbrella and a little dog in a raincoat walked through the door and disappeared through the wall.

"You see that?" Doralee asked.

"What?"

But the itching distracted Doralee, and she didn't answer. She pushed back the sleeve of her raincoat and scratched hard at the rash on her arm.

"You're making it bleed." Francine got a tissue from a box on the counter and dabbed at the bloody spots.

"You're a nice woman, Francine, even if you drag my ass to the doctor."

Francine smiled, and the way her mouth turned up reminded Doralee of a man she might once have been married to.

"There, that's better." Francine pulled down the sleeve of Doralee's jacket.

"I'm not letting them take my kidneys or nothing like that."

Francine looked sad. "I don't think there's a big demand for seventy-eight-year-old kidneys. Dr. Goldpin is going to give you a physical. See if she can give you something for that rash. Maybe something to help with your memory."

"Not a damn thing wrong with my memory. Why, just yesterday, Officer Grandin stopped in to visit my mother. See, I remember."

"Mm-hm. Officer Grandin?"

"Yeah, he's on the police. He brings Momma a bottle of shine, stays a while, then leaves. He come yesterday."

Francine rested her head in her hands and muttered, "Oh, dear Lord."

Doralee's eye fell on a bottle labeled *alcohol* on the counter next to the Band-Aids and those wooden popsicle sticks. What were they called?

Nothing stayed in her brain. Best medicine for that was vodka, but good old mouthwash would do. Sometimes doctors' offices had mouthwash. If Francine left her alone for a minute, Doralee could look right quick in the cabinets.

When she'd come up here—wherever here was—Doralee remembered the shakes and chills, sweating, puking, how her joints and muscles and head hurt all at once, like she was on fire, then in a freezer, the bugs crawling out of her skin, her eyes and nose and ears. How she couldn't get out of bed. She didn't want to go through that again, ever.

The people in the wall screamed and scratched and cursed. Why didn't they go to some other room?

"I'm so thirsty. I need a drink," Doralee said.

"I'll wait until the nurse comes in and ask her for a cup of water." Francine crossed one leg over the other, her foot kicking up and down, up and down.

Doralee laid a hand on her knee. "You wound tighter than a drum. You're the one who needs a drink to loosen up."

"Thanks, but I'm off the sauce."

"That's too bad."

There was scratching and scrabbling in the wall. Voices whispered and screamed. Doralee gripped her purse and drew her raincoat closer. "I got to get out of here 'fore those people come in here after me." She stood and made for the door, but her feet had a mind of their own. They didn't set down the way she wanted.

Francine stood up and put her hand on Doralee's arm. Her touch was kind, rather than trying to hold her down. "Please wait. The doctor will be right in. This won't take long."

A woman came in. "Hi, Doralee. I'm Amy. I'm the nurse." She washed her hands and dried them on a paper towel. "I'm going to get your vitals before Dr. Goldpin comes in and examines you." She pulled out a stethoscope. "Do you need help climbing up on the exam table?"

"I'm not getting up there."

Doralee tried for the door again, but Francine got a hold of her purse strap. Doralee struggled and yanked, but Francine was stronger, and Doralee couldn't go anywhere without her purse.

The nurse took a few steps back. "Maybe the doctor can do the vitals."

"Easy, easy," Francine said in a soothing voice. "It's okay. Nothing's going to happen. I'm right here."

She put her arm around Doralee's shoulders and held her tightly like a little kid. It was nice, actually.

The nurse laid a package on the exam table and said, "Maybe you can help her put the gown on. Have her sit on the table. Doctor will be right in." She practically ran out the door.

Doralee turned back to Francine. "Why are you making me do this? I'm perfectly fine."

"Let's get this gown on you," Francine said in a way that made it impossible to refuse. "Can we set your purse down right here?" Francine helped her get undressed and draped the paper gown around her.

"Thank you," Doralee said. "Nobody's ever been this nice to me."

Francine made a noisy sniff. "Okay, let's get you up on the exam table."

Hard as she tried, Doralee couldn't lift her foot high enough, and the step kept wiggling this way and that. "Can't seem to manage."

Then, Francine knelt and lifted first one foot and then the other onto the step. She steadied Doralee with her other hand. When Francine stood, tears spilled down her cheeks.

Doralee patted her cheek. "Thanks, dearie, but see? That's

why you shouldn't be around me. I make you sad, and I don't want to do that."

Francine turned away and wiped her face with her jacket sleeve. "I want to help."

Nobody could help.

There was a knock on the door.

Francine said, "Come in."

"I'm Dr. Goldpin. How are you today, Doralee?" The doctor shook her hand, and Doralee felt a little calmer.

Dr. Goldpin was a White woman about the same age as Francine. She had bright blue eyes and long brown hair twisted in a clip. Her smile was sweet, her voice kind, and the wrinkles at the corners of her eyes were from happiness.

Doralee said, "Don't know why I'm here. It's all a waste of time and money. I want to go home."

Francine's face had a pinched, worried expression.

"Your daughter brought you because she's worried about you" Dr. Goldpin sat on a stool and started making notes in a folder. "Is it okay if I do a simple exam to help calm Frankie's worries?"

Doralee crossed her arms. "You can examine me if I can have a drink afterward."

"That's out of my area of practice." Dr. Goldpin smiled. "You'll have to discuss that with Frankie."

Doralee held her purse tightly as the doctor used the blood pressure cuff and took her pulse. Then the doc looked in Doralee's ears and nose, pulled her lower lids down and looked into her eyes, and then listened to her heart and lungs. Finally, the doctor had Doralee lay down, then pressed on her belly, making her insides slosh back and forth.

"Ow!" Doralee said.

"Sorry," the doctor said, frowning. "There's quite a fluid wave there."

Whatever that meant.

Dr. Goldpin asked, "Can you sit back up?"

But Doralee couldn't so Francine helped her sit back up.

"Can you squeeze my fingers?" the doctor asked.

Doralee tried to squeeze, but her hands felt all rubbery, as if the muscles didn't work. "That's the best I got."

"Pretty good. Now, can you get down and walk a bit for me?" Dr. Goldpin asked.

Francine helped her climb off the table.

"Walk in a straight line, will you?" Dr. Goldpin stood and crossed her arms and watched Doralee walk.

Keeping her feet moving straight was harder than Doralee thought it would be. "Nothing works the way it should."

"What do you mean?" Dr. Goldpin asked.

"My feet wander around. And my hands feel like they're made out of noodles."

"When did you first start noticing that?" Francine asked.

"Oh, maybe couple years." Lately, Doralee's brain felt like someone was taking sandpaper to the inside of her skull, but she wasn't going to tell them that.

Francine traded a look with the doctor.

Dr. Goldpin nodded. "I see." She held her hand out. "Can I see your arms?" The doctor gently ran her fingers along the burning, itchy patches. "I'll give you something for the rash, Doralee, but there are some things you'll need to do to get your health under control."

"I keep telling you I'm fine. My health is fine," Doralee insisted. Why didn't they believe her?

"How many drinks do you have a day?" Dr. Goldpin asked.

"Oh, 'bout as much as I can get, I guess. But my sister, Evelyn, she won't let me drink anymore."

"That's probably a good thing."

"Says you."

Dr. Goldpin smiled. "Maybe it's time for you to get some help with that."

Doralee shrugged. "Naw, I don't think so. I'd do pretty much anything for a drink right now."

Dr. Goldpin wrote something in her file. "Do you mind if I talk with Frankie a bit and see if she has any concerns?"

"Sure, go right ahead."

"Thank you." Dr. Goldpin turned to Francine. "Are you noticing anything that concerns you, Frankie?"

Francine clasped and unclasped her hands. "She's pretty forgetful, and you saw how unsteady she is. I'm worried about how yellow her skin and eyes are. Her tremors are quite pronounced."

"Oh, who cares?" Doralee laughed, but the other two didn't.

Dr. Goldpin stood. "Why don't you get dressed? Then I'll meet you in my office, and we can chat?" She left and closed the door softly.

As Doralee pulled on her clothes, she felt a broken heartedness in Francine. It was hard to make other people happy when you wanted to be left in peace to drink.

"Ready to talk to the doctor?" Francine asked as she bent to tie Doralee's shoes.

Doralee hugged her purse and took her cane. "She's going to say my drinking's killing me, and you know what?"

Francine's voice shook. "What?"

"All I want is another drink before I die."

CHAPTER 34

If it were possible to heal sorrow by weeping and to raise the dead with tears, gold were less prized than grief.
Sophocles

Frankie had never been in Dr. Goldpin's office before. It was light and sunny with an antique desk, bookshelves with family photos and an orchid, and a window that looked down on a row of shops.

She knew the news would be bad because the doctor didn't meet her gaze. Ominous finality filled every corner of the room. Frankie knew Doralee had cirrhosis. She hoped they might have a year or two left. Her heart was beating so hard she couldn't catch her breath.

Dr. Goldpin said, "I'm sorry to tell you, Doralee, but I think you're pretty sick."

Doralee clutched her purse closer. "Yeah, I guess I know that."

Frankie's mouth was dry, and her hope teetered precariously.

Maybe if Doralee heard it from a doctor, she'd be willing to get some treatment or take some medication.

"What's wrong?" Frankie asked.

Dr. Goldpin said, "I have my suspicions, but you need some tests—"

"No tests, no doctors, no hospitals," Doralee said flatly.

Doralee possessed a wealth of decisiveness, considering her befuddlement, the ranting about doctors taking her kidneys.

"That's your choice." Dr. Goldpin shuffled some papers on her desk. "Tell me, Doralee, do you ever hear or see things that might not exist?"

"I ... I ... I don't know," Doralee said uncertainly.

Frankie nodded. "Yes, she does. And she's forgetful, can't remember recent or past things. She gets confused, her moods swing rapidly, and her face, well, she doesn't have much expression."

Frankie felt badly describing Doralee's symptoms so bluntly, but she wanted to get as much information as possible. That way, maybe Doralee would take things more seriously.

Dr. Goldpin folded her hands. "Those are all symptoms of long-term alcoholism."

"How'd you know?" Doralee asked belligerently.

"My mother was an alcoholic," Dr. Goldpin said without defensiveness.

It was a stunning admission, but Frankie saw no trace of shame, resignation, or helplessness on Dr. Goldpin's face. Only acceptance. But Frankie wasn't there yet.

"There's medication that can help, right?" Frankie asked.

Dr. Goldpin shook her head. "Cirrhosis is chronic and irreversible. It's not my area of practice, so I can't give you hard facts, but I can refer you to a hepatologist who treats liver and pancreatic diseases. They can perform more definitive tests and prescribe the right medication if they think it will help."

Frankie squeezed her eyes shut and pressed her fingertips to her temples. Her head swam. The bright sunlight pinwheeled. Dust motes throbbed and exploded like supernovas. A door closed somewhere outside. She had known but forced her gaze from the truth the way one turns from an animal struck and killed by a car. There was no deluding herself any longer. She clasped her palms between her knees to keep her hands from shaking. Deciding it was best to be prepared, she asked, "What's this going to look like as we, um, go along?"

"As things progress, you might see paranoia, anger, greater mood swings, combativeness, confusion, word loss, increased forgetfulness, hallucinations, inability to walk and speak and eventually to breathe."

Frankie sat back in her chair. She was a strong, capable woman, but she could not do this. She couldn't.

Dr. Goldpin opened her desk drawer, scribbled something on a business card, and handed it to Frankie. She took it numbly and stuck it in her pocket.

Dr. Goldpin's eyes filled with sympathy. "There are some medications that might help ease the discomfort."

"Best thing for my discomfort is a bottle of vodka," Doralee said drily.

Frankie laid a hand over her mother's hand and felt the spindly bones. She had to get Doralee to the specialist, get her to take medication they might prescribe, and get her to accept available treatments. They would never be like other mothers and daughters, but they might weave some friendship in the time she had left.

"How long I got?" Doralee asked.

It was the first sign she seemed interested in the fact she was sick. Frankie realized that her mother had known all along how sick she was.

"That's hard to say." Dr. Goldpin tented her fingers.

Frankie could tell she was hedging.

Dr. Goldpin was sensitive but intent. "One of the main things to watch out for is esophageal hemorrhaging. If you begin to bleed from your nose or mouth or have blood in your stools, get to the hospital immediately."

Doralee's face remained expressionless, but the words hit Frankie with the force of a sledgehammer dropped from thirty stories. The ache made Frankie want to double over, but she held herself together.

Her mother was going to die, not in a few years, but in a few months, maybe less.

Frankie's desperation to feel loving and forgiving was still only a mirage shimmering on a distant horizon. She needed time to understand herself and Doralee, to untangle and reweave who they were to one another, but there might be little time left.

Dr. Goldpin went on as if Frankie weren't falling apart. "You need a procedure at the hospital to drain your abdomen to help with your breathing."

"What's my stomach got to do with my breathing?" Doralee asked.

"When the liver and kidneys begin to shut down, fluid builds up in the abdomen. It's called ascites. The doctors can drain it so you can breathe easier. Your other internal organs will function better too."

Frankie roused herself. "And the rash?"

"The rash is also caused by toxins building up in the blood," Dr. Goldpin said. "That's also the cause of the mood swings and forgetfulness. They'll test the ammonia levels at the hospital, but I suspect they're quite toxic."

Doralee shook her head from side to side. "No doctors or hospitals. No, no, no."

Frankie asked, "Will she get better after they drain her abdomen?"

"Her thinking and moods will probably stabilize somewhat," Dr. Goldpin paused and fiddled with a pen on her desk. "But long-term drinking causes irreversible neurological damage." Dr. Goldpin cleared her throat. "Her disease is quite advanced, and things will only worsen."

Frankie forced air into her lungs and blew it out. "What else should she do?"

"It's important not to drink, Doralee. Can you do that?" Dr. Goldpin asked.

"I don't got a choice 'cause nobody'll let me," Doralee said in her scratchy, flat voice.

Frankie couldn't move. Every joint and muscle hurt like her body was coming apart. They all sat in silence as the sun crept across the carpet.

The world was not going to stop.

Finally, Frankie said, "Let's go home, Mom."

CHAPTER 35

When you are at your last, there is nothing for it but to keep going.

Anonymous

In the van, hollowed out and numb, Frankie stared out the windshield at the unforgivingly sunny day. Her mom sat without any expression as though unaware of what had just occurred.

All these years, she had needed her mother, but now her mother needed her. Frankie could stick it out or walk away and let Evelyn deal with it. When Doralee reappeared, Frankie stepped up the way she always did, and God kicked her in the teeth. The entire mess wasn't fair, which only added to her frustration.

She banged her fist against the door. *Hit it with the biggest fucking hammer! Find a cure, get another opinion, do research on the Internet, and look for drug trials.* Anger, she realized, was the hammer she reached for when fear or hurt threatened to knock her off her feet. This time, anger was not going to get her through. The only thing she could do was let her raw heart take a pummeling.

"What's wrong?" her mom asked.

"I was just hoping to hear something different."

Not wanting to talk, Frankie turned on the radio. She chose an oldies station because she thought Doralee might like the playlist. Her mother's face brightened, and she hummed along, tapping a rhythm on her knee.

Some of Frankie's loveliest memories were of her and Doralee dancing together in the living room. Or watching her throw her head back as her dad whirled her around. The way she sashayed around the kitchen while she cooked. It seemed impossible that this woman, once full of life, piss, and vinegar, now faced a miserable death.

"I'd like to make an appointment with the specialist the doctor suggested."

Doralee flapped a hand. "*Pppft*. Why bother?"

"Don't you want to feel better?" Frankie did not say, "Don't you want to live a little longer?"

Her mom shrugged. "What for? Can't drink, so what's left?"

"Me! Me! I'm left," Frankie said, trying not to lose it. "My boys, Dad, life, sun, rain, and flowers are all here on this beautiful earth." She paused to catch her breath. "Why didn't you come back sooner? I could have helped you."

Her mom reached into her scrappy purse, pulled out a tissue, and handed it to Frankie. "Francine, you were always better off without me. You didn't need me when you were little, and you sure don't need me like I am now. I stayed away because it was better for you to be without me than with me."

It was upside-down logic. Frankie couldn't believe there wasn't some way Doralee could have stayed and been her mom. Frankie said quietly, "Every child needs their mother."

Her mom laid her hand on Frankie's arm. "Children need to feel loved, and I loved you when you were little. I still love you."

Finally, the words Frankie had waited all her life to hear. She wanted the monolith of love her dad gave her. Love she could lean into when and as much as necessary. The kind of love she hoped her boys felt from her. Booze had cut the legs off her mother's ability to love her when, and in the way, she needed.

"I'm sorry," her mom said.

Frankie wanted her to be specific, to apologize for leaving, for making her grow up without her, for screaming at and slapping her, for abandoning her at the Catrambones', for throwing dishes and broken promises, for lonely birthdays. Something to let Frankie know she deeply understood how her absence had affected Frankie.

"For the things I did that hurt you."

There it was: an apology. No unicorns, fireworks, or rainbows.

Frankie had believed a heartfelt apology would heal her hurt and anger. For years, she'd held her breath like a swimmer heading for a distant shore when there was no shore.

"Wish there was something I could do to make it up to you," Doralee said.

It was a tiny offering as big and wide and deep as Doralee could give. It didn't feel like enough, but it was all there was. Frankie drew a deep breath. "Do you remember I invited you to my house to meet my boys? That you didn't show up?"

Doralee shook her head. "No, I don't remember."

"I want you to meet them before it's too late. We only have a little time left. I want to spend as much time together as we can. That's what I want."

Once she'd said the unspeakable, Frankie felt a sense of calm. She'd been stuck on an emotional roundabout, but now she knew which direction to go. A relationship with her mom didn't have to be like winning the lottery. Her mom didn't even have to love her in return. Frankie wanted a chance to love her mom and practice forgiving her so that when she died, Frankie would feel she'd done everything she could.

Her mom turned and stared at her. "You sure 'bout this?"

"One hundred percent."

Doralee nodded her head. "All right."

CHAPTER 36

Let us Build a House, Hymn No. 301

Let us build a house
where all are named,
their songs and visions heard
and loved and treasured,
taught and claimed
as words within the Word.

Marty Haugen

Frankie accomplished the miracle of making a family of Doralee, Javier, and Jordan. It was good enough. They chatted about basketball, school, the difference between étouffée and gumbo, Jordan's college plans, and Javier's playing basketball at the Carver Center. She had given the boys a pep talk about her mom's shortcomings. She had warned them that she might be argumentative, but everything had hung together.

She felt the marathoner's triumphant exhaustion, close enough to see the finish line but with a few crucial feet to go. When Evelyn came to pick up Doralee, Frankie would sail through the yellow tape, arms, and neck outstretched, gasping with relief.

After dinner, her mom said, "Where's the little girls' room?"

"Just down the hall." Frankie smiled at the quaint expression.

Javier moved to the living room while Jordan helped clean up. He closed the dishwasher. "I need to go upstairs and study."

She was tempted to give him a break since he'd endured the meal on his best behavior, but only she knew Doralee's time was short. In a low voice, she said, "Please can you stay and talk to your grandmother for a few more minutes?"

He imitated his grandfather's irritated growl. "For the thousandth time, Mom, she's not my grandmother. She's just some random old White lady who showed up. Seems like you're the only one who wants her here. You even kicked out Grandpa so she could come over here."

"I did not kick your grandpa out," she said. "He left of his own accord. I'd like to make her feel welcome. Ten minutes tops, then you can go, okay? I want her to see what great kids you are."

He rolled his eyes and slouched into the living room.

Frankie followed him.

He flopped into his grandfather's Barcalounger, his long, muscled arms dangling over the armrests toward the floor. Beasley laid down next to the chair, hoping Jordan would drop a scrap of something.

Doralee sat melted into the sofa, slumping to one side. Her eyes were at quarter-mast. The pink lipstick on her mouth was smudged.

Frankie experienced a moment of panic and checked her

watch. Fifteen more minutes until Evelyn picked Doralee up then she could exhale.

Javier knelt at the coffee table, his colored pencils laid out in order of color, dark to light, ends in a straight line, next to his elbow. His face was placid and relaxed. Only when drawing would he get lost in what he was doing.

"You like drawin'?" Doralee asked Javier, her words softly slurred.

Frankie's exuberance deflated. Her mother was drunk in front of the boys. She had to get them out of here. "Boys, you can go upstairs now."

Javier, hyper-focused, bent further into his drawing.

Jordan raised his eyebrows.

"Oh, let 'im stay. I like watchin' him draw," Doralee mumbled.

Where had she gotten booze? All night, she'd carried her purse with her. Frankie knew she wasn't smuggling a bottle because her purse was flat. She'd been sober when she'd arrived, and the liquor cabinet was locked, the key in Frankie's jewelry box upstairs.

Javier spoke into his bent elbow. "I got a certificate from the library once for drawing."

"Um hmmm," Doralee hummed. Then she patted his shoulder.

Javier violently shrugged her hand off. His eyes were furious pinpoints of fire, the tendons in his neck taut.

Alert, Beasley felt the tension in the room and raised his head.

Jordan shot Frankie an anxious look.

Frankie rose. "You can go upstairs now, Javi."

"That a buildin' you drawin'?" Doralee mumbled.

Javier didn't answer.

With an extra dose of ebullience, Jordan answered for

Javier. "Oh, yeah, he really likes drawing buildings! Skyscrapers, castles, mansions. Keeps his mind calm, you know, occupied."

Frankie smiled at Jordan, grateful for his effort to smooth things over.

Jordan bent forward in his chair, elbows on his knees, poised for intervention. "Javi, dude, let's go upstairs."

It was as if Javi didn't hear anyone except Doralee.

"Why do your hands shake like that?" Javier asked Doralee without looking at her.

Doralee held up her gnarled, shaking hands. "Dunno. I'm sick, I guess. If I could have a drink, they'd stop."

She glanced slyly at Frankie and smiled as if they were trading a private joke.

Her mom's tremors, confusion, and bloated stomach were all worse. Neither she nor Evelyn had been able to convince her to have the procedure Dr. Goldpin told her was necessary, but Frankie wasn't giving up yet. She didn't want Doralee to die alone. There wasn't much runway left, but Frankie was determined to go to the end, however long it took.

Her mom made a noisy inhale. "How 'bout lil' pitcher of your momma for me?"

Doralee didn't seem able to form her words clearly.

Frankie's sense of panic rose. "Javi," she said, more firmly this time.

"No, I don't draw people," Javier snapped.

Beasley sat up, watchful.

Jordan intervened. "He only draws buildings and stuff." When Jordan spoke to kids who were bullying his brother, Jordan's voice carried an undercurrent of menace that threatened a pounding. His tone carried the same acid combativeness now. Frankie was proud of how fiercely protective he was of Javier.

"Javier, it's time to get ready for bed," Frankie said. She wanted to take him by the arm, but she knew better.

"Javi, let's *go*!" Jordan insisted.

"What's wrong with you? Why don't ya look at me?" Doralee demanded, her words sliding together as she slumped further sideways on the sofa.

Fire shot through Frankie, and she took a step closer to Javier. "He's tired. He needs to go to bed."

Beasley stood up and paced nervously, his amber eyes fixed on Javier.

"Nothing's *wrong* with him. He's got autism, for God's sake. Get over it!" Jordan ground out.

And then, her mom made the fatal mistake of laying a hand on Javier's neck.

Everything happened simultaneously.

Javier scrambled away and shot to his feet. "Leave me alone!" he screeched.

He kicked over the coffee table and sent the colored pencils flying all over the living room. He hurled his sketch pad into the glass-fronted china cabinet, and glass shards sprayed across the rug.

Frankie leaped out of her seat, but she was too slow.

Jordan placed himself between Doralee and Javier with arms wide as if blocking a pass.

Beasley barked madly at Doralee.

She drew her legs up on the sofa and held a pillow between her and the dog.

The doorbell rang.

Javier dashed up the stairs.

Beasley followed.

Jordan charged up the stairs after his brother. "Bro, it's okay; she doesn't know what she's talking about."

"What's wrong with that boy?" Doralee said. Her raw-bacon

eyelids drooped. The purple-red spider veins in her face seemed to pulse.

Every time Frankie thought she understood her mom, something happened that told her she was clueless. Frankie wanted to make everybody happy, but she had failed to do the most important thing: protect her boys.

Heart racing, Frankie whirled on her mom. She managed to keep her voice even, but just. "Why did you get drunk in my house? I invited you for a nice dinner, and you spoiled it."

Doralee looked as though she didn't know where she was or who Frankie was. "I ... I don't ... I'm sorry."

"I have to clean this mess up." Frankie knelt to pick up the pencils. A sliver of glass pierced her left forefinger. "Ouch!" Blood trickled down her finger.

The doorbell rang a second time.

FUUUCK! She forgot it already rang once.

Frankie stood and, grabbing a tissue from the end table, wrapped her finger in it. "That's Evelyn. You should go now."

"Yeah, guess so."

Her mom struggled to her feet.

Frankie took her upper arm to steady her. The last thing she needed was for her to fall on the glass and cut herself. "See yourself out, will you?"

She could have spoken to Evelyn, but getting her family settled and cleaning up the glass right now was more important.

When she heard the front door close, the tightness in Frankie's chest released. She hadn't even realized how tightly wound she was. She took the first deep breath she'd taken all night.

The living room was a war zone with glass and colored pencils everywhere. Blood was smeared on the carpet, her pants, and shirt. Taking care of the cut was her top priority.

In the guest bathroom, she examined the cut and decided

stitches were in order, but she didn't have time, energy, or money for that. A squirt of alcohol, a Band-Aid, and a paper towel would do. She'd had worse.

Looking for the rubbing alcohol, Frankie rifled through the medicine cabinet: Band-Aides, toothpaste, hand lotion, antibiotic cream, athlete's foot spray, hydrocortisone cream, baby aspirin, hair cream, plastic razor, but no bottle of alcohol. She remembered buying mouthwash last week. That was usually mostly alcohol. That would work.

Next to the toilet was the chrome trash can, its lid propped open by something. She stepped on the lever, and inside the can, was the empty bottle of mouthwash. She picked the bottle out of the trash and turned it around in her hand.

Smeared around the neck of the bottle was lipstick the same shade her mother had worn this evening.

Frankie's heart stalled.

Doralee drank the mouthwash to get drunk.

CHAPTER 37

Home

Here is a thing my heart wishes the world had more of:
I heard it in the air of one night when I listened
To a mother singing softly to a child restless and angry in the
darkness.

Carl Sandburg

"So that's what happened," Frankie said after filling in the details of the previous night's dinner for her dad.

Jordan leaned against the kitchen counter, his enormous body occupying space enough for two. Javier sat at the table, drawing and muttering. Her dad was rubbing his balding head. He had a look on his face she'd only ever seen once before when, high as a kite, one of his employees ran the work van into a client's yard and knocked down the porch they'd just put up to the tune of $10,000.

"But Javi, bro, everything turned out okay, right?" Jordan said.

He was so easygoing and upbeat that it was hard to remember that sometimes he made her so frustrated she wanted to ground him until he was thirty.

"Yeah," Javier said. "Bitch is crazy."

Using his calm, this-is-your-last-warning voice, her dad said, "I know last night she upset you, but the rules still hold. No cursing."

"Yessir," Javier said, not looking up from his drawing of an Italianate villa he'd seen only once, a year before, in a magazine.

Frankie heard him mutter "fucking bitch" under his breath. She could hardly blame him. She took a deep breath and said, "I want to apologize to you all."

"What for?" Jordan said as he rummaged in the snack cabinet.

"Don't snack," her dad said. "Dinner's in a minute."

Jordan rolled his eyes, sighed, and shut the cabinet. "But I'm *starving*."

The aroma of roast chicken with rice and vegetables filled the kitchen with a hominess that made Frankie so grateful for these three men. She loved them so much that sometimes it felt like her chest would explode.

"I'm sorry I exposed you to her when she was drunk. I thought I'd made sure nothing like that could happen. I'm sorry I pushed you guys so hard where my mom was concerned. I shouldn't have tried to create a fantasy family or anything."

"S'not really your fault," Jordan said. "But I gotta say, it was you who wanted more family, not us." Jordan slung his arm around his grandad's neck in a show of loyalty.

Frankie felt a deep sense of gratitude for her dad's help in raising them to be the kind of man he was. "You're right, and I'm sorry. I did exactly what my mom did to me: I thought I was doing what was best for everybody without realizing how it affected you all. I know that now, and I'm sorry."

Jordan let go of his granddad and moved to her. He wrapped her in one of his massive bear hugs. "It's okay, Mom. You're the best mom we could ever have, even if you didn't have a good mom yourself."

"Thanks." She was so moved by his words she barely got the words out.

Jordan rubbed the back of his neck, and she could tell what was coming. "Can I have twenty bucks for the movies tomorrow night?"

She laughed, happy that all was right with her and Jordan. "Yes."

He grinned and disappeared upstairs.

Javier, not wanting to be left out of cashing in, said, "Can I play a video game until dinner?"

"Yes," she said, feeling shame slice across her heart. If Javier had asked for a plasma screen TV, she probably would have caved. He scooted out of his chair, pushed it in three times, and headed off to the TV.

Her dad's back was to her, but she could tell by the set of his shoulder blades that he was still angry with her. This was the most serious part of the conversation.

"I never thought she'd drink the mouthwash, for heaven's sake. But you were right about her," she admitted.

"I know I was." He slipped his knuckly hands into the oven mitts, removed the chicken from the oven, and set it on the counter. "You done with her now?" He slapped the mitts on the counter. He spooned rice into a serving dish.

She set the bowl of steaming rice on the table. "No, but I'm done involving everybody else. I'm going to love her as best as I can, even if she can't love me. You ruined me, you know?"

He rested a hand on the counter, his bad leg bent at the knee to relieve the pressure. "How's that?"

She stuck the serving spoon into the rice. "I thought every parent loved their kids as much as you loved me, and I thought she would love me like that. Love me the way I love my boys, which is the way I learned from you."

His eyes softened, and a smile brightened his tense, worried face.

"She's just not able to do that and never was. It's not her fault. I've always understood alcoholics are different, but my heart didn't know that. Now it does."

"Oh, Frankie," he murmured, his face sorrowful.

She wanted him to know how much she loved him, how grateful she was to him. "You ruined me in another way, too. I always thought some man as good as you would come along someday, but all those guys I dated? They never stood a chance."

His eyes glistened. He opened his arms wide, and she walked in to hug the man whose love had made her the woman and the mom that she was.

CHAPTER 38

Be kind and compassionate to one another, forgiving each other, just as in Christ God forgave you.

Ephesians 4:32

Frankie hung the dress on the hook in the dressing room. "I think this dress might look nice on you."

It was probably a fool's errand, but Frankie cuddled hope to her heart. From what she could gather, her mom's life had been rough, bleak, and hopeless. That she was alive at all was a bit of a miracle. Frankie wanted to give her mother one fine, memorable afternoon. To buy her the last pretty dress she would ever have.

Because Doralee was weak, Frankie knew they would have to make the trip quick. She had scouted out the store ahead of time, so she knew how far away the dressing rooms were and they were located. She looked at dresses that might look nice on her mom and had asked the store to hold a flowing, rose-colored shift-style dress in a soft fabric. The dress had no waist, allowing it to fit over Doralee's belly, whether big or small. When she saw the color, Frankie knew it was *the* dress.

The first Easter after Doralee had left, Frankie's dad, of all the things he had to worry about, decided his little girl needed a new Easter dress and bonnet. She had chosen a dress in this color.

Even in his collapsing muddle, her dad had put her first.

Her mother's ratty navy coat flapped about her like crow's wings. The drooping neckline of her flimsy blouse showed her cleavage, age-spotted and wrinkled like crumpled old wax paper that had been smoothed out.

She also hoped a new dress might soften her mother's resistance to having the procedure the doctor had suggested. No cajoling from Evelyn could persuade Doralee to consent to the procedure to drain her stomach cavity. Her distended belly reminded Frankie that toxins were swimming around her mother's body.

A bigger hammer couldn't fix that.

A perpetual ticking clock and intense sorrow that subsided and returned unexpectedly accompanied Frankie's every thought of her mother. In the middle of the night, she awoke with a start, gasping from a weight on her chest. Her mother's face would flash before her, eyes yellow, skin sallow, and Frankie would feel the panic of a lost child.

Doralee said, "I don't need clothes where I'm goin'."

The cords in her neck tensed as she struggled for air.

Frankie leaned against the dressing room wall to steady herself. She fixed her eyes on the gold buttons marching down the front of the dress.

Frankie said, "I want you to have a pretty dress, Mom."

"It's real pretty, but you think it'll go over this?" She patted her tummy.

"I think you need to see the doctor about your belly. They can drain it so you can breathe easier. And yes, I think it will fit."

Doralee inhaled. A choky, tight sound. "Oh, I don't want to bother with no more doctors."

"*I* want to bother. I want to take you. Will you go for me?"

"Why?"

A clot of emotion gathered in the back of Frankie's throat, and she didn't hold back. "Because we don't have much time left, and the procedure might buy us a little more."

Doralee blinked her yellow eyes, which shone. She glanced aside. "All right then. You can call the doctor. Next week maybe?"

Frankie's whole body smiled. "Okay, then. I'll see what needs to be done."

Things weren't bad yet, but they would be soon enough. Frankie knew that she would grieve less—afterward—if she cared for her mom as much as she could.

"Nice color," Doralee said of the dress. Her chest rose slowly and collapsed quickly.

Frankie worried this shopping trip had been too much. "Looks like you're having some trouble breathing. Let's try this on quickly and get you back home."

"Oh, I'm just old. I'll be fine if I sit down there." Doralee sat on the bench in the dressing room. She balanced her gnarled hands on her cane, gazing at the dress.

Frankie helped her off with her clothes, soft from many washings, then she held the dress while her mom wormed her arms into the sleeves.

In the closeness of the dressing room, the ravages of her mom's life were painfully evident. Her arms were spotted with the rash. The knobs of her spine, each one a tiny fist, stacked down her age-spotted back. Her knobbed knees seemed too fragile to bear her weight. Her freckled shoulders lifted and dropped as she fought for each breath. The unhuman hue of her skin made it impossible to ignore that death was filling her mother with poison.

Frankie had to turn away to get her heartbreak under control.

The internet said that death from cirrhosis was not a pretty death. Looking at the naked, frail, damaged body, Frankie knew she had to do whatever she could to make the end as comfortable, kind, and gentle as possible. With her strength and determination, she could push most jobs over the finish line, but she didn't know if she had what it took to help her mother, a virtual stranger, die.

She forced herself to turn back, witness, and let grief brass-knuckle her in the chest. Kneeling in front of her mom, she began at the lowest button and worked her way up. She closed the buttons over her mom''s weary sagging breasts. Frankie sniffled, and for once, she didn't let shame or strength or resilience keep the tears back. She wiped her face with the back of her hand.

Even though she had never had a chance to be her mother's child, now she would be a good daughter. It would be the last, best gift she could give her mother. "As things come up, I want to help you. Schedule and drive you to doctor visits, fill your prescriptions, help you decide how ... things should go."

"I don't know how many doctors I'm gonna see, Francine."

"You don't have to know right now. You can decide as you go along. After the doctors take care of your tummy, you might feel differently."

Frankie stood, took her mother's two bird-claw hands, and pulled her to standing. They stood side-by-side, closer than ever before, in the cramped dressing room. The backs of their hands brushed against one another. In the mirror, they looked into one another's eyes.

Frankie saw the eyes of a stranger.

"Looks real nice, don't it?" Doralee's smile transformed her face into joy.

Frankie felt like shouting with triumph. She tried to speak, but her voice quavered. She cleared her throat. "Shall we take it then?"

Her mother looked back at her in the mirror. "Maybe it's too expensive," she said tentatively. "I told you I don't need no new dress."

In the mirror, Frankie fixed her eyes on her mother's and reached across the inches between them. She took her mom's hand. "I know you don't need one, but I want to buy it for you because it makes me happy."

Her mother stared back at her. "All right then. You deserve some happiness from me. And thank you. I sure don't deserve it."

She looked down at the floor as Frankie held her hands, easing her back onto the bench. Her mother tried to work the buttons, but the tremor in her hands made unbuttoning the dress impossible.

"Let me do that." As Frankie undid the buttons, she promised herself she would remember everything about these minutes; the shiny metal of the buttons; the soft fabric of the dress; the age spots on her mom's shoulders; the ridges of her collarbones; the female smell and intimacy of the dressing room; her mom's eyes in the silver flash of mirror; the sound of her breathing.

Her mother's breastbone rose with the effort of breathing.

Frankie pushed the buttons through the holes faster.

"I don't know why I remember this 'cause I can't remember squat, but do you remember one Easter, I made us matching dresses?"

Frankie smiled, her chest filling with sun. "I sure do. I still have that picture Dad took with us standing on the porch steps together."

Her mother said, "I thought that was what good mothers did." She paused to fight for a breath. "Dressed up like each other. I thought it would make up for a few of the times I was drunk."

Frankie eased first one, then the other of her mother's arm, out of the sleeves. She braced her mom as she leaned forward, which allowed Frankie to tug the dress from beneath her. Her mother sat on the bench in sad cotton panties and a too-big bra, grey from age while Frankie hung the dress back on a hanger.

"But that didn't make up for it, did it?" Doralee asked.

"No," Frankie whispered. "No, it never did."

Those were the truest words she had yet spoken to her mother. Frankie's honesty had the effect of satisfying some hungry animal inside of her.

Their eyes met in the mirror again, and in Doralee's eyes, Frankie saw regret, sorrow, and something like acknowledgment for what her daughter had suffered. This one look in her mother's eyes touched Frankie more than any words her mother had said.

Her mom's mouth gaped.

Her chest heaved and strained.

She gripped Frankie's arm.

"Help me." She panted. "I can't get enough air."

CHAPTER 39

The Sarum Prayer

God be in my head and in my understanding.
God be in my eyes and in my looking.
God be in my mouth and in my speaking.
God be in my heart, and in my thinking.
God be at my end, and at my departing.

Frankie sat in the ER waiting room, her veins vibrating with adrenaline, every thought short-circuiting. She felt like a scared little kid who'd caused an accident by running out in front of a speeding car. She had almost killed her mother by loving her.

Evelyn came out of the double doors of the ER, her features bent into anguished lines. "What happened? I thought this was going to be a quick trip." Leaving two chairs between them, Evelyn plopped into a chair and closed her eyes.

Frankie didn't know her well, but she could tell Evelyn was scared. "I'm sorry. We were only in the store about twenty minutes. I called the ambulance as soon as I realized something was wrong."

"At least she's finally agreed to have the procedure the doctor recommended, so I guess something good's come out of it."

"Can I go in and see her?"

Evelyn shook her head. "Paracentesis is not something you want to watch. They'll be done in an hour or so. The doctor wants to keep her in the hospital until she's better mentally and physically. The accumulated fluids were pressing on her lungs and heart. That's what caused the shortness of breath. She'll feel better after they drain her abdomen."

The image made Frankie nauseous. "Drain her" like a clog in a sink. "I'm glad she's agreed to the paracentesis."

"Sick as she is, she has said over and over the one thing she didn't want was to end up in the hospital." Evelyn sighed with a weariness that sounded bone deep. "

Her half-moon eyes, the same as Frankie's, reminded her they were family. If she had stepped in as an aunt, her presence might have gone a long way toward patching the hole left by Doralee's absence. Because of this history, Frankie felt no affection for Evelyn whatsoever. She wanted to fire Evelyn from her life, the way Evelyn had fired Frankie from hers. Frankie hated to admit it, but they would have to work together as they saw Doralee to the end.

Frankie moved one chair closer to her aunt. "Why didn't you tell me how sick she was when I knocked on your door?"

Evelyn's body contracted. She shrank in her chair. "I'm sorry, Francine. I wanted to tell you, but Dorie's always been stubborn and secretive. She absolutely refused to let me contact you."

"How do you think that makes me feel?" Frankie shot out of her seat and stood facing Evelyn. "All these years, and you never fucking told me? My dad called you, I called you, and you never responded." With every word, Frankie jabbed a forefinger at

Evelyn. "Not. One. Fucking. Time. I didn't know if she was dead or alive."

Evelyn swiped the back of her hand across damp cheeks.

Frankie saw how anxious and drawn her face was for the first time. How the deep shadows beneath her eyes were.

Evelyn whispered shakily, "I promised her, and we've always kept our promises to each other. It was the only thing she's ever asked of me, and she's given me so much."

Frankie wanted to grab Evelyn by the shirt front and shake her eyeballs out of her head. "You could have thought about how a little girl felt, how my dad felt."

"You're right, and I was wrong. I tried to do what was best for Dorie, but it hurt you, and I'm"—Evelyn glanced away—"I'm sorry. I'm so sorry."

Frankie turned her back on Evelyn and her too-late regrets. She strode across the waiting room. She stared out the window and tried to wrestle her anger into forgiveness. She had only ever considered what her mom's drinking had done to her and her dad, but Evelyn had also taken an emotional battering.

Frankie returned and sat next to Evelyn. "All right. Apology accepted. How was it that she finally came back?"

"The police in Lafayette knew her, and they called me. They told me she was very sick. They told her she had to come here or go to jail for vagrancy, so she agreed, but only if I promised no doctors or hospitals. When she got here, it was clear she didn't have long. As soon as they're done, she wants to go home."

The words pierced Frankie. "She can't just die at home."

"People go into hospice and die at home all the time," Evelyn said matter-of-factly.

Hospice: a word that sounded like the final swing of a wrecking ball.

Frankie's words came out sounding like her eight-year-old

lonely self. "I knew it was coming, but ... I thought she would get to be my mom just a little while longer."

Evelyn's smile was mournful. "Francine—Frankie, honey, she stopped being your mom when she left, but that didn't keep her from loving you the best she could. She loved you from a distance."

"How?"

Evelyn tilted her head. "Over the years, I sent her copies of the newspaper ad for your company, Women's Work, and pictures of Jordan playing basketball. I even got a picture of Javier holding his certificate for winning a drawing contest at the library. Before she got so bad, she would call me and crow about how big your boys were, how successful your business was. She was so proud of you." Evelyn pulled a tissue out of her purse and blew her nose.

"But she never called me." Frankie's throat tightened around a sob.

"Dorie's love hasn't been dependable, but she wanted to spare you having a drunk for a mother like ours."

"I don't know anything about your parents."

"We never knew our father, but our mother ..." Evelyn drew a breath and exhaled between pursed lips. "... was the town drunk and the town whore."

The shadow of pain behind Evelyn's eyes was the same Frankie had seen in Doralee's. Liquor had derailed three generations and caused so much damage, loss, and pain. What if her mom had stayed? If Frankie had seen her mom drunk day in and day out, she would have despised her. Frankie might have become a drunk herself. There would have been more slaps, screaming, and recriminations. Her dad might have left. Frankie might have been broken. She wouldn't have her business, her friends, her boys, her house, or her dad.

Her mother had saved her by leaving.

Evelyn's face flared crimson. "Strange men came to the house at all hours, so we used to push furniture up against our bedroom door."

Frankie's skin crawled as she recalled the few hints of the tortured childhood that her mother had let slip. Her life might have been just that grim if her mom had stayed.

"We had no relatives and no friends except each other. Dorie never told a soul about our mother, and she swore me to secrecy, too. We got good at lying and keeping secrets. We kept up a fake life along with our real one."

Evelyn heaved a sigh. Her face sagged, but she looked relieved, too. It was as if she'd been waiting all these years to tell Frankie the truth.

"You must have been terrified all the time," Frankie said, her new understanding giving rise to compassion for Evelyn.

"With Dorie by me, I wasn't. She was so capable and dependable. You'd never know it, but she did whatever needed doing. Problem with lying and keeping secrets is that she ended up trusting only me and, maybe your dad."

Those characteristics matched Frankie's personality more than she liked to admit. She'd thought they came from having been without her mother, but perhaps these characteristics came from her mother.

Either way, Frankie was beginning to see that total self-reliance could be a two-edged sword. She had convinced herself that she was strong and independent, so she had never honestly shared the depth of her pain with her friends. It was sin of distrust, a failure to acknowledge how much they loved her. A failure to recognize that she deserved love *just because*. "Didn't anyone know?"

Evelyn continued, "When Momma was sober—which wasn't very often—we attended St. Barnabas, the Episcopal Church in

Lafayette. The priest there was Father Francis. It was the only place we really felt safe."

Frankie felt a click of recognition: that was why she felt so safe and welcome at St. Paul's. Why she wanted to share that with others. That, too, came from her mother.

"Sometimes, if Momma was on a bender, we'd sleep outside the church in a little alcove."

"Outside?" Frankie gasped.

Evelyn nodded. "One night, Father Francis found us." Evelyn smiled and laid a hand on Frankie's. "You know, you're named for him, don't you?"

Frankie didn't know whether to laugh or cry. "She never told me."

"Because then she would have had to tell you why."

"How old were you when he found you?"

Evelyn squinted, thinking. "Mmm, I was nine or ten, and Dorie was eleven or so."

Frankie's heart broke for those two little girls, alone and lost. They had been on their own nearly all their lives. No one held them, comforted them, or kept them safe. *Thank God for Dad.*

"Dorie wouldn't even tell him what was going on, but Father Francis knew. He arranged for parishioners to take us in until Momma showed up to claim us. The Vascolis, the Thrupps, the Narbonnes, the Derbannes, the Freemans." Her voice was warm, charmed by memories and scraps of happiness.

"The congregation was Black. White people thought we were trash and wouldn't have anything to do with us. We'd never been around Black folks, but our experience changed our thinking. You could say that's the one good thing that came out of Momma's drinking. The people who saved our lives are all gone now. They were like family." Evelyn shook her head, a faint smile of sadness on her lips. "Dorie thought she was keeping secrets, but everyone knew."

"Dad doesn't even know. Why didn't you tell him or me?" Frankie asked.

Evelyn lifted her chin, her neck rod straight. "Dorie made me promise never to tell. She dropped out of school and supported me so I could go to nursing school. That's why I have a career and a house. I did what I did to protect Dorie because she protected me. I owe her my life because she gave up hers."

The sisters' secrets had left them hurt and scarred. Their pain had driven Doralee to drink and Evelyn to a misguided loyalty. How could Doralee love her daughter after that kind of childhood?

Evelyn turned her palm up. "What do secrets matter now?"

Frankie answered, "Not one damn thing."

"She believed she was protecting you by staying away. She wanted to spare you the shame of having a drunk for a mother. For you to have the life she never had. She refused whenever I begged her to come home to live with me. Same with letting me talk to you. Said it was best for everyone."

"I wish she had sent me a note or called me. Something to let me know she was alive. I would have known she at least thought about me, even if she didn't love me."

Evelyn swiveled in her seat and faced Frankie. "I don't know about you, but I can't imagine what it must be like to love your child so much you force yourself to stay away. If anything will make you drink, that would."

Frankie had been unprepared for the raw honesty of this conversation. Everything she felt, thought, wished, and yearned for was meaningless in the face of what Evelyn and Doralee had endured as children. She felt foolish and selfish for having spent so much emotion alternately loving, hating, and longing for her mother. "Why did she start drinking if she saw what it did to your mother?"

Evelyn's eyes followed a nurse pushing an empty wheelchair

to the door. "She told me it made her forget." Evelyn blinked and blinked. "She tried to be invincible, lied, kept secrets. If only she had told people how much she was hurting, things might have turned out differently."

They sat in silence for a few moments, each with their bruised and aching hearts.

"You're a nurse. You must have some idea of how ... how long?"

"No one can predict, but I'd say not more than a couple months."

Frankie felt as though her hopes had been given a death sentence. After almost a lifetime apart, a couple of months was all that was left. She rubbed her temples. "I know she doesn't like the doctors, but we need to see how we can prolong her life."

Evelyn raised her eyes to meet Frankie's. "She's signed a living will refusing any more treatment than they're doing today."

Cold spread through Frankie. Her insides jerked up as though she'd been yanked to a standstill.

There was nothing left to do but wait.

CHAPTER 40

For life and death are one, even as the river and the sea are one.

Kahlil Gibran

Frankie went home and told her dad and the boys what had happened at the store about the ambulance. They took the news soberly. Jordan cleared the dinner dishes without being asked. Javier walked Beasley without having to be nagged. For the first time in ages, it felt as if they noticed she was an actual person, not just a mom.

Once they were alone, her dad opened a bottle of wine and poured each of them a glass. He waved her into the living room. She settled on the sofa, and he in his Barcalounger.

She couldn't remember when she had ever felt so exhausted and heartsick. It was an effort just to breathe.

"I'll check on Marina's job tomorrow if you want," her dad said. "That way, you can do whatever needs to be done at the hospital."

"Thanks," she murmured. "At least now that they've been able to do the procedure, she might improve."

"Frankie," he said in a gently chiding tone. He meant, "Stop kidding yourself."

"I know," she said wearily. "I just keep hoping for a miracle."

"Kind of a miracle she came back here at all. Don't think we can ask the Good Lord for any more than that." He sipped his wine and gave a little lip-smacking sound of enjoyment. "I waaas thinking ..." He set his glass down. "... Maybe I'd go see her."

She was as shocked as if he'd said, "I think I'll fly to Mars."

While she'd been on her journey with her mother, he'd been on his, without letting on that Doralee's return had touched him in any way. Or more likely—more like him—he'd let her have enough room to let her heart settle however she needed.

Like always, he put Frankie first.

She didn't say anything. He had his own broken heart to mend, and she hoped he might do it before it was too late. Her burden of loss had been a ball and chain, but his burden must have been the size of a cement truck.

"Good idea," was all she said.

He picked up his thriller, put on his reading glasses, and ended the conversation.

The next evening after work, she stopped in to see her mom. When she got to her room, her dad was sitting next to her bed, holding her mom's hand. Frankie froze in the doorway. He was so intent on speaking to her mom he didn't notice her arrival.

Doralee's eyes were closed, but he was murmuring lovingly to her. The bend of his body, the angle of his head, and the tone of his voice were achingly intimate as if no time at all had passed. As if Doralee loved him as much as he still loved her.

Frankie didn't want to eavesdrop, but it was impossible not to. He had remained single all these years, his love for Doralee wrapped around his heart like barbed wire.

She stood quietly, not moving.

"Aren't you proud of how she turned out? She's real smart, like you, and stubborn like you, too. She's a good mom." He sighed. "It wasn't easy raising her alone, but I loved being her dad, watching her grow up. I wish you coulda' seen her. I'm"—he sniffled—"I'm sorry ... sorry you didn't get to see her grow up, but you understand why I did what I did."

He pinched the bridge of his nose. "I didn't know how bad things would get for you, but I just couldn't ... I'm sorry," he said hoarsely. He cleared his throat noisily, pulled a tissue from a box, and swiped at his cheeks.

Frankie bit her lower lip to keep from crying.

"Well, anyhow," he went on. "Aren't her boys nice? Jordan"—he paused to laugh, lovingly and amazed— "I don't know if you could tell, but he's got a good head on his shoulders. Really smart." He lowered his voice secretively. "I kind of wish he'd try for a basketball scholarship, but he likes math and science, too, so I guess the engineering thing will be what he does." His voice became lighter, almost jovial. "I've been saving for the boys for college. Frankie doesn't know—don't tell her now—but I have near seventy-five saved up for each of the boys. Javier, he'll probably ..."

Frankie backed out of the room because she was afraid he'd hear her crying.

CHAPTER 41

The glory of friendship is not the outstretched hand, not the kindly smile, nor the joy of companionship; it is the spiritual inspiration that comes to one when you discover that someone else believes in you and is willing to trust you with a friendship.

Ralph Waldo Emerson

Frankie let herself into Flicka's condo. She could hear the Marriage Survivors Club in the living room, cackling up a storm. She wasn't in much of a mood for that, but as usual, it was time to set her feelings aside and get on with the tasks which living required.

In front of the gilded hall mirror, she smoothed her practical black skirt and checked her makeup in the hall mirror. She'd applied a little makeup, pinned her hair back, and added a glob of that tightening cream at the corners of her eyes. She was no beach bunny bikini babe like she supposed Cam Simpson was used to, but she looked nice. She had chosen her understated outfit so that Cam Simpson wouldn't think she was hurling herself at him when, really, that was precisely what she wanted to do.

Flicka appeared in the hallway. "I thought that was you." She gave Frankie an appraising look which wasn't very encouraging. "Don't you look like a church lady!"

Flicka's black beaded gown hugged every medically-sculpted curve and dove low at the neckline to show the twin hillocks of her fake boobs.

Wasn't the woman worried about a wardrobe malfunction?

"I am a church lady." Frankie opened her shawl to show the silky maroon blouse she'd found languishing in the back of her closet. "With a touch of sin mixed in."

"We're Episcopalians; we don't believe in sin." Flicka waved a red-manicured hand at Frankie. "Come on, we have some work to do." She paused and kindly said, "I'm sorry about your mom ending up in the hospital."

"Thanks. It's the best place for her. But I don't want to think about that right because I have other things on my mind."

Like Cam and the house. Or just Cam.

The Marriage Survivors lounged in Flicka's living room. A sweating silver bucket held an open bottle of Dom Perignon Champagne. Bianca, sprawled across the sofa with one leg hanging off the edge, was watching baseball with the sound off, her black and white dress rucked up around her thighs. Without taking her eyes off the game, she waggled her fingers hello at Frankie.

Olivia greeted her. She wore a pale green silk dress and low heels, giving her a prim, classy mother-of-the-bride look. As usual, Olivia dove straight to the heart. "Are you up to this with your mom in the hospital? We can manage it if you want to bag it."

Frankie said. "I couldn't miss this after all our work. And Cam's expecting me."

"How is your mom?" Carolina asked.

Frankie suddenly felt enormously weary. "She's stable. The good news is, they've convinced her to stay in the hospital until they get her to a better baseline." Something flung itself at Frankie, and she fought the impulse to sit and cry. *No time for that. You have a job to do.*

Carolina turned her back to Frankie. "Zip me?"

Carolina had accented her demure lapis blue dress with a fabric belt woven with images of colorful tropical birds. She wore a string of pearls and small pearl earrings. Her hair and makeup were subtle but elegant.

"How are you feeling?" Olivia asked.

"I understand why she left and that she loves me in her own way, however lame that is."

"You don't sound convinced." Hélène wore a white, Grecian-style gown and black elbow-length gloves. With her dramatic sweep of black and white hair, she looked like a dove caught in mid-flight. She expertly poured a glass of champagne, not spilling a drop, and handed the glass to Frankie.

Frankie said, "She had her own history, and it's hard to fault her for her decisions and logic."

Bianca lifted her head. "You were planning on wearing that?"

"Sssss!" Hélène hissed at Bianca.

Heat rose in Frankie's cheeks. She should have asked for fashion advice from one of the women, except Bianca, of course.

Frankie held her hands out from her sides. "This is it. I wore these low shoes so I can work the room and introduce Cam to everyone. I want to make sure he gets to know who we really are."

"You look very nice," Carolina said. "Very serious."

Frankie said, "Thanks. That was my intention. So Cam will take me seriously."

Flicka said, "Quit worrying about what Cam Simpson will think of you. You just kick his ass with a moral argument about how good this is for the whole town, and he'll cave like a bad soufflé." She headed to her bedroom and called over her shoulder, "Be right back."

Frankie said, "My plan is to introduce him to Father Gabriel and people who could have used a place like this. I want Cam to meet the other people behind the project. He'll see how committed we are and maybe reconsider his position." She sighed with exhaustion. What she really wished she could do was go home and sleep. "Tonight's my Hail Mary."

Hélène said, "Try not to be, you know, your usual stubborn self. Charm him, talk to him, get to know him."

"Show him your boobs," Bianca muttered.

"And get him good and liquored up," Flicka said as she reappeared from the bedroom. She carried a long dress made of filmy fabric. "Okay, take that stuff off," she ordered.

Frankie asked, "Why?"

"I got you a little convincer for this evening." Flicka held the gown up to Frankie.

It was a fire engine red, floor-length, one-shoulder gown with a sparkly belt.

"I'm not wearing that! It makes me look like a beauty queen wanna-be."

"Oh, yes, you are going to wear it."

Her tone told Frankie she'd already lost the argument.

"And what's wrong with looking like a beauty queen?"

"If I looked like you, nothing," Frankie said.

Bianca craned her neck back to look at the dress. "Makes you look like a high-class hooker." She added quickly, "Not that there's anything wrong with sex work! Sorry, didn't mean to sound all judgey." She turned off the TV.

"It's gorgeous," Olivia said admiringly. "Try it on, then decide."

"Why'd you do this?" Frankie asked.

"You were busy with your mother, and I knew you wouldn't think of getting anything for yourself," Flicka said. "Besides, I have better taste than you. I thought I'd help you out and save you the trouble."

Hélène raised her champagne glass. "This is your evening, Frankie. You deserve to look like a queen."

"I can't afford this." She couldn't resist touching the gown. In her fingers, the sheer drapery felt girly and sexy in a way she forgot she enjoyed.

Her dad had always made sure she had frilly dresses for church, a new Easter hat until she got too old for hats, and Mary Janes in black or white. He'd encouraged her girliness in her bedroom, with fluffy bedspreads, lacy curtains, and every Black Barbie he could find. But she'd always donned work boots, jeans, sweatshirts, and hard hats to work with him after school. In the world of men, and construction, those duds were necessary, and she'd gotten used to that uniform.

"We all chipped in. It's a present from all of us for everything you've done," Carolina said.

Frankie's heart swarmed with love; they had considered her important enough, loved her enough, to do this. She was unused to feeling this fragile, as though she might break down and weep at any moment. Only their presence buoyed her up. "Thanks, guys," she mumbled, blinking away tears.

She shed her skirt, shapeless blouse, and boring flats. Here she was, in sexy Flicka's living room, in panties and a bra with worn-out elastic. She recalled helping her mother in the store dressing room. Like mother, like daughter.

Flicka unzipped the gown and held it for Frankie to step into. Olivia adjusted the single shoulder strap and pulled up the zipper. Carolina fastened the rhinestone belt around Frankie's waist while Bianca made swoony noises.

When she'd seen the dress on the hangar, Frankie had expected the gown to feel wrong. But the chiffon whispered against her skin. The proportions were perfect. She felt glamorous. Beautiful. Cinderella-ish. Frankie felt a glow of pleasure. "You guys are transforming me into a princess."

Flicka stood back and twirled her finger circle.

Frankie complied and made a turn.

"Excellent. Perfect size," Flicka said. "Can I pick 'em, or can I pick 'em?"

"Except for husbands, evidently," Bianca said.

Flicka threw her a withering look.

The rest of them laughed.

"Where's the mirror?" Frankie asked.

"No looking yet. We're not done." Hélène gestured to a straight-backed chair.

Frankie sat while Hélène applied her makeup. Carolina swept Frankie's hundreds of tiny braids into a French twist, fixing it in place with rhinestone pins. Olivia painted her nails with a quick-drying polish in a red that matched the dress. Bianca kept the champagne glasses filled.

Flicka fixed her again with a critical eye. "All right, you can go take a look."

They trailed Frankie as she swept into Flicka's *boudoir*—as she called it—to behold herself.

When she saw herself in the mirror, Frankie felt a gush of astonishment. The gown flowed in molten red over her breasts, her hips, and her butt. The rhinestone belt caught sparkles of light and accented her waist. The make-up job took ten years off her face. Well, maybe five. She was beautiful. And awestruck.

"Look at those biceps!" Flicka said. "You have Michelle Obama arms."

"All that carrying sheet rock and power tools," Frankie said. "I feel like a fraud. Like I'm trying to sell Cam Simpson a bill of goods."

"There you go, being self-deprecating again," Olivia said.

Bianca flopped onto the bed on her stomach. "If only he were lucky enough to nail you."

They laughed again.

"It's not overkill?" Frankie said, feeling undeserving and insecure.

"If you want to catch bees, you have to sweeten the pot," Flicka said, giving Frankie a hip bump.

"I bet he's got a fine stinger," Bianca said, and they all laughed some more.

"You're who God meant you to be. A beautiful Black princess," Carolina said sweetly and with such feeling that Frankie almost believed her.

She held her arms out and gave a swift pirouette making the light-as-fog fabric swirl around her. "Thanks, guys. I didn't know I could look like, well, this great!"

Flicka said, "Because you work with men all the time, you forgot you have a vagina."

They all laughed uproariously.

"Let's see if it gets used tonight," Bianca said.

More laughter.

Hélène said, "Oh, wait, one more thing."

She poured a pile of glittering rhinestone jewelry onto Flicka's bed from a velvet drawstring bag.

Olivia gasped. "Where did you get all these?"

"Oh, you know," Hélène hedged, a red flush creeping across her sharp cheekbones.

Flicka dangled an earring in the light. "These are excellent fakes."

"When did you ever wear this kind of stuff?" Bianca asked.

Hélène kept her gaze fixed away from the boodle as though they were too sparkly to look at. "Ah, no occasion. I just had them for fun."

Something mournful and regretful in Hélène's expression made Frankie question her words.

Hélène slipped a wide rhinestone cuff on Frankie's wrist and a chunky cabochon ruby ring on her left hand. Holding two different earrings up to Frankie's ears, Hélène debated, then decided on a pair of chandelier-style earrings.

Frankie put the earrings on, then stared down at her bare feet. "Will the dress be too long with my flats?"

"Do you think I'd let you wear flats with this dress?" Flicka opened a box and pulled out a pair of red skyscraper-high stilettos.

Frankie raised a skeptical eyebrow. "Are those some kind of medieval torture devices?"

"Jimmy Choo's. You just have to forget you have feet for the evening." Flicka placed them in front of Frankie. "Put 'em on."

Frankie slipped on the shoes, which had pointy toes and needle-like heels. "I'll have to amputate my toes for lack of blood supply when I take these off."

But they were exquisite and unbelievably sexy.

"It'll be worth it for the look," Flicka said. She kicked out a foot, displaying her own weapon-grade shoe. "After a few hours, they stop hurting because you no longer have any sensation in your feet."

"Just pull them off when you're not dancing. They complete the outfit," Hélène said.

Frankie gazed at herself. Overcome by wistfulness, she spoke without thinking. "My mom's never seen me all dressed up like this, I mean, even to go to a school dance or anything."

Olivia held Frankie by the forearms. "Why don't you stop by the hospital and show her how gorgeous you look?"

Frankie glanced at the bedside clock. "But the gala starts in an hour. I need to be there."

"What, you think we can't do anything without you?" Bianca said. "Go show your mom and get one of those mother-daughter moments."

"Are you sure?" Frankie asked.

"Go," Hélène said.

Flicka snapped her fingers. "All right, girls, let's go knock 'em dead and wring every cent out of them we can!"

"One for all, and no bullshit for any!" Bianca said.

CHAPTER 42

Let us Build a House, Hymn No. 301

Built of tears and cries and laughter,
Prayers of faith and songs of grace,
Let this house proclaim from floor to rafter.
All are welcome, all are welcome,
All are welcome in this place.

Marty Haugen

On her way through the lobby, in her gala finery, Frankie got plenty of stares, and at first, she wondered who everyone was looking at until she realized with delight that it was her. As the elevator doors closed, she reached back to make sure the flowing skirt wasn't stuck in her butt crack.

She swanned past electronic medical equipment on wheels, supply carts, and laundry bins cluttering the hospital hallway.

The door to her mom's room was open. Frankie slipped in quietly, not wanting to wake her. The room was dark except for the red and green LED lights blinking and winking on the monitor. Frankie could still see the leathery skin sagging in deep loops of flesh below her mom's sunken eye sockets. Under the covers, her belly was oddly deflated, which only made her appear gaunter. Her rash-spotted arms lay atop the hospital blanket, and the blanket outlined her knobby, withered legs.

This was not what Frankie had signed up for, but love seldom was, she supposed. Loving could be boring, gut-wrenching, exhilarating, breathtaking, terrifying, and devastating. So far as her mom was concerned, Frankie had lived on the careful edge of those emotions. Loving her boys kept her aware of the danger of a shattered heart every day.

But here was death come to call.

This was what it meant to be loving: doing it even if you knew it meant walking into a buzzsaw. You found the courage to do the hardest thing you could imagine: love someone you knew would leave you, who couldn't really love you back the way you wanted and needed because they needed you.

Frankie stepped into the room and crossed to her mom's bedside. She brushed a strand of white hair from her mother's forehead with its map of blue veins.

Her mom spoke on an exhale of breath, "Who is that?"

"It's me, Frankie," she said. "Your daughter."

Her eyes flickered open. "You come to see me? Turn on the light." Her voice was strong, and her diction astonishingly sharp.

Frankie flicked the switch for the light. Despite how ravaged her mother's body looked, her eyes were clear. She seemed alert.

"You look so much better, Mom."

"I feel better, too, now that I can breathe. My mind feels clearer too."

But Dr. Goldpin had said the onset of dementia was permanent, so her mom's self-assessment couldn't necessarily be trusted.

Her mom's eyes widened. "What have you got on there?"

Frankie stood back, giving her mother a full view. Proudly, arms extended, palms up, like a mannequin in a window, Frankie displayed her finery.

"Oh, look at you!" Her mom's crinkly mouth formed an *O* of surprise. "My, my, my! Turn 'round so I can see my beautiful girl."

Her pleasure was like a pearl Frankie caught and tucked away in her pocket to remember later.

Her mom patted the edge of the bed.

Frankie perched there tentatively. Under blue, translucent lids, her mom's eyes were bright. At this minute, one more year didn't seem unthinkable to Frankie.

"The boyfriend taking you tonight is one lucky man," her mom said.

"Oh, he's not my boyfriend. I'm going to the gala with the developer who bought 61 East Avenue." Frankie described how she and Cam had met and how he volunteered at the Carver Center.

When Frankie finished, her mother said, "Something about the way you talk about him tells me you think a lot of this man."

Frankie was surprised that her mom, after all these years, could still read something in her. Was it their weaving a relationship into being that made that trick possible? Or was there some vestigial thread that made it possible for her to do it? It made Frankie feel seen and heard in a way she didn't know she had missed.

"Well, I guess I do, sort of." She quickly added, "But not in a romantic way."

Her mother snorted softly, a smile appearing on her cracked lips. "You sure went to a lot of trouble to dress up for someone you don't like too much."

Caught out, Frankie laughed. "My girlfriends ambushed me. One bought the dress and shoes, one did my hair, and another one did my makeup."

"They sound like good friends. Is he handsome, this guy you don't like?"

Thinking of Cam, a wire sparked in Frankie's blood. Those slate gray eyes, silvery hair, and square chin, the ropy arms she'd seen at the gym; his sense of humor and the way he danced around the court in his beat-up sneakers; his kind, effortless connection with Javier. There was more to him than the RWM real estate developer: someone lovely and thoughtful.

"He's handsome enough," she said. With a grin, she added, "For a White guy."

"He's White?"

"Yeees."

"Long as he treats you nice, don't matter what color he is."

"It's just business, Mom."

Her chuckle sounded wet and stuffy. "You know, that's one thing I'm sorry about. Never seeing you get married. Me and your dad had a rushed, kinda secret wedding at St. Paul's. Only Evie came as the witness." She sighed. "Back then, we were still afraid somebody'd come burn a cross in the front yard."

"Not much has changed," Frankie said.

"Never does. Never does," her mom said.

"You guys were incredibly brave to make a biracial marriage," Frankie said.

"Love'll do that to ya. We were crazy about one another."

This brought a question to Frankie's mind that she had long thought of but only now felt permission to ask. She focused on the fabric's hem as she threaded it through her fingers. "Do you think, maybe ... do you think marrying a Black guy put so much stress on you that you drank more heavily?"

Her mom's knotty fingers came to rest on her arm. "Your father was the best thing that ever happened to me. I loved him, and he loved me." She put her hand back on her chest. "But booze got ahold a me, and I couldn't fight back." She turned her wizened face to Frankie. "All these years, how come you never found anybody who drove you crazy the way Vic did me?"

Frankie shrugged. "I used to date when I still had time and energy. There's always plenty of single men around a construction site, hardworking, a little rough around the edges, nice guys, but I kept telling myself I was waiting for a guy like Dad." Frankie sighed and tugged at an earring. "Anyway, that was how I protected my heart from getting broken. Now, I guess I'm too old to find true love."

Her mom smiled, her voice chiding. "Oh, Vic was one of a kind, but it's never too late to fall in love."

Cam had jiggled something hot and springy loose in her. And it was more dangerous than a blowtorch. But he was an opponent, and she still wanted the house. She had to keep her head about her tonight.

"You deserve somebody nice." Her mother wagged a motherly finger at her. "Listen, you find a nice guy and work hard to make it stick. I didn't try hard enough."

The words hung in the awkward silence between them.

Then her mom said, "You turned out beautiful and fine. Wish I'da had more to do with it."

Another pearl to hold on to.

"You did have a lot to do with how I turned out, but I'm sorry you didn't see it happen."

"Me, too, honey. Me too." She sighed. "Don't keep that lucky fella waiting."

Frankie's phone showed six o'clock. She would be late if she didn't leave now for the gala, but so many questions filled her head. She was torn between going and talking to her mother. What was it like growing up without her own mother? How had she found the courage to marry her dad? How had she and Evelyn managed to stay alive?

Frankie leaned down to kiss her mom's cheek. It was cool and wrinkly, like a piece of fruit that was past.

Her mother lifted a crooked finger. "Wait a minute. Let me fix your hair. You got a braid come loose."

Frankie sat on the bed with her back to her mother. The sensation of her mother's fingers poking and prodding her hair provoked a sensation of such force Frankie couldn't breathe for a moment. She was flooded with the memory of her mother fixing her hair when she was a child, the intimacy of her mother's touch on her head, in her hair, her fingertips brushing her neck as she gathered loose strands. She felt every tug, stroke, and pull again. She smelled the scent of a special oil her mother used to keep her hair soft. She heard the story she told.

"There, that's it," her mom said. "Now you ready for the ball, Miss Cinderella."

When her mother's hands left her hair, Frankie felt such a sense of loss she nearly asked her to touch her hair again. She put a hand to the spot on her scalp where her mother's fingers had left the ghost of her fingerprint. Frankie had to sit a moment longer, gathering her equilibrium.

"When I was little and you fixed my hair, to keep me still you told me about how you and Dad met."

"Yes, I did."

"Will you ... will you tell me again?"

Her mother's expression was one of amusement. "Why you want to hear that?"

She touched the back of her mom's hand. The bones felt like

twigs held together by parchment. "Tell me, please, for old time's sake?"

"'Course I will." Her mother folded her hands and closed her eyes. Then, she took a breath and began the story, the details of which Frankie remembered. "I met your daddy when I was waitressing in a diner off I-95, and he come in for breakfast. We were real busy, but he starts talking to me, hears my Louisiana accent, asks where I'm from, so we struck up a conversation. Men used to chat me up all the time, but he was different." Her white eyebrows knitted together. "Serious, like he was on a mission."

"Back then, it was a big deal for a Black guy to ask out a White woman, wasn't it?" Frankie asked. As a child, she always asked this question when her mother got to this point because it was her part to tell in the story.

"Yes, it was, and that was one thing I liked about him right away: his courage." She cracked an eyelid and looked at Frankie with one eye. "You know, I was quite a looker in those days. I was tall and had slender hips, like you." Her voice grew lazier as she became lost in the memories, but she showed no sign of losing her train of thought. Whatever the doctors had done was the answer to Frankie's prayers. "Finally, my boss come up, and he said to Vic, 'Mister, stop pestering my waitress and order something or get out.' So he ordered a cup of coffee and drank that and asked me some more questions."

Frankie laughed here like she always had.

"Then he ordered toast, and he asked me more questions, and I asked him some. Then, he ordered two eggs, over easy," she paused and opened one eye again. "He still like his eggs that way?"

"Yup, but now without the yolks because of his high cholesterol," Frankie said.

"Guess he got old, too."

They chuckled.

Her mother closed her eyes again and continued. "He kept on talking to me. Ooo whee! My boss was fuming, but he couldn't say anything because Vic kept on ordering things starting at eight, and he kept it up for two hours."

As she talked, the feeling of sharing a family story settled in Frankie. It was as though the past had not broken but kept moving through time and space, the years falling away. She felt the physical closeness she had felt as a child, her mother's hands working in her hair. Her breath on her neck, her hands sweeping the hair off Frankie's nape, her laughter vibrating in Frankie's ear, the tug and pull of the comb, the snap of the hairbands at the ends of her braids, the click of plastic barrettes. Every movement and sound burned bright and hot in Frankie's memory. Those tiny sensations in the space between them had been her mother's love. That was why the memory was so vivid, why she wanted to hear it again. Her mother had loved her—not well, but now and then—as much as she could.

"Then my boss—he was laughing, and he didn't know your dad—he said to Vic, 'If you just ask her out already and get outta my place, I won't make you pay for all this food.' Your daddy stood up, and the whole place," she lowered her voice to a hoarse whisper, "went quiet. I don't know if people were waiting to see if he was going to or hoping he wouldn't. But he asked me if I would go out with him every Friday night for the next six months. We knew pretty much everything about each other by now, so I said 'Yes.' The whole diner, customers, waitresses, my boss, everybody who'd been watching clapped and cheered. After about three dates, we both knew we was meant for each other, and that was that."

"And that was that," whispered Frankie, repeating her part.

"And that ... was that," echoed her mother.

Her eyes fluttered closed, and Frankie held her hand until her breath was steady. Then, she kissed her mom's forehead and left.

CHAPTER 43

Let us Build a House, Hymn No. 301

Let us build a house where love is found
In water, wine, and wheat:
A banquet hall on holy ground
Where peace and justice meet.

Marty Haugen

Frankie left the hospital filled with a sense of serenity and peace, but when she arrived at Norwalk Inn, the ballroom was rocking to "YMCA," by Village People. It made her wonder if the time spent with her mom was another one of her fantasies.

The music pulsed through her, made her breastbone vibrate, and crushed her thoughts into white noise. Under a sparkling disco ball, couples gyrated shoulder-to-shoulder, men with men, women with women, guys in drag, older couples, Asian men,

African American couples, and straight couples jammed together.

This, *this,* was what St. Paul's was about.

It filled her with pride that she and the Marriage Survivors Club had made it happen. She wished she could have shared her feeling of success with her mom.

Frankie tottered to the table where Flicka and Carolina checked in guests at the ballroom door and directed them to their seats.

Frankie scanned the room. "Has Cam checked in yet?"

"Nope," Flicka said. "But don't worry. He'll be here."

Frankie's internal seesaw bobbed. He was probably just blowing smoke when he agreed to come. He didn't have any interest in St. Paul's. He only wanted to ease his conscience. She didn't want to admit it, but she would be disappointed if he stood her up. Here she was, all beautified, and he would miss the show.

Sam Wanamaker and Darren Houser strode in with an incredibly handsome man in tow. Darren and the gentleman paused at a distance to admire the decorations. Sam came up to the check-in table.

"Who's that?" Flicka asked Sam.

"Dr. Octavio Martinez," Sam answered. "Friend of ours."

"Gay?" Flicka asked.

Carolina and Frankie looked at one another and exchanged eye rolls.

Sam nodded. "Yeah, sorry, Flicka."

She laughed. "Yes, but is he single?"

"For now," Sam said with a grin.

Flicka said, "Let me check on your seats. I want to make certain you have interesting table mates."

"Thanks. I'll get a drink and be right back." Sam wandered off.

Carolina leaned over the seating chart and pointed to a table. "They're with Carol and the McElhones."

Flicka eyed the seating chart. "Put him next to Father Gabriel and move Carol over to that table."

Carolina said, "You're trying to set up Father Gabriel with the doctor!"

"He's hot, gay, and single," Flicka said. "What could be better?"

"I'm havin' no part of this," Frankie said, unwilling to be implicated in Flicka's perpetual scheme of trying to set up Father Gabriel.

A few minutes later, her arm hooked through the man in question, Flicka waltzed the doctor, Sam, and Darren, to Father Gabriel's table.

When Flicka came back to the check-in table, she wore a smug smile on her face.

"You are bad," Carolina said and laughed.

"Father Gabriel!" Flicka crowed as he walked through the door.

"Good evening, ladies," he said. "This looks fantastic. Thank you for all your work."

"Oh, we're getting some playtime in tonight." Flicka pointed to his newly assigned table. "Your table is right over there."

Flicka grinned. "I'm going to see him married off if it's the last thing I do."

"You are the most meddlesome woman I know," Carolina scolded, but she was laughing.

"I know!" Flicka said gleefully.

Frankie bent and pulled off one of her killer shoes. She groaned with relief. "If Cam wasn't going to show up, he could have called me."

"Put those shoes back on," Flicka ordered.

"Please, just a minute more," Frankie begged.

"No! He's here." Flicka nicked her head toward the door.

Frankie almost fell over. He paused at the doorway, looking over the room. In his tux, Cam looked as delectable as whipped cream. He was his jaw was taut, his shoulders were thrown back, and his eyes narrowed. He was unsmiling, as though steeled for battle.

How could she keep her priorities straight with him looking like that?

If she couldn't persuade him to sell them the house, she would simply have to own up to the fact she wasn't good enough to pull this off. The church and her friends deserved to have someone shove this project over the finish line. If she couldn't do it, she'd gracefully let someone else take the helm. She'd been the one to sell everyone on 61 East Avenue. She didn't have it in her to face another flop.

He spotted her, and his eyes flared. An enormous grin, which she'd only seen when he was playing basketball with the kids at the Carver Center, spread over his face. He made his way to her. "You look fantastic."

"You look pretty fantastic yourself." She grinned. His smile made it hard not to flirt with him.

He leaned close so she could hear him, and she didn't find his proximity unpleasant. He smelled like pine trees, new leather, and money.

He said, "I don't mean to sound insulting, but I expected to find a bunch of gossipy old ladies in orthopedic shoes, sitting around eating cheese and soggy crackers, but this! This is like a flashback to the '80s. And it's with the church!"

"You must be thinking of some other church. Episcopalians know how to party."

Father Gabriel, wearing his clerical collar and a staid charcoal suit, jived passed with Carol Baxter. She wore a white powdered wig and a sleeveless, neon-orange dress. The head of her dead, stuffed Lhasa Apso, Winnie, protruded from her backpack.

"Is that your *priest*?" Cam's shoulders bounced with laughter.

"Oh, yeah." Frankie laughed too. "He dances a little like Elaine on *Seinfeld*, but don't tell him that."

"And who's he dancing with?"

"That's Carol. She's a little weird, but we love her. Everybody watches out for her. That's what we do at St. Paul's."

They each took a glass of wine from a passing waiter. Cam's body bopped along with the music as he sipped his wine. His movements stirred the air between them, and every inch of Frankie's skin felt alive. Her bones vibrated in tandem with the jamming rhythm of "It's Rainin' Men."

She had only finished half her wine when Cam knocked back the remainder of his. He set his glass on a table and pointed to the dance floor. "Ready to dance?"

How was she going to dance in these shoes? With him? Together? Dancing was the furthest thing from her mind. He wouldn't take her seriously if she danced with him.

She stalled. "I wanted to introduce you around. Have you get to know us. See why you should sell us the house."

"You don't give up, do you?" He was still smiling.

"No, it's one of my better qualities."

"You promised not to bring up the house tonight, remember?" His eyes flicked toward the door.

She needed to keep him engaged, or he'd leave. But she didn't want to sleaze her way to a deal either. Not that she wouldn't like dancing with him, but that smacked of consorting with the enemy. She wanted him to see who the people of St. Paul's were. What the house meant to them, to Norwalk, and to her. "It's been ages since I've danced."

"That's okay. Out there, it will be too loud to have you sweet-talking me about the house. And I'm a pretty good dancer if I do say so myself."

His confidence wasn't arrogant but playful, with an edge of challenge.

She was trying her damnedest to be friendly without flirting, but his slate gray eyes, and the curve of his lower lip, didn't make it easy. She raised her eyebrows and smiled. "Haven't you heard? Straight, White guys can't dance."

He tipped his chin up and jerked smartly on the lapels of his tux jacket. "I am about to disprove that stereotype."

He grabbed her hand, short-circuiting her brain, and led her onto the dance floor. The feel of his hand on the small of her back made a whiskey-like warmth spread through her body. If dancing with him was her only move, she would sacrifice her toes for the cause. Anything for St. Paul's, for the house, for the people she loved, for her friends, for Father Gabriel.

They danced to "Celebration" by Kool and the Gang, and her creaky body reminded her that she should slow down. Without warning, Cam took her hand, twirled her out, and reeled her back in, pinning her to his chest.

"Holy shit!" she muttered, terrified of falling or looking like a fool.

But Cam knew what he was doing, so she loosened her limbs and let him whirl her around the dance floor. Her long skirt furled and unfurled around her legs like a silken cloud. She felt the firmness of his grip, the heat of his body as it bumped against hers. Spinning in and out of his arms, every cell in her body fired at top voltage. When he looked directly into her eyes, whirlpools of desire whipped up inside her.

It was like being drunk or high.

A slow dance came on, and he held her to his chest. Their eyes met, and for an instant, their gazes fused together like melted glass. She felt the sharp intake of his breath, the minute tensing of his fingers on her waist as he pulled her closer. His eyes were all fire and about as dangerous. Cam Simpson was eye-smoldering her.

She looked around the room for one of the other Marriage Survivors. She should swap with one of them because his smile and smoldering eyes muddled her head. She laid her palms on his chest and shakily stepped back from his embrace. He let her go but rested his hands on her hips. She found herself wanting to close the space between them again, to lean against his chest or lay her head on his shoulder. *What I need is some fresh air. Or a cold shower.*

The music was too loud to speak over. Frankie hooked her thumb toward the lobby, and he nodded in agreement.

As she stepped away, his fingers dragged across her hip.

She didn't step away too fast.

In the lobby, she said, "I need a breather. That was quite a workout."

He had a sheen of sweat on his forehead and was grinning his fun-guy grin again. "Me, too."

They grabbed some seltzer from the bar and escaped to the darkened, deserted patio,

Now he stood close enough to her that the sleeve of his jacket brushed against her forearm, raising goosebumps along her skin. Inside, there were lights and other people, but if they went back in, it would be too loud to talk about the house, but out here, the lines framing his mouth when he smiled made it hard to think about anything else.

Over Donna Summer hammering away in the background, he said, "The music is giving me a headache. How about we take a stroll. It's nice out." He smiled.

Delicious shivers and chills and hot flushes ran through her. She was in menopause. Her body wasn't supposed to do this anymore. But, glory, hallelujah! She was glad it did.

He offered her his elbow.

She linked her arm through his.

They passed Flicka, who had a smutty smirk on her face.

Frankie sent her a look that said *Don't even think what you're thinking.* Except Frankie had smutty thoughts of her own. Perhaps the dancing had set her blood to the edge of boiling, not the arc of his forehead or the seductive curve of his smile. Maybe the cool air would sort her brain out.

She would take their time alone to share stories about the people of St. Paul's. Describe the sort of refuge, support, and community a shelter and the church could offer. She wouldn't ask him to sell them the house. She'd just tell him who they were and hope to touch his heart.

Outside, the wind blew her dress against her body, outlining every lump, bump, and bulge. She noticed Cam checking her out when he thought she wasn't looking. For a few moments, she tilted toward embarrassment, but then she thought, *What the hell? I'm not a sporty model. I'm built for comfort.*

He loosened his tie and unbuttoned his collar.

At her van, she slipped on a spare pair of work boots she kept in the back. When she lifted her skirt to put the boots on, she caught him staring at her sturdy legs. She was tickled she could still inspire ogling at her age. Once she had the boots on, she held her arms wide and said, "Fashion fail."

He tilted his head and surveyed her. "Oh, I don't know. I think it's a pretty sexy combo."

For the first time, she noticed that his voice had a smoky, sinuous quality, an ear caress.

What was she letting him do to do her? This wasn't an actual date, just a dance. They weren't drunk, out past curfew, or high. They weren't young and horny. Except he made her feel horny. She shivered and rubbed her arms.

He slipped off his jacket and draped it around her shoulders. "That'll warm you up a bit."

"Thank you." His gallantry flattered her. The most gallant thing the current men in her life did was take out the garbage without being asked.

"If I'd have known St. Paul's threw parties like this, I'd have joined the church long ago." He laughed, and his face had a new set of lines and contours she'd never seen before.

"See, I told you that you'd like us!"

"I do like you." He drew out the *do.*

A hot shiver ran through her.

They started walking, and she realized he was headed toward 61 East Avenue. She had promised not to discuss the house, but he hadn't. That gave him some advantage over her. But she still had stories to tell him about her people.

"Let me tell you about some of the folks you saw at the dance," she said.

"Is this meant to soften me up?"

"No, just break your heart," she said. "Remember Vera Cruz, the girl in white go-go boots and a purple wig?"

"A memorable outfit if there ever was one."

"Her parents threw her out when her name was Vern Cruces. She was homeless until one of the parishioners took her in. She started attending St. Paul's, and she credits us with giving her the courage to transition from Vern to Vera. She's got a job as a vet tech and a safe place to live. Says she's never been happier."

He came to a stop and stared at her. "Seriously?"

She felt, more than saw, Cam's surprise.

"You're the real deal, aren't you?" He took her hand and the pulse at the base of her throat quickened.

She gave him a half-smile. "Not me. All of us. St. Paul's takes everybody. The congregation is full of stories like that."

She told him about the people whose families rejected them

when they came out and who were now happily married, some with kids. About the high school kid who needed a safe place to live. About Carol and her dotty antics. About high school kids who grew up in the choristers' program and, against all odds, had gone to college. About a pair who'd finally been married at St. Paul's after having lived together as partners for forty years. She told him about the women who'd married one another after long marriages to men and households full of kids.

As they walked, he listened with his head bowed, and she couldn't tell if she was reaching him.

"Those are amazing stories," he said finally.

She could tell by the serrated edge in his voice he hadn't changed his mind.

They walked a bit further, his silence sandpapering the quiet. She was afraid she'd ruined the evening.

"I talked forever. Tell me about you. I want to know as much about my opponent as I can."

He stopped in his tracks. Squinting into the dark, he stared past her shoulder. "Is that what I am, your opponent? Because back there on the dance floor, in the parking lot, it sure didn't feel that way to me."

Gulp! To her own surprise, she admitted, "Me neither."

"I'd love to be able to help out the church, but I need the development to save the business I inherited from my father. He taught me everything about real estate development that I know. When he died, he left me the company. I owe him everything. If I can't make this development work, I'll have to close the doors on a sixty-year-old business. The house was such a wreck I never imagined anyone wanted it besides me." He lowered his voice, the silk of it twining into her ear. "But then you came along and, well, the rest is history."

She had been ready to press her case, but now, she considered the impact on him. "How did a smart businessman go broke?"

He sucked air through his teeth, and she heard chagrin in his voice. "I failed to heed the advice of my lawyer and let my 'nads do my thinking. I didn't get a prenup. One day when I was in my forties, I looked up and realized all I had was the business. My parents were dead. I was single and spent every minute I wasn't asleep or working out at the office. I was burned out. I married a significantly younger woman whose one desire in life turned out to be the only thing I couldn't give her." His voice tightened. "Kids."

She squeezed his hand, and he squeezed back, like a little heartbeat passed between them. The evening wasn't going at all as she had planned. Her attraction to him made her feel like she was betraying her friends and church.

Why couldn't she be as mercenary as Flicka? Bonk and bail.

CHAPTER 44

What is to give light must endure burning.

Viktor Frankl

Holding hands Frankie and Cam stood on the sidewalk in the shadow of 61 East Avenue. In the moonlight, her outer walls seemed to tilt inward. Someone had cruelly kicked out more of her pickets from around the porch railing, making the old girl look even more toothless. Peeling paint chips littered the overgrown grass like dandruff. She looked so lonely and forlorn that it broke Frankie's heart.

The only bright spot was the gnarled old lilac bush, which was beginning to bloom, the fragrance as intoxicating as Cam's smile.

"Why did you bring me here?" she asked.

"So maybe you"ll tell me the real reason this house is important to you."

She grew irritated at his obtuseness. She had made all her

reasons clear. "I've done nothing but tell you. The church. The shelter. The need in Norwalk. For the kids."

His eyes scared her with their intensity. "I think there's more to that than you're admitting." He rearranged his jacket on her shoulders, and the back of his hand brushed against her jaw, sending sparks of fire up her cheek. "I want to know why this house turns you into an Amazon warrior."

She pulled back, not sure if she was insulted or flattered. "Is that what I turn into?"

"That, and bullheaded." He smiled his brain-melting smile.

She laughed. "Why should I tell you why it turns me into an Amazon?"

"So I know how to stay out of the way when I see it coming."

She threw her head back and laughed harder. "Why should I tell you if it won't change your mind?"

He dragged his knuckles across her cheek. "Because I want to know what makes you so passionate about something."

Her heart tumbled.

He pulled a key out of his pocket. "I've never seen the inside. Let's go in." He started up the walk.

She didn't move. Softly, regretfully, she said, "This house will always be a barrier between us."

He paused and looked back at her, his gaze like a magnet drawing her in. "It doesn't have to be," he said, climbing the stairs.

Blood rushed from her hands, her feet, her head, to her heart. The night air felt thick and enveloping, but her every nerve ending was hot as an ember. Even her earlobes burned.

He put the key in the lock, jiggled, and turned the knob. The hinges squealed as the weathered oak door swung open. He stood there, one hand on the knob, the other extended toward her, waiting. The magnet of him pulled her up the creaking stairs.

A musty, dead-air, closed-up odor drifted out of the house, the scents of death and despair and broken hearts.

She stood on the porch. The streetlamp cast her shadow onto the floor inside. She knew every nook and cranny of the house and didn't need reminding of what it looked like inside.

He stepped inside and held out his hand to her. "Coming?"

She hesitated. She was giving in to his charms. She really shouldn't trust him because they both wanted the same thing, and right now, she was losing. Losing the house and her head. She couldn't lose her heart, too. The intensity of his gaze and the warmth of his voice told her she was safe.

She placed her hand in his and stepped over the threshold. He shut the front door, and the click of the latch echoed through the empty house.

Inside, she put her palms together and held them to her lips. The cold of the place assaulted her bones and made her ache inside. Aside from being filthy, everything else was as she remembered it. The oak handrail gliding up to the second floor. The wide plank oak floors now warped and stained with age. The stone fireplace.

Memories rushed back at her with such force and immediacy she felt a pressure deep inside herself, as though the past was trying to get out. The wine had worn off, and the surge of energy generated by dancing with a handsome man had dimmed. In its place was the weariness that comes when you realize you have gone far but gotten nowhere.

"Are you all right? Do you want to sit down a minute?" He pointed her toward the window seat.

That was the last place she wanted to sit because that was where she sat on the last day she'd seen her mom. She'd watched the snow falling so fast that the sidewalk, the trees, and the yard disappeared under a blanket of white. She had waited for her mom to pick her up, but she never did.

Frankie drew back from him, and he looked hurt. "No, no. I'm fine."

Moonlight streamed through the grimy window, casting half his face in light. "Let's take a look around."

"I'll wait here." She pulled his jacket closer.

He didn't move. "C'mon, there's nothing to be afraid of except maybe a rabid raccoon or some bats in the attic. Let's take a look around, and you can tell me what this house means to you."

She moved to the fireplace and ran a hand over the cool, dry stones, the scent of woodsmoke clinging to them. To her left, in the kitchen, she recalled her mother at the kitchen table, stripping the strings off sweet peas, a glass of orange juice and vodka at her elbow.

Cam followed her as she opened the corner cabinet in the kitchen where her mom had hidden her Mason jar of vodka.

She paused and stared at him in the low light. He made her doubt herself. Vulnerable was not who she was. She was capable, independent, tenacious, hardworking, bright, and, right now, terrified.

Considering telling him about her past and her mom was like standing at the edge of a three-story roof, looking down, knowing if her safety harness broke, it would hurt like hell if she landed on the cement below. But, sometimes, walking around the roof was the only way to finish the job. "When I was a kid, I came here with my mother. She was the babysitter and housekeeper for a friend of mine."

His silence was as solid as the stone fireplace, as serene as a drifting cloud. He followed her as she wandered from the kitchen, through the dining room, and back to the living room.

She stood in front of the window seat, unable to move, remembering the cold terror when she realized that her mother wasn't coming.

"What was she like, your mother?"

"She was ... complicated."

"That's it? That's all you can remember?"

She drew a long, slow, deep breath. "Aaaand an alcoholic." Exhale. "She drank here when she was babysitting. She always picked Bettina and me up at the bus stop. One day when it was snowing, she didn't. At first, I wasn't worried. Bettina and I walked home together. I let us in because I knew where the spare key was. I poured glasses of milk and made peanut butter crackers, and then we waited and waited."

"How old were you?"

"Eight."

"Jesus," he murmured. "You did all that by yourself?"

She nodded and, for the first time, realized how much that was for a little child to have done. "The snow turned into a blizzard, and Bettina's parents were stuck in the city." She gestured to the window seat. "I sat right here, watching out the window, for my mom to come, but I never saw her again."

He sat on the window seat, took her two hands in his, and gazed into her face. As she spoke, his attention bent toward her, wrapping around her like his arms on the dance floor. Rather than feeling exposed, his fixed attention made her feel safe and heard. She couldn't bear to meet his eyes as she told him the story of her mom's abandonment, reappearance, cirrhosis, the hospitalization.

He pulled the jacket closer around her and smoothed it down her arms. She found herself leaning into his shoulder. "That was a rough beginning, but you've overcome your past. I can tell by the way you talk to Javier that you're a good mom. You're a smart, successful businesswoman. You're ambitious, not just for yourself but for your community. You're a sexy hard ass with a heart." He brushed his lips against her temple.

Oh, God. Her eyes practically rolled back in her eye sockets.

Her chest cavity filled with a tornado of fear, lust, happiness, and joy. It had been so long since she'd felt so alive, but she hadn't expected him to be the one to reignite her. "And you are a dangerous man," she whispered, looking up into his penetrating eyes.

"I'm a man on a mission that has little to do with this house," he said in a way that made the hair on her nape stand up.

He lifted her hand and rubbed her knuckles against his cheek, which felt smooth and soft and stubbly all at once.

The gesture made the floor wobble beneath her feet. He took her in his arms, and though every inner alarm bell was ringing, she kissed him back when his mouth found hers. Her insides turned to butter, and her limbs felt as though they were coming unglued from their joints.

When she came up for air, she waved a hand in the general direction of the Norwalk Inn. "We—I think we'd ... let's walk ... the party—I have responsibilities."

"Yes," he murmured, nuzzling the spot under her left earlobe.

She got a dipping, gravity-defying rollercoaster sensation in her stomach.

He locked the door behind them, and hand in hand, they strolled down the front walk. The streetlamp cast a veil of light around him. His profile stood out against the darkness, a beacon in and of itself. He tipped his head back to look at the house. "This house means a lot to both of us."

"It's a big part of my past, and I'd hoped it would be part of my future, too," she said.

"Who knows? It might still be."

The weight of his palm resting at the small of her back sent shock waves up her spine to the base of her skull.

Despite the house's sagging gable roof, wheezy shutters, and potbellied porch, Frankie felt like a new season was revealing itself. She heard the grass making crinkling sounds as it pushed out of the ground. New constellations pivoted into place in the blue-black sky. The humming breeze carried the scents of lilacs, fresh grass, and an open road.

"I thought this place was going to solve my financial problems." He turned to her, and even in the dark, his gaze emitted a kind of blue light found at the heart of a flame. "But it seems that falling for you," he said, angling in to kiss her again, "has led to a bigger problem than either of us realizes."

CHAPTER 45

From Yearnings for Home

Oh, let me go I'm weary here
And fevers scorch my brain,
I long to feel my native air
Breathe o'er each burning vein.

Frances Ellen Watkins Harper

Frankie stopped the doctor coming out of Doralee's room. "How is my mom?"

His eyebrows rose.

She knew he was thinking *a Black woman is the daughter of a White woman?*

He straightened his features out, closed his clipboard, and then extended a hand in the direction of a small conference room.

She stepped into the room. Her hope was like a team of wild horses which she had to yank the reins back on. They sat in padded armchairs in a room meant to be comforting but still smelled of antiseptic, pain, and grief.

He glanced at his watch in a way he assumed was surreptitious. "Doralee's deteriorating, but that's the only direction a case like this goes"

His bluntness struck Frankie as callous, and her anger flared. "Well, what else can you do for her?"

He looked at her strangely and continued more compassionately. "When someone has late-stage alcoholism, there isn't much that can be done but palliative care. That can be done here in the hospital or at home. I've explained all that to her. She's expressed—as much as she's able—that she wants to go home to her sister's."

That word again: hospice. Frankie felt as though she'd run headlong into a stone wall.

He waited until she spoke.

"But she was doing so well after the paracentesis. I thought … I thought we had bought a little more time."

"Paracentesis is only to make the patient more comfortable. It can't reverse the damage that's been done over the years." He glanced at his watch again. "I apologize, but I have to go. I'm expected—"

She waved him away. "Just go."

"Hello, Francine," Doralee said when her daughter entered the hospital room.

Doralee's mind was clearer than it had been in ages. She remembered Francine, that Evie was her sister, and that Vic had been her husband once upon a time.

Whatever the doctors had done was like wiping some dirt off her brain. There were still holes and gaps, words she couldn't bring up, and talking was a slippery job. It hurt to talk. Her bones hurt. The needles hurt. The medicine gave her nightmares. The stupid tubes going in and out hurt. The noise in the hospital was terrible. She hated the medicine, the poking, and prodding. She wanted to go home, and she wanted a goddamned drink.

But she clung to what she wanted most: to protect Francine from more of what she had already done to her dear girl.

"Hi, Mom," Francine said with her pretty smile. "You look great."

"I'm going home."

Francine's face fell. "But Mom, I think you should stay a while."

"I want to go." The words scratched the back of Doralee's throat. "To Evie's."

Francine took the water from the bedside table and held its straw to her mother's lips.

Doralee sipped and then swallowed with a grimace. Even that hurt.

"Please, Mom, it's too soon for you to leave," Francine pleaded.

"It's getting too late to stay," Doralee croaked out. After all, what else was there to do? She'd seen her daughter and grandchildren, her sister and Vic.

Vic Carter. He had been in earlier in the day, sat with her, and held her hand. He was old with not too much hair, but he was still a big, handsome man with the same smile she'd fallen in love with. He told her about their grandsons—his boys, he called them—their dog, Beasley, his business, his bum knee. He had cried, and so had she. She didn't remember exactly what he'd said, but she remembered how he'd made her feel. He seemed sorrowful but resigned when he left. She didn't expect to ever see him again.

Francine caressed her hand and brought Doralee back into the hospital room. "But Mom—"

"Francine, it's ... no use," she whispered.

"I don't want you to leave the hospital," Francine said a little angrily. "You have to stay. We need more time."

The words started in Doralee's mind but stopped and went up in smoke before they reached her mouth. "Francine, my mind ... don't work ... s-s-so good. But I know one thing"— Doralee held up a single finger—"I know I don't want to hurt you."

Francine pushed back Doralee's hair. "I don't like your doctor, and I thought we could ask another doctor for a second opinion. What do you think of that?"

Francine was such a kind woman, so pretty and strong-minded. But she wanted something Doralee was out of. Time. She fought to put the words together. "I don't want ... die ... here."

"You're not going to die yet, Mom," Francine lied.

"When I go ..." Doralee closed her eyes.

"What is it?"

"No ... funeral. No service."

"Oh, Mom."

Everything was a lot of work. Just lying in this bed took work. Sorting the words was work. Even dying was work. Her greatest regret when she left this world would be not loving Francine like she deserved. Doralee wanted to tell Francine that, but it was too hard.

But the words had feelings: staring over the ocean with the sun dancing on the waves. The sound of little Frankie laughing. Sun warm on your eyelids. Soft wind at night making the leaves sing. Wet grass sparkling at dawn.

The smell of lilacs.

CHAPTER 46

The Self-Unseeing

Here is the ancient floor,
Footworn and hollowed and thin,
Here was the former door
Where the dead feet walked in.
She sat here in her chair,
Smiling into the fire;
He who played stood there,
Bowing it higher and higher.
Childlike, I danced in a dream;
Blessings emblazoned that day;
Everything glowed with a gleam;
Yet we were looking away!

Thomas Hardy

Sitting with the Marriage Survivors Club at La Paella, Frankie related her experiences with Cam Simpson and their side trip to the house. She was glad to have something to take her mind off her mother.

"I saw how he looked at you when you took your little walk," Flicka said slyly. "I don't think all you two did was look at the house."

Heat rushed to Frankie's face. "Well ..." She cleared her throat and brushed a braid back. "Looking at the house wasn't all we did, but that's not the point."

Flicka lifted her wine glass. "Would have been the point if I'da taken a midnight stroll with that man."

Snickers rolled around the table.

"But the important thing is, I couldn't convince him to sell the house back to us," Frankie insisted, trying to return some seriousness to the conversation.

"What did he say?" Carolina asked.

"He suggested maybe we could buy one unit below market rates, but that's not enough." Frankie set her wine glass down. "We need more space. We needed that house." She glanced around at her friends. "Look, that was my Hail Mary, and I failed. I let that house slip through my fingers, so somebody else has to lead now. I'm going to resign from the shelter committee."

"You're not quitting the committee," Bianca said. "Or I'll have to—I don't know—sue your ass or something."

Frankie's misery felt like cold, moldy darkness she was hauling around inside of her. "It's not just the house. I feel like I've failed everyone. You guys, the church, my mom."

"That's crap," Olivia said, using a word she rarely used.

Carolina touched her wine glass to Olivia's.

"Nobody cares as much about 61 East Avenue as you do." Bianca dragged her roll through a puddle of olive oil. "We'll all be happy to fundraise and back another house. Time to let go."

"You're busting your own balls too much, Frankie," Flicka said. "You did what you thought was best for everybody, but really, you wanted the house to win your mom's love and admiration."

Frankie said, "No, I didn't."

They all rapped their knuckles on the tabletop and chanted, "No bullshit, no bullshit, no bullshit," until Jaime, the owner, shot them a distressed look, and they stopped.

"Okay, well, maybe a little," Frankie admitted.

With narrowed eyes, Bianca poked her roll at Frankie. "'Fess up."

Frankie leaned back and sighed. "I thought she would be proud of me if I redid the house." Frankie poked her own roll back at Bianca. "But I didn't think it consciously."

"Who cares," Bianca snatched Frankie's roll, chomped a bite out of it, and handed it back. "Same difference."

"How is your mom?" Carolina asked. "I've been praying for her several times a day." She patted Frankie's hand. "And for you."

A ball of emotion threatened to choke Frankie's words. "Bad, but she's planning on leaving the hospital today or tomorrow to go home to her sister's. It's frustrating that I can't get her to stay longer."

An arm looped over the back, Flicka slouched elegantly in her chair. "Look, I've been divorced four times, and none of the relationships ever turned out the way I expected, but I took what love and companionship I could. You haven't got much time left. Use it wisely."

That sort of wisdom coming from Flicka made Frankie listen closer.

Flicka went on in her acid, loving, confrontational way. "You're kind of a fucking amazing woman, Frankie, and your biggest failure is your failure to acknowledge *that*. That and realize you can't have the relationship you wanted with your mom. You've focused on rebuilding the house instead of rebuilding a relationship with the woman who left you there. You're trying to patch the wrong hole because you're scared shitless to really open yourself up to being abandoned again when your mother dies. The train's going to leave the station, and if you don't catch it, your mom's going to die without you. People are imperfect. Love's imperfect. She did the best she could for you, even if it sucked. Even if you think that your own love for her sucks."

It was like a pie to the face. Flicka was right. It wasn't much different than they'd been telling her since her mom showed up. But this time, everything lined up like a row of two-by-fours.

A deeper relationship with her mom wasn't going to happen. What Frankie could have was love in a lumpy, crotchety, broken way. She was human with her own cracks, her own shortcomings, her own blind spots. The real test of love was the willingness to love without expectations or demands. Kind of the way Jesus told people to love one another, the way the Marriage Survivors Club loved one another. *Duh.*

The background music in the restaurant filled Frankie like a hymn. The seafood paella on the table smelled of salt and fish and the great wide ocean. The faces of her friends were filled with the love and acceptance she had wanted from her mother. She opened the fist of her heart and let the yearning for that love slip away.

"It's just a house, Frankie," Hélène said in a way that sounded as though she was humming a tune.

"Not for long," Bianca said. "The demolition is scheduled in two days."

"Let's all go and watch." Carolina's enthusiasm sounded as if she secretly liked watching buildings get wrecked.

Flicka said, "That'd be cool. Then we all know there's no

turning back." She looked pointedly at Frankie. "We all have to push ahead to find a new place for the shelter."

Their talking ceased, but Frankie felt their eyes on her, waiting for her reaction. These women knew her best and her worst, yet still loved her the way she wanted to love her mom.

In turn, Frankie waited for some emotion to surface and poke her in the heart. Instead she felt no twinge of regret, no aching loss, saw no haunting memory, no sense of abandonment, disappointment, or failure. Her friends had opened the cage of expectations she had locked herself in, and now, she felt free.

Frankie smiled. "Okay, let's do it." She grinned and raised her wineglass. "Burn the fucker to the ground."

CHAPTER 47

From Property

Old House! You've never known a death,
Well, now's your hour to know.

Robert Service

On a luminous morning beneath a pristine periwinkle sky, Frankie and the rest of the Marriage Survivors Club stood on the sidewalk behind the high chain-link fence surrounding 61 East Avenue. A backhoe crouched on the gravel driveway, and a dump truck rumbled in the rear of the property.

Frankie hooked her fingers into the fence and stared at the lifeless shell, which was no more than four walls and a sagging roof. Nothing about the house called to her or demanded attention.

What a freeing feeling.

Cam Simpson stood beside her in shirtsleeves, wearing well-fitting jeans and newish work boots. He radiated excitement, confidence, and compassion at the same time. He approached Frankie.

The others moved off a small distance.

"You're certain you don't want anything from inside?" he asked Frankie.

"I'm sure."

"And you're sure this won't be too painful for you?"

His concern for touched Frankie. "Nope. I'm over it." She tilted her head at him. "Unless you're having second thoughts and want to sell it to us."

He laughed. "That's what I like about you; you don't give up."

"I take it that's a *no*?"

"It is," he said. "But I'm still trying to find a way to help."

"Unless you have an answer right now, let's go," she said, eager to get on with it.

Turning to the Marriage Survivors Club, he said, "Ladies, would you like to go inside the fence and have a go at it before the backhoe starts the job?"

Frankie nodded. Flicka led the way, tottering along on stilettos in the tracks left by the dump truck. Inside the fence, they clumped together on the driveway.

"Bianca, you go first because you have the best aim," Olivia said.

"All right. Lemme see if I still have my arm." Bianca bent over and chose a softball-sized rock. She stretched her arm, bent her neck from side to side, wound up, and let the rock fly. Her back leg came off the ground like a Major League pitcher. The rock sailed through an upper-story window. The sound of shattering glass could be heard over the noise of the dump truck.

Frankie went next and took out the front living room window. Some part of her took flight out that window.

In an air of celebration, the women hurled stones that

dinged off wooden clapboards, chipped paint, knocked off a shutter, and smashed a few windows. Each time a stone landed, they all cheered and clapped.

Cam stood next to her, and Frankie felt him watching her closely as though ready to catch her should she stumble or weep. She didn't give one damn about the house because it wasn't important any longer. She was well and truly done.

Behind them, the backhoe growled to life. The driver trundled into the side yard and stopped directly over the spot where they'd buried their treasures and talismans for luck.

Cam took her callused, work-battered hand into his flawless fingers.

She felt a catch in the base of her throat. Her heart did a jig. She looked up into his thoughtful face and considered that perhaps the talismans had brought her a different sort of luck.

"I think we'll all be going now, Frankie," Flicka said.

Frankie glanced over at the Marriage Survivors Club. They were all staring and smiling at her and Cam, except for Bianca, who was weighing another rock in her hand.

"But I want to see the backhoe make the first smash," Bianca said, oblivious as usual.

Itty-bitty Olivia looped an arm around Bianca's plump waist and steered her toward the gate at the end of the drive. "C'mon, slugger, I hear your mom calling."

When she saw Frankie and Cam holding hands, realization lit up Bianca's eyes. "Oh, right, sure. Coming." She waved. "Bye, Frankie. Have fun."

They all trooped off, leaving Frankie and Cam alone in the front yard. He laughed and said, "You have great friends."

"I know," she said and laughed. "And they know better than I do what's good for me."

When the massive mustard yellow backhoe raised its bucket, vibrations rose through the soles of Frankie's feet. Diesel fumes stung her eyes and nose. The backhoe treads made a metallic clanking sound as he maneuvered into position.

"How do you feel now that you're about to see your dream busted into matchsticks?" he asked.

"Actually, right now, it feels marvelous," she said on an exhale. "I thought my mom would feel proud of me if I rebuilt this house. Turns out, I just needed to rebuild a relationship with her in the time I have left."

"I'm sorry about your mom. About the house."

"I know you are." She looked up into Cam's attentive eyes, which held a mosaic of emotions. Emotions she wanted to understand, to hold, and to be a part of.

It struck her as ludicrous that they were at a demolition site with gigantic noisy equipment, and she was falling for the man who had killed her dream. Vulnerability wasn't as scary as she had always thought. Surviving a broken heart didn't have to leave you with a hard heart.

In the cab of the backhoe, the driver, looking for a signal, waved to Cam. He held up his hand to stop the driver. Gazing at her, Cam's eyes were all steel and silk, and she felt the breeze of possibility sweep through her.

"Last chance," he said. "Are you sure you don't want anything from the house?"

Lightly, she bumped against his side. "No, I'm done with it. Thanks for letting us come to watch, though."

"When you called to see if you could come, I thought maybe you were going to try to talk me out of tearing it down one more time."

His smile made her want to put a hand to the back of his neck and pull his face to hers; instead, she laughed and dug at a weed with her boot. "I'm moving on."

"I hope not from me." He angled his face to look into her eyes.

She felt a tickle in her belly and smiled up at him. "No, not from you."

He lifted her hand and brushed his lips across her knuckles.

The driver sounded his horn to get their attention.

Cam tucked her hand into his elbow. "You give him the go-ahead."

She raised her arm and waved him on. The bucket rose in the air, swung back, and with one great smash, the porch crumbled to the ground. He cocked the bucket back and clawed at the chimney, which collapsed in a shower of stone. Extending the bucket arm to its full height, he brought it crashing down through the upper story and punched a hole in the roof. A breeze caught a spiral of dust, whirling it upward until it disappeared into the sun-soaked sky.

CHAPTER 48

The heart will break, but broken live on.

Lord Byron

Frankie was stretched out on the sofa, laptop on her lap, as she estimated a kitchen renovation for a previous client, muttering to herself about the costs of floor joists, two-bys, and dump fees. It was as far from hospital beds, hospice, and doctors as she could get for now.

As he did most days after the boys were in bed, her dad eased back in his Barcalounger with his tortoiseshell half-glasses perched on his nose to read a thriller by one of his favorite authors. Beasley flopped beside him on the floor.

He closed his book, holding his place with a finger between the pages. He looked at her over his reading glasses. "I went to the hospital the other day to see Doralee," he said somberly.

She stared at him and pretended surprise.

Avoiding looking at her, he schooled his face into a set of

features that were still his but held together by sheer force of will. After all the years of loving his wife, waiting for her to come back, and years of lonely nights, he had finally made his peace with Doralee. Maybe now that his heart was breaking for the final time, he would find someone to help him put it back together.

"She's going home to Evie's tomorrow morning," he said.

Frankie had known it was coming and thought she was prepared, but her world telescoped into a burning circle of pain at her very core.

"And since we're talking about it," he said, "I might as well tell you now, I'm going tomorrow morning to move her in and stay over there ... until she's gone."

She knew he still loved Doralee, but even this surprised her. "You're going to help see her off?"

He looked at her with a withering glance. "She's not taking a cruise, Frankie. She's dying."

She had no answer to that.

"I hope you'll do what's best for me, not you when it's my time."

"You're not going to die, are you?" she asked, half-seriously, unable to even consider losing him.

His smile was gentle, and he continued with his usual calm. "I loved your mother more than anyone I ever knew. Until you came along, but that was different, of course. She was my whole world. When she walked into a room, it was like the sun turned on. Just looking at her across the kitchen table, I felt like I'd won the lottery."

His sudden vulnerability forced Frankie to realize that he was more breakable than she had been willing to acknowledge. His softness, a result of Doralee's reappearance, was a good thing.

"Not many people get the chance to love like that, ever. I was lucky. I've idolized her all these years, wondering if she could still do that to me." He sniffed and knuckled a tear from the corner of his eye.

Frankie closed her laptop quietly and sat up slowly, afraid he would retreat into his usual patient, beleaguered silence. "And did she?"

He made a noisy sigh. "You know, even as broken as she is, after all the hurt she gave me, I still love her."

God had made some kind of miracle that her dad's heart was so enormous that he still held so much love for Doralee.

If Cam and she lasted, Frankie hoped her love would be as forgiving, deep, and expansive as her dad's.

"All the time I was growing up, you never wanted to talk about her, so I thought you hated her; you were still angry at her."

"I was. I am. But I love her, too." He laid his book and glasses on the side table and folded his hands over his tummy roll. "I've done you a bigger disservice than she did by leaving. I never let you see me move on, find anyone else. I wanted to give you stability, be both mom and dad, but ... I guess I waited too long." He held out his palms. "At some point, I should have let you have your own life. Maybe you'd have met somebody else if I'd been out of the way."

She blinked back her tears. "I only ever wanted to meet a guy like you, but there weren't any."

"There are," he said with a chuckle. "You just never gave 'em a chance, honey."

"I think Cam Simpson might be that kind of guy," she said shyly.

He nodded sagely. "I been hoping so."

His smile settled his face back into the warm, solid, reliable man she had always counted on to keep her safe, be her parent, help her with the business, and help raise her boys.

To be her rock.

She went to him, kissed his bald spot, and laid her cheek there. He smelled of shampoo, flannel, and his unique Dadness, a combination of wood glue and dryer sheets.

He took her hand resting on his shoulder and squeezed. "She needs to know it's okay with you for her to go."

He had been able to put the past behind him at last. Her mother was made up of broken bits and putting her back together again wasn't possible. Frankie had to grieve what they would never have.

Because there was no more time.

CHAPTER 49

God will wipe away every tear from their eyes;
here shall be no more death, nor sorrow, nor crying.
There shall be no more pain, for the former things have passed away.

Revelation 21: 4

Frankie stepped into Evelyn's entryway and barely had time to move her bouquet of lilacs out of the way before Evelyn gave her the first hug Frankie remembered ever getting from her.

Evelyn held her by the shoulders at arm's length. "She can barely talk. Be patient."

Even though her dad had warned her what to expect, the news hit Frankie with an almost debilitating pain, like she'd shot herself in the thumb with a nail gun. She gathered herself.

"Dad told me when he came home. I just want to be with her."

"He's been a big help, your dad."

"I know he didn't want to leave, but the boys needed a palatable meal, so it's nice he came home to cook for them. I think he missed them as much as they missed him."

Evelyn nodded and called out, "Dorie, Francine's here. Come on out. You don't have to be afraid."

When she peeked around the corner of the hallway, her mom's confused gaze made it obvious she didn't know who Frankie was. Even more frail and shrunken, her mom had deteriorated significantly since coming home.

"It's me, Mom. You don't have to be scared." Frankie held out a bouquet of lilacs to her. Even if her mom didn't know who she was, she would recognize flowers, and maybe their inherent meaning would return to her scattered mind.

Her mom came shyly out of the shadows with wobbly steps and took the bouquet. "Pretee! Wha?"

"What kind of flowers? They're lilacs," Frankie said. "They've always been your favorite."

Seeing her mom so debilitated made Frankie want to weep. Her heart wanted to give up, to grieve and howl. She took her by the elbow and led her to the sofa and eased her down. She was almost childlike, and Frankie felt again the inversion of their relationship.

Her mom's eyes looked confused. "Oh? Wel ... come," she said, meaning *thanks*.

Frankie knew what her mom was trying to say. "You're welcome. You and I used to cut and bring them in the house when I was little."

Her expression remained blank. "We?" She paused. "Do?"

"Yes, we did." Frankie fought the tears stacking up behind her eyes. "One of my favorite memories of us."

Her mom buried her nose in the bouquet and inhaled. "Smell ..."

"Yes, they smell wonderful." It was remarkable her mom still had a sense of smell. Frankie had read that it often disappeared as alcoholic dementia progressed.

Her mom squinted and cocked her head to the side. "Where? Big ... big ... build?"

"Where did we cut them? Yes, we cut them by a big building, a big house." Frankie was surprised at the flicker of recollection. If they sat together, perhaps more memories would float up. *Stop having expectations. Just listen and love.*

Frankie held the takeout bag aloft. "I brought dinner so we could all eat together."

Evelyn said, "I'll put the flowers in water, Dorie."

"Many vase," her mom mumbled.

"Many vases?" Evelyn asked. "You mean more than one vase?"

Her mom nodded.

Frankie waited to see if she could articulate her thoughts.

"Why?" Evelyn asked and looked to Frankie for an explanation.

"Re ... member?" Her mom's mouth moved, fighting to form words. "Lot vase."

Frankie silently gave thanks for this scrap of shared past and let the memory fill her with the images of armfuls of flowers, of her own childish excitement and joy over a house full of flowers.

"She's remembering that we used to put them in a lot of vases and put them around the house so the whole house smelled of lilacs," Frankie explained as she watched her mom's face.

Her mom smiled and nodded, and Frankie pressed a kiss to her cheek.

Evelyn's eyes were shiny when she said, "I'll take the food while I'm at it, and you two can sit in the living room while I get the table and flowers set." She slipped away into the kitchen.

Frankie was inclined to fill the silence with the clatter of words, plans, and her own needs. Instead of giving in to those urges, she let her jagged, vulnerable feelings settle in. Her heart throbbed with tender pity, knowing her mother had tried to be sober. The demons of her own childhood had dragged her under.

Pulling her mom into a careful embrace, Frankie held her close for a long while, feeling the *tap tap tap* of her mom's hand patting Frankie's spine. When she let her mom go, tears shone in her eyes.

Love, small, but enough.

They sat on the sofa and faced one another.

Her mom looked quizzically at Frankie. "Me ... you ... you?"

Frankie wasn't sure of her question, but she decided to speak her own truth with kindness. "I remember having some good times when I was a kid. I've been trying to create more of these times with you, but I should have waited and listened instead."

"Ooooh ... kay," her mom said sweetly.

Frankie doubted her mom had understood what she meant, but that was okay because it was what Frankie needed to say.

Her mom stared blearily at Frankie. "Preet-tee eyes."

Frankie felt her heart collapsing behind her breastbone. It took a minute until she could say, "Thank you. I got them from my mom."

Evelyn poked her head around the corner of the kitchen. "Food's on the table if you two are ready."

"Shall we?" Frankie asked, relieved.

She put her hands under her mom's arms and lifted her gently off the sofa. Her mom was nearly weightless as she tottered into the kitchen, leaning heavily on Frankie's arm.

Evelyn had set the table with china. The lilacs' glorious fragrance mixed with the aromas of the tomatoey, cheesy, garlicky Italian food.

This was the way heaven would smell.

As her dad had taught her, Frankie took her mom's and aunt's hands, bowed her head, and prayed, "Dear Lord, thank you that we're all together again and that you love us and provide us with what we need, even though sometimes, we want more. Amen."

Frankie opened her eyes and saw her mom watching her, eyes glowing with pride. Evelyn's face was red as she sniffled and wiped her eyes with her napkin, but she recovered enough to dish slabs of lasagna onto the plates.

Frankie spooned parmesan cheese on her lasagna and offered to sprinkle some on her mom's plate.

Her mom nodded. "What ... name? Who?" she asked, pointing at Frankie.

Frankie and Evelyn exchanged worried glances. Her mom's mind was slip-sliding all over the place, but there was no point in upsetting her.

Frankie smiled and said, "Oh, don't worry. It's not important."

Her mom tried to cut a bite of lasagna, but her hands shook so badly she couldn't.

Frankie said, "Here, Mom, let me cut that for you." She cut the lasagna into child-sized bites on her mom's plate. The sight of her struggling to bring the fork to her mouth gave Frankie a hollow ache in her chest. "Let's push your chair in a bit further." Frankie rose, eased her mom's chair closer to the table, and sat again.

As though someone flipped a light switch, her mom's eyes brightened as they had after the paracentesis. She stammered, "Thank ... you ... ssssspecial me."

It had to be enough.

Frankie rubbed her mom's back, the sticks of her shoulder blades poking through her thin shirt. "I love you, and you are more than special to me. You're my mom."

CHAPTER 50

"It takes courage to grow up and become who you really are."

E. E. Cummings

Cam and Frankie stood side by side in his office, looking at the plans for the Essex condominium project on his desk.

With her so close, his cranky old body—bad prostate and all—felt filled with electric sparks. Since they'd met, she'd only burrowed deeper and deeper into his thoughts. He wanted more from her but wasn't sure she wanted the same thing. A few stolen kisses in the house, which they watched being torn down, wasn't much to build a relationship on. He loved making her laugh, her smile, seeing her dark eyes dance, feeling her in his arms. He loved her determination and her fierce love for her children and friends. He wondered if she could fall in love with an old fart like him.

"What will the church do now?" he asked.

"Probably put the project on hold while we look into

different properties and do more research. We have to find a house where we won't get pushback from the neighbors, but ..." She squinted as if going through the options. "I'm not optimistic that'll be possible."

"I'd like to help you."

"Thanks, but I can do it my—" She stopped.

He saw her reconsidering her reply.

She continued, "Thanks, I'd like that."

"Me, too. I've gone over the figures several times, and I've been thinking. Maybe St. Paul's could buy one of the one-bedroom units before it goes on the market, at cost. Would that help?"

Her lovely eyes widened. "You'd do that for us?"

He wanted to help make her dream come true. Of course, the last time he'd tried to do that for a woman, it nearly cost him the company. He'd repeatedly reviewed the figures and thought his idea might work.

"Not for them, for you."

"Wow, wow," she whispered. "That's ... that's an amazing offer."

She paced around the office, frowning, thinking, and arrived back at his side. "It's very generous, and we were thinking of asking you about that. But we need more room than a single unit. We want to house at least four to six young people for two to four years. That's the agreement St. Paul's made with our other non-profit partners, so we have to keep looking for something that fits the bill."

"I tried," he said, disappointed his offer had fallen short. He wanted to do something, but money wasn't enough.

She recognized his disappointment because she caressed his arm. "Show me the rest of your drawings."

Cam glanced up at his father, glowering down at them from

the painting behind his desk. "The old man would be proud of this project."

He unfurled another page of the plans. Pointing out the floor plans for the different types of units, he told her about the gym, the pool, and what the condos might sell for,.

Frankie's brows came drew together. "These are great, but what about more community spaces? Places for people to gather, have a cup of coffee, drink some wine, and share a meal? Maybe cabanas and a fire pit around the pool."

Cam waved his hand over the plans, slightly annoyed. "This is a standard condo design. I've used this to build more than six projects over the last twenty years."

"Yeah, but life is different now, isn't it?" she said thoughtfully. "This is based on the way people used to live and work. I'd suggest you update this in a few ways. On the lower level, build community rooms, which people can reserve for private events. Maybe put in a coffee bar." She pointed. "And over here, some desks and workspaces. People need one another. Need to connect. You've put them in cubbyholes that take a lot of effort to break out of. If people are going to live together and accept one another, they have to bump up against one another."

She had trusted him enough to share the details about her mother's imminent death. Now he wanted to return her trust, so he decided to lay out his financial situation. "Your suggestions make sense, but I have to maximize profits so I can pay the last alimony payment to my ex, pay off the second mortgage on my condo, and set aside a cash reserve for Simpson and Sons. It's what my dad would have wanted, and it'll put the business on a solid financial footing."

"I see," she said, nodding.

"A bottom floor of community space instead of units will lose money," he said. "I'd have to go up another story to maximize profits. And zoning would never approve that."

"You don't know that about zoning. And you could charge more for the units because you're offering amenities that no one else has." With her palm, she smoothed out the page of drawings. "These changes would establish you as forward, not backward, looking."

He rubbed the back of his neck. "If I did that, I'd need new drawings. It would delay the project by several months, which I can't afford. Plus, I'd probably have to make concessions to zoning if I go back with a completely different set of plans, which they might not approve anyway."

She frowned. "What if you offered to make some of these low-income units as a swap for approval for another story?"

"This old vision has served this company well for more than fifty years," he said, clipping his words as he rolled a rubber band around the drawings.

"Let me ask you something."

She had that Amazonian look in her eyes that had loved and which now predicted a slugfest that might end the tenuous relationship they had.

"How much money do you need, anyway?"

The eyes of Cam Simpson, Senior, bored into the back of Cam's head. The old man always said money made the world go round, made people respect you, gave you power.

Cam answered the way his father would have. "A lot."

Except Frankie didn't seem to give a damn about any of that. Her currency was connection, and he wanted to connect with her in the worst way, but he could not afford to do it at the cost of his project.

With a mischievous sparkle in her dark eyes, she playfully flipped up the end of his silk tie. "So you can buy more silk ties? More of those fancy-ass suits you wear? You worn out all your Italian shoes?"

The affection he felt for her was coming up against his long-held values. The history of Simpson and Sons and his work determined who he was. She was asking him to throw that out the window for a coffee bar and community room. And for her.

She nudged her chin at the painting. ow much money will it take before you chart your own course, use your own gifts instead of living up to the old man's legacy?"

He stepped away from her and put the drawings on a shelf. "My dad taught me to work hard, find every nickel on a project, plan, get things past reluctant zoning boards, find land nobody else wanted, and cajole people into selling empty lots. How to make money," he said more snappishly than he wanted to. "I've worked for what I have and don't have anything to apologize for. Before he died, I promised my dad I'd make sure the business lasted."

"So you could hand the business down to the next generation?" she said gently.

He glowered at her. "That's a low blow, Frankie."

"Sorry." She nodded to the empty bookshelves. "Aside from this picture of some of the kids at the Carver Center, I don't see a single photo of a friend, relative, or co-worker. Why are you working so hard? What do you have to prove?"

The tendons across his shoulders tightened. She was right. He had worked all the time and only made time for relationships once it was too late. If he'd tried to start a family earlier, maybe he would have a son or daughter to pass the business on to. He was the end of the line. In a certain way, he'd failed his father because he tried to live up to the old man's unreasonable expectations.

Deflated, Cam dropped into the chair behind his desk.

She placed her palms flat on the desk and stared at him. "You don't have to let your old man or some promise you made years ago determine the rest of your life. Those don't make you who you are. I've seen you with the kids at the Carver Center."

She came around the desk and perched on the arm of his chair. She patted the spot over his heart, that rusty organ she had resurrected. "The most important assets you have are right here: knowledge and love. You can slave over the business and earn pots of money or earn enough to be happy and spend your life making other people happy."

"I've always tried to make as much money as possible, and I'm good at it. I don't know exactly how else to run a company. My dad was proud of the company he built—and of me."

"Be proud of yourself."

He laughed. "Are you always right?" he asked, chagrinned but not annoyed.

"Only if I'm not arguing with a teenager." She laughed.

"If I build a couple of low-income units, the other tenants won't be too happy," he said, thinking aloud. "And I'd still have to get approval for a fourth story."

"I'm not suggesting you do this to sell those units to St. Paul's. We'll find another house in Norwalk. Do with them whatever you want."

"What I want is to help make your dream come true," he said. "I want to do it for you. For us."

Her brows raised. She tilted her head to the side as if making sure she'd heard him right. "You don't have to do it for that reason either."

"I know, but I want to." Looking into her green eyes, his heart filled with hope and longing and certainty. She—not money, not a legacy, not a company—was what he wanted.

She dropped from the chair arm into his lap. Cupping the back of his neck, she brushed her lips against his.

Holding Frankie felt more right than anything he'd ever experienced. He kissed her long and hard.

She sat up and looked into his eyes. "I want you to know I'm not just smooching you up so you sell us the low-income units," she said in a voice heavy with desire.

"If you were, it would work."

Her lips lifted into a smile. "I'm smooching you because I like doing it."

"Me too. Let's do it some more." He directed her mouth back to his. She tasted like raspberries and sunshine.

When they parted, he said, "Frankie, I've never met a woman like you. If you told me to crawl across East Avenue during rush hour on broken glass to get to the other side, I wouldn't hesitate."

She grinned down at him. "You're serious, aren't you?"

"Damn straight."

They sat for a moment, the air electric between them, staring at one another. Neither could believe that this was what they'd both been waiting for.

Her eyes flicked toward the painting.

With her in his lap, he swiveled his chair to glance up at his dad's cast-iron face. Cam set her on her feet. He took the canvas down and leaned it backwards against the wall. He gathered her into his arms and felt as though he'd won the lottery. "I want to take care of you."

"I don't need taking care of," she said, laughing against the side of his neck. "I'm an Amazon."

With a single, swift motion, he swept everything off his desk and lifted her onto it. "Oh, yes, you do."

CHAPTER 51

Never tired pilgrim's limbs affected slumber more
than my wearied sprite now longs to fly out of my troubled breast:
O come quickly, sweetest Lord, and take my soul to rest!

Thomas Campion

Three days after he'd left to go to Evelyn's, Frankie got a text from her dad: *She's had a stroke. Come now.*

"But don't you think she'd be more comfortable if we take her to the hospital," Frankie said, leaning against Evelyn's kitchen counter.

Her dad sat on a straight-backed wooden chair at the kitchen table. Exhausted, he answered as if he'd forgotten she'd asked a question. "You know she didn't want that. We're not moving her."

Deep grooves carved either side of his mouth, and she worried about how helping his wife die was affecting him. But then, his never saying goodbye had exacted even worse consequences.

Opposite him, Evelyn sat with a steaming mug of tea. "Vic and I have taken care of her. There's nothing more to be done. The hospice nurse was here an hour ago and gave Dorie a shot of morphine. The nurse left some, so I can give it to her again if she needs it." Evelyn blew across her tea. Curls of steam, like minute ghosts, rose and disappeared into the air. "It won't be long now." She sipped her tea and looked over the top of the mug at Frankie.

"I kept hoping we'd have a little more time." Frankie sank into a chair beside her dad.

Her dad said, "Time for miracles is over."

The doorbell rang.

Evelyn set her mug down and excused herself to get the door.

From the glance Evelyn and her dad exchanged, it was clear they were expecting someone else.

Evelyn returned to the kitchen with Father Gabriel, his eyes grave but certain.

Frankie stared at him, her mouth tasting like cement dust. "Father Gabriel," Frankie managed to say.

Father Gabriel carried with him the light and the dark. His arrival left no question of the end. He, if not comfortable with the end of life, was more experienced than the rest of them. Without uttering a word, his presence filled the room with dignity and compassion that wafted about him like an angelic shroud. He had come to shepherd them to the threshold of death's door where they couldn't follow. "Peace to all of you."

She didn't want peace. She wanted sirens and paramedics and beeping machines and doctors and time. She wanted time.

"How is Doralee?" he asked.

"We've already said our goodbyes," her dad said. "She's only waiting for Frankie."

When he looked at Frankie, his eyes said he wished he could protect her from this, but he couldn't.

Frankie rose and took two steps down the hallway toward the bedroom, then stopped, unable to go any further. It wasn't death that frightened her. She feared the drowning loss and the sense of relief, the emotional whiplash that her mom had always stirred in her, which had affected her as a child.

Father Gabriel spoke again. "Would you like me to come with you, Frankie?"

The words wouldn't come. She nodded.

In a west-facing bedroom, the shell of her mother's body lay beneath a light blue cotton blanket. The rise and fall of her chest were minuscule, each breath a whisper. The room smelled of a dusty old person, of stale breath and freshly laundered sheets, of dying.

The window shade was halfway down to block the radiant mid-day sun. It seemed wrong for her mother to die on a day of effervescent light, on a day when cloud-scented breezes fluttered leaves in a thousand shades of green, when high-flying birds rode updrafts into azure skies.

Frankie braced her palms on the seat and lowered herself into a chair next to the head of the bed. She had worried that she would be afraid, but she wasn't.

Evelyn had combed Doralee's hair away from her face, revealing every plane and curve of her skull. Jaundiced skin stretched over her skeletal cheekbones, pointed chin, and high forehead. Her mom's eye sockets were two pits in a gray face. Her lips were colorless, as though life had already drained from them.

Frankie lifted the blanket, took her mother's hand, and kissed it. The paper-dry, weightlessness of the hand shocked her.

The way incense smoke spirals upwards, life was evaporating from the body that was once her mom.

She forced out the words, "Mom, it's me, Francine." Then she pressed her lips against her mom's forehead. The back of Frankie's throat filled, her eyes burned, and her body sagged over onto her knees. It surprised her, this bone-crunching grief. It clawed and tore at her, shredding her from throat to belly, wrenching away every strength she possessed. But her hollowed-out heart clung to the complicated love she had found with her mom.

Father Gabriel took his white stole from his suit pocket, looped it around his neck, and crossed himself. From his pants pocket, he took a tiny silver chrismatory which contained frankincense anointing oil. With the ointment, he made the sign of the cross on Doralee's forehead. He opened a copy of the Book of Common Prayer, and as he read, his wooly baritone voice comforted Frankie like a warm blanket.

He murmured, "Eternal God, grant to your servant Doralee, and to we who surround her with our prayers, your peace beyond understanding. Give us faith, the comfort of your presence, and the words to say to one another and to you as we gather in the name of Jesus Christ our Lord." He closed the Book, pulled up a chair, and sat opposite Frankie on the other side of the bed. He bowed his head and waited, praying quietly.

Bent double, Frankie unfolded herself. No matter how hard she tried, she felt her face crumpling, her mouth sticky with tears. "I don't know if she'll hear me."

He said, "It doesn't matter if she does. I'm sure she senses your presence, and I think it means a lot that you're here."

The words tumbled out unplanned, little rocks excavated from her heart. "I feel like I didn't love her as much as I wanted to. As much as she needed."

"Trying to love someone who hurt you deeply isn't easy. It

means opening yourself up to hurt all over again. You loved your mom as well as any human could." He moved the Prayer Book from one hand to the other. "We're all broken, weak, disappointing, and frail, as she was. But that doesn't make her death any less painful."

"She came all this way to die, and I never actually said I forgive you. What does that make me?"

"Human," he said simply.

"I thought there was ..." She swallowed. "A little more time. Time to forgive. To figure this out."

"There is no time like the present. Would you like me to leave you alone?"

She wiped away her tears with the sleeve of her jacket and nodded. "I think I'm ready."

"You know where to find me."

Father Gabriel stood and left, closing the door softly behind him.

Frankie took her mom's hand. She searched her heart for the words she wanted to say, but nothing seemed sufficiently honest. Her words came out awkwardly choked. "Mom, I'm sorry I didn't love you better. Sorry I didn't understand how awful your childhood was. I'm sorry it took me so long to accept you for who you were."

She smoothed a white strand of hair off her mom's face. Sobs wrenched from deep inside Frankie. She caressed her mom's hand. "It's okay. You don't have to stay. It's okay to go."

There was a hiss, a low gurgle of air, and her mom's chest went still.

"Francine, I loved you every day I was gone, every day I was with you. Every day of my life. You are the only thing I'm proud of. You're a good mother. Do the best you can. I loved you the best I could. I'm sorry I hurt you. Thank you for forgiving me."

As Frankie imagined her mom speaking these words, her hand grew cold.

CHAPTER 52

... a time to weep and a time to laugh,
a time to mourn and a time to dance.

Ecclesiastes 3:4

Frankie knelt and placed a bouquet of lilacs next to her mom's brass grave marker set flush into the ground. The Marriage Survivors Club had gathered with Frankie in the memorial garden behind St. Paul's.

The night was warm and humid. Clouds obscured the stars, yet moonbeams silvered the tall pines that created a protective circle around the garden. From a brass bowl, incense smoke spiraled up into the dark night. The candles they each held illuminated their laugh lines, wrinkled foreheads, sagging cheeks, and double chins, all of which Frankie adored.

Her entire body felt leaden, her hands weak, her knees like jelly. She choked out the words, "Mom, you didn't want a funeral or memorial service, but I need this. I need my friends around me, so I hope you understand us all gathering here to think about you and what you meant to me."

"It's kind of like when we put all our wishes into the ground at 61 East Avenue." Flicka kicked off her stilettos and groaned in relief.

Bianca blurted out, "Yeah, but that goofy ritual didn't have the desired effect."

Olivia said, "Oh, I don't know. I think the outcome was pretty good. Frankie got Cam out of it, and we'll get brand new condo units."

"They're going to cost way more, which means more fundraising, but hey, anything for a party," Flicka said.

"Frankie might never have arrived at this point if her mom hadn't shown up," Hélène said, her voice the song of a night bird.

"And you might not have fallen in love with Cam," Carolina said. She added one of the Marriage Survivors Club catch-phrases, "God works in mysterious ways."

Carolina slipped a supportive arm around Frankie's waist. She was glad of the support.

"I couldn't have gotten through this without all of you. You taught me to love the mother I had, not the one I wanted."

"Goes to the heart of being a Christian, I think," Carolina said. "That's grace."

The moon fell across the spire of St. Paul's, lighting it in a warm, welcoming glow. The lilacs in Frankie's bouquet smelled as lush and dense as love.

"But we're here to talk to Doralee, not the shelter," Carolina reminded them.

Carolina, the spiritual heart of the Marriage Survivors Club, had said *to*, not *about*. Everything Frankie never got to say washed through her with the force of a waterfall. She promised herself that when she got home tonight, she would tell the three—no, four—men in her life how much they meant to her.

"Should we sing?" Hélène asked, but she was the only one who could carry a tune.

"Only if you want to wake the dead," Bianca said.

Shaking her head, Flicka looked skyward and muttered, "Oh, Lord, Bee."

"What? What'd I say?" Bianca asked.

"It's okay," Frankie said, laughing and crying at the same time.

Hélène said, "We're here for you. Not just for tonight, but for good."

At that, Frankie's legs gave out, and she dropped cross-legged on the grass in front of her mom's grave. Tears flowed down her face, and the sobs she'd struggled to hold back wrenched out of the deepest part of her being and tore the through the silence.

In her designer dress, Hélène sat on the dew-wet ground next to Frankie and gathered her into a hug.

After a bit, Carolina said, "I was thinking that maybe we could talk about our moms and what we got from them, or things we remember, or are thankful that they taught us."

They joined Frankie on the grass, planted their candles in the soft grass, and joined hands.

"I'll go first," Carolina said. "I'm glad my mom took a chance and married my dad at a time when, like Frankie's parents, mixed marriages were looked down on. She was quiet and reserved, and I always wondered why. Eventually, I realized it was because she was paying attention to how God was working in her world." Carolina, her voice filled with emotion, paused to look at each of them. "She gave me a kind of faith that makes me curious and wonder, so thanks, Mom."

Someone handed Frankie a tissue, and she blew her nose. She wanted to lay down on the dirt, dig her fingers into the soil, pull out the grass, and hurl it into the darkness. She wanted to scream at the moon for being so brilliant because her mother would never again see them, never feel the magic of living, loving, and being loved. Because she would never have the chance to love her mother the way she wished she had.

Olivia's voice broke through Frankie's sobs. "I'm thankful that my mother helped me to adjust to having a child with Down Syndrome. She accepted Ariel before I did. I've been so lucky because Ariel made me the kind of mom I wanted to be, the kind of mom my own mother was." She looked up at the canopy of sky. "Thanks, Mom."

Hélène rubbed small circles on Frankie's back, bringing back a memory of her mother doing that when she was little and sick. Her mom sang softly until Frankie fell asleep, the darkened bedroom, her mom taking her temperature, spooning chicken broth into her, the enveloping love which made her feel safe. She had forgotten this precious memory, but now it was as vivid in her mind as if it had happened yesterday. The recollection hurt so deeply that Frankie's bones ached, and her heart irreversibly cracked open.

Hélène said, "I'm grateful my mom insisted I take piano lessons because now I can support myself teaching piano to little kids. Music is a huge part of my life, and it wouldn't have been if she hadn't made me practice every day. Merci, Maman."

"Okay, I think I have something," Bianca said. She inhaled and launched ahead without waiting for an acknowledgment. "As you all know, Ma lives with me, and she alternates between driving me crazy and making the best Italian food this side of Italy. But one thing I'm grateful for is that my mom always said that even if your life isn't filled with true love, you can still be a good person, and you can still do good in the world." She paused to clear her throat, but the emotion in her voice came through anyway. "So thanks, Ma."

"Thanks for always doing a lot with not too much, Mom. You always made me feel like I was special and loved no matter what." Flicka tipped her chin up and spoke to the sky. "When I was a little kid with boney knees and carroty hair, the other kids made fun of me, but you promised me that someday I'd be beautiful, and all I had to do was wait." Her voice cracked, and she paused to gather herself. "I thought I would die waiting to become pretty, to get hips and boobs, but it finally happened."

"I'll say," Bianca muttered, and they all laughed softly.

Flicka said, "So thanks for teaching me to hope."

They were all quiet for a while, waiting for Frankie's sobs to release their grip, but she couldn't find the words or strength to say what was in her heart.

Then, a balmy wind kicked up and swept through the circle and lifted a single, tiny braid from her forehead.

In the moonlight, the silvery pines swayed and made soft, whispery sounds. The clouds finally revealed the stars which seemed to multiply, flashing and spinning against the velvet dark, and the night air felt charged with tender sweetness, and Frankie felt wrapped in an embrace.

The words came as if they had been placed in her upturned palms. "Thank you for loving me enough to leave me and let Dad raise me. He was the best dad in the world, so thanks for having the courage to marry him. He loved me so much and made me feel like I was the most important person in the world. I didn't understand why you couldn't do it. Even though I knew it in my brain, I know now in my heart that it was because of your disease. And because of your own childhood. That you could love me at all was a miracle." She brushed her sleeve across her eyes. "I got my stubbornness and determination from you. I always thought I got those because you were gone, but now, when I remember how you marched right down the center aisle of the church with all those people staring at your mixed-race family, I can see how your example made me determined to make sure everybody belongs. Thank you for having the courage to come back to see me one last time, for apologizing, and for telling me why you left. I know that must have been hard for you. Thanks for loving me as well as you could, and I hope you can forgive me for taking so long to love you back."

Frankie glanced around the circle. Warmth flowed through her as though a fire, stoked by the Marriage Survivors love, burned in the center of their circle.

"If you had friends like mine, maybe you would have been able to get sober. I guess that's what I'm most sorry you never experienced, Mom, because I'm finding that friends can make all the difference in your life."

EPILOGUE

Sunday morning, Olivia bowed her head and thanked God again for all the people at St. Paul's who loved her daughter. She knew that whenever she brought Ariel here, people would greet her, hug her, and make her feel that she belonged here. No one stared past her or walked by. They acknowledged her just like they would any other member of the congregation.

In her broken speech, Ariel said, "Who man? Why kiss Frankie?"

Cam sat with his arm around Frankie in her usual pew, and Olivia could practically taste their happiness, as dense and rich as a flourless chocolate cake.

But like cake, Olivia never allowed herself to indulge in the fantasy of having another great love like she'd had with Derek, Ariel and Taylor's father.

"That's Cam Simpson, her new, special friend. And church is a good place for a kiss, don't you think?"

"I want kiss, too, Ariel said in her burbly voice that carried three pews forward, causing several people to turn around and smile.

"Someday," Olivia said.

But for the millionth time, her heart broke. Ariel would never know what it was like to be the love of someone's life, to be cherished and adored, the way Derek had adored Olivia. Loving someone put the sparkle and dance in life, put the spurs on your boots. But protecting Ariel and Taylor came before everything else, including love.

"Me have boyfriend?" Ariel asked.

Olivia patted her daughter's hand and smiled to herself. "You'll always have me."

Cam's breastbone vibrated when Wat Crabtree cranked the volume on the organ up to the "jet engine" setting. But then, that tremor in his chest could have something to do with the woman beside him. He brought Frankie's hand to his lips, and she smiled at him with a smile like salvation itself.

When Javier passed, he raised his eyebrows and smiled at Cam. Jordan passed their pew and gave Cam a grin so wide it was like a sunbeam shot out of his face.

Cam was still sore from having shot hoops with Javi and Jordan the night before. Aside from making love with Frankie, Cam thought it was the most fun he'd ever had. This afternoon, he was supposed to help Javier with his math and had promised to take him miniature golfing if he got through the entire time without a meltdown.

It astonished Cam that it wasn't too late to find love, "have kids," and start over with something that felt right. Most men his age might have been intimidated by taking on another woman's teenagers—African American young men, at that—but he was raring to prove to them he could love them, that he adored their mother and would love her as long as she let him. She was his home.

. . .

Frankie and Cam sat hip-to-hip in her usual pew, the air between them trembling. Frankie would have sworn the floor was shaking under her feet, but since she'd let herself fall in love with Cam, her feet had yet to return to Earth.

Frankie had buried the box of her mother's things, which she kept in her closet, in the gaping hole dug for the foundation at 61 East Avenue. It had felt right to put it there. Cam had comforted her and shoveled in the dirt for her when she couldn't.

Afterward, his lovemaking had been the most exquisite experience she thought she could ever expect for the rest of her life.

Vic, fallible and doting, sat on her other side. Released from the grip of his heartache, he seemed perkier than he'd been in ages. He'd never expressed the slightest interest in Carol Baxter, but she sat beside him, dead Winnie wedged between them.

Flicka, Olivia, Bianca, Hélène, and Carolina sat in different spots around the church. The Marriage Survivors Club had saved her from herself and helped her understand that her mother had loved her as well as she knew how. Cam squeezed her hand. Their love was as surprising, glittering, and brilliant as the stained-glass window above the altar.

Frankie, in her unfocused alto, and Cam, in his waspy tenor, sang, "All are welcome, all are welcome, all are welcome in this place."

Dear Reader,

Thank you for reading. Writers love to hear from readers, and I'd love to hear from you. To find out when the next Marriage Survivors Club Book drops, sign up for my newsletter:

https://annettenauraine.com/contact/

. . .

If you haven't read the Prequel for the Marriage Survivors Club series, here's a link to a free download.

https://storyoriginapp.com/giveaways/dba20524-1760-11ee-95dd-47a650f45331

CHAPTER 1 OF AFRAID TO LET GROW

MARRIAGE SURVIVORS CLUB BOOK 2

Olivia Maxwell, her arms weighed down with four heavy grocery bags, staggered up the steps to the front door. The door was slightly ajar. If the door was open, the alarm wasn't on.

Her heart lurched. Whenever she wasn't watching, terrible things could happen.

She had dropped her daughter, Ariel, off only thirty minutes ago. She was twenty-two and had Down Syndrome, but she knew to lock both locks, turn on the alarm, and not answer the door.

Olivia mentally bludgeoned herself. What had she been thinking? How could she have been so irresponsible to leave Ariel home alone? What if someone had walked right in and kidnapped Ariel? Or did something worse to her baby girl?

She did everything she could to keep her children, Ariel and nineteen-year-old Taylor, safe from burglars, fires, floods, thieves, airplanes falling from the sky, nuclear waste, lead in the water, chemicals, kidnappers, drowning, earthquakes, and molesters.

Olivia shouldered the front door open. Juggling the bags, she kicked the door closed behind her and dropped the bags on the kitchen table.

"Ariel," she called, her anxiety rising. "You're supposed to keep the front door locked and the alarm on. Otherwise, it's not safe."

No answer.

Olivia's mouth went dry. "Ariel?" she croaked.

Olivia had left Ariel at home because she had complained of being tired. Maybe she had fallen asleep in her room. Heart pounding, Olivia ran upstairs to Ariel's bedroom, but her bedspread lay neatly smoothed over the mattress with her collection of *My Little Pony* characters neatly arranged against the pillow. Olivia pulled aside the curtains and scanned the backyard, but it was empty. Her lip twitched the way it always did when she was nervous.

"Ariel?" Olivia tried to keep her breath even as she checked her bedroom, Taylor's bedroom, and the bathroom. She yanked open every closet even though she knew Ariel wouldn't hide in the dark.

Nothing.

Ariel was missing! What had happened to her baby girl? Where could she have gone? Olivia's palms grew sweaty. She was shaking and close to tears.

It was one of May's first lovely, warm days, so maybe Ariel had decided to take a walk. But she knew only to leave the house if she first asked Olivia or Taylor for permission.

Olivia raced back to the kitchen. Her hands shook as she clawed her phone out of her purse and speed-dialed Ariel. "Pick up, pick up, please, pick up."

Ariel's phone lay on the charging pad, ringing and ringing and ringing.

Panic set fire to Olivia's veins. Ariel never went anywhere without her phone because if she ever left the house without it, she wouldn't be able to watch *America's Got Talent* for a week. She lived for that show.

Olivia's mind ramped into panicked-mom mode. Someone must have convinced Ariel to open the front door and kidnapped her. Someone must have been watching the house and knew a vulnerable person lived there. Olivia charged back to the front porch. Shielding her eyes from the late afternoon sun, she looked up and down the street, hoping to see Ariel come trudging down the sidewalk.

Nothing.

How could Olivia have been so lax? So trusting? Even a few minutes was too long to leave Ariel alone. Olivia was about to dial 911 when Taylor's Subaru pulled into the drive. Ariel sat in the front seat, eating an ice cream cone.

The knots in her stomach gave way, and she blinked back tears of relief.

Taylor climbed out of the car and waved. "Hi, Mom!"

She forced a smile despite her impulse to wring Taylor's neck. "I was terrified when I came home to an empty house with an unlocked door. But welcome home, anyway."

The grin on Taylor's face hardened. He adjusted his baseball cap.

Ariel climbed out of the car. "Tay Tay buy ice cream cel-brate home." With an ice cream-covered hand, she held out a dribbling cone. "Lick?"

Olivia said, "No, thanks, Honeybun. You forgot your phone, young lady, and you know what that means no *AGT* this week."

Ariel stomped a foot. "Crap."

Taylor bent and enveloped Olivia in his arms. "Gotcha!" He lifted her off her feet and jiggled her up and down, the way he did when he wanted to tease her about their size disparity.

Her friends teased her about being the size of a twelve-year-old, which was about right. It was a mystery how she'd given birth to a six-foot-three hulk like Taylor.

Feet dangling in mid-air, Olivia laughed helplessly. "No matter how big you are, I'm still the mom." Olivia knocked his hat off and ruffled his hair.

Taylor set her down, picked up his hat, and settled it back over his lush curls. "Don't blame Ariel. She was so hyped to see me she forgot her phone."

Olivia straightened her clothes. "I'm glad you're home, but I thought you had finals for two more days, so I wasn't expecting you." She wrapped her arms around her son's waist and pulled him in for a mom hug.

The way all mothers can identify their babies, she recognized his smell: young man, leather, and gym socks. Having him near was like breathing again. She didn't have to worry when he was right there with her.

Olivia let go and looked up at him. "Next time you take her, please leave me a note."

"I did. It's on the kitchen table." He arched an eyebrow at her.

He looked so much like his father, Derek, that her breath left her for a minute. Taylor was as strapping as his father. He had his dad's jumble of dark brown curly hair springing out from his baseball cap. His angular face was defined by the fatless cheekbones of someone who played a lot of sports. Bulkier than when he'd left for school after Christmas, she noted that he had an unfamiliar swagger. Taylor was a good man. After finishing his medical residency, he would make someone a good husband. Until then, she had to keep him safe, make sure his grades would get him into medical school, and he would be fine.

Olivia tugged at her sleek ponytail. "I looked all through the house and thought she'd been kidnapped."

He easily hefted a pair of duffle bags out of the trunk of his car. "My phone's out of gas, or I would have texted you. And besides, you shouldn't get so bent out of shape if Ariel's not home."

His devil-may-care-attitude made the hair on the back of Olivia's neck stand up, but she held back on reminding him about Ariel's safety. He was a great brother but clueless about what it felt like to be a parent. He would understand when he was sweating bullets over his own teenager coming home late or a missed period.

She said, "I thought finals weren't over until Friday."

Taylor's gaze slid away. "I finished up early. I'm going to take my bags in. I brought all my stuff home."

Olivia knew the look in his eyes, like that of a naughty little boy who, too busy playing to stop, had peed his pants. "How did your finals go?" she persisted.

Taylor seemed not to hear her. He pushed the front door open and headed inside. Had he done poorly on his finals? She would have to stifle her worries until the letter with his grades showed up.

Olivia and Ariel followed him into the house.

Dropping his bags in the entrance hall, he headed immediately to the kitchen. He lifted a grocery bag on the kitchen table and pointed to a bright pink sticky note. "There it is. I told you we left you a note." He pulled it off and shoved it at Olivia. "Here, read it."

She read the note and tossed it in the trash under the sink. "I'm glad she's safe and that she was with you."

"Mom, I. Left. You. The. Note. Just admit you didn't find it, okay?" Taylor opened the fridge and pulled out three sticks of string cheese.

Sorry they'd already gotten off on the wrong foot, she sighed. "All right, I'm sorry. You left me a note. Thanks. But you know how I worry about your safety."

"Well, stop worrying already." He grinned.

Ariel sat at the table licking the dripping ice cream cone.

Olivia said, "Wash your hands, honey."

"Okay." Ariel rose and laid the remnants of her ice cream cone on the counter.

Over the sink, Olivia soaped up her daughter's hands.

"Mom, she can wash her hands," Taylor said snottily.

Olivia shot him a look but let Ariel finish washing her hands on her own. Interfering with Ariel was a new twist in his being her brother.

Ariel said, "I'm going in to watch *The Wiggles*."

"I'm making salmon for dinner. That okay with you?" Olivia asked.

"Anything's fine," he mumbled around the cheese in his mouth.

She bit back the words *don't talk with your mouth full*.

Olivia pointed to the fire alarm above the sink, its light still glowing green. "Now that you're home, maybe you can change all the fire alarm batteries. It's only been six months since we did it last time."

"You only have to change the batteries once a year." He took a mug from the cabinet, set it under the coffee maker, inserted a plastic pod, and flipped the switch. "Why are you so safety obsessed?"

"I'm not safety obsessed. I like the batteries changed twice a year, that's all." Kids were oblivious to all the dangers lurking in the world. She hoped he'd never have to confront that reality the way she had.

He rapped the coffee machine with his knuckles. "Why isn't this working?"

"You know I always unplug the appliances when I leave the house."

He gave a noisy irritated sigh. "Oh, right. You act like every day is Armageddon just waiting to happen." He plugged the coffeemaker in and flipped the 'on' switch again. He leaned against the counter.

She flapped him out of her way. His body seemed to crowd her out of her kitchen, but she was happy he was home again. "I'm just cautious, is all." She set the slab of salmon in the sink. "How did your spring semester go?"

"Fine." The coffee machine hissed as the liquid dribbled into his cup.

Fine? Fine? That was it? He'd been gone three months, and all he could say was fine? "You stopped texting or answering my phone calls, so I had no idea how things were going. It was very worrying."

He said nothing, but she felt his annoyance like a cold front rolling in. She tried a softer approach. "I like hearing from you." And she worried less about him if he texted. There were dozens of things she had to watch out for: concussions in lacrosse, mass shootings on campus, hazing or drinking, blackouts, car wrecks, snake bites, or Lyme disease.

"Mom, I'm nineteen. I'm in college. You don't have to check on me every day. It's like you're the Gestapo or something."

She didn't try to disguise her hurt. "I am not the Gestapo because I want to hear from you."

Above all, she had to make certain that Taylor never fell into Derek's all-consuming hobby of cheating death. Derek had loved daredevil sports: rock climbing, surfing, scuba diving, paragliding, board sailing, cave diving, and off-trail skiing. Dutifully, she patched up his scrapes and bruises and nursed him back to health. When she asked him why he tempted death so often, he said it was because he saw so much death in the ER. He felt alive, living on the edge. She fought her terror and accompanied Derek to keep him from slipping off the edge.

Until she failed, and he slipped anyway.

AFTERWORD

The Marriage Survivors Club Series has been a labor of love and joy inspired by St. Paul's on the Green in Norwalk, CT. Please stop by either in person or virtually and experience the love and acceptance that makes it such a special place.

All are Welcome

If you can't visit in person, join us virtually for a Sunday morning live stream service at:
   https://www.facebook.com/stpaulsnorwalk

Or take a virtual tour at:
   http://www.stpaulsnorwalk.org/who-we-are/on-our-grounds/

ACKNOWLEDGMENTS

No book is born without a lot of help—usually pulled kicking and screaming from the author!

For helping this baby into the world, I have my crit pals, Lelah, Sara, and Tara, to thank.

You guys are the best!

ABOUT THE AUTHOR

Annette Nauraine is a wife, recovering opera singer, mom of two, and Doodle mom. She loves chocolate, blood orange sorbet, classical music, Chinese food (eating, not cooking), gardening, gardens, writing, reading, history, opera, her dog, Beasley, and cat, Wolfie. When she has a spare minute, she enjoys period movies and TV series like *Versailles* and *King*. She spends her time trying to keep ahead of everything life has to offer and enjoying love and laughter.

Find her at www.annettenauraine.com or on any of the Social Media links below.

ALSO BY ANNETTE NAURAINE & SOFIA BARROW

Kissing the Kavalier

A steamy historical romance based on the opera, *Arabella,* by Richard Strauss

Auto-narrated book available exclusively here:

https://books2read.com/u/mBoKry

Masquerading as a man wasn't a problem. Until she met the man of her dreams.

Countess Zdenka Waldner dreams of a future on her ancestral farm, free of Viennese Society's rules or expectations to marry. But her dream depends on saving the farm from her father's gambling debts and finding her sister, Arabella, a rich husband. Tasked with chaperoning Arabella, Zdenka masquerades as her younger *brother.*

Falling in love with a handsome and passionate Kavalier was *not* part of the plan.

Lieutenant Matteo von Ritter, veteran of the Austro-Prussian war, vows to spend his life caring for his injured men. He has no tolerance for ordinary women, but Arabella Waldner appears to be extraordinary. In need of a messenger, Matteo recruits her charming *brother*, Zdenko, to deliver a series of love letters.

Unbeknownst to Matteo, he is trading letters—*and* falling in *love*—with Zdenka.

When her deception unravels, can Zdenka save her dream, her sister's engagement, Matteo's honor, and his love?

Print book and ebooks available here:

https://books2read.com/u/mBoKry

Kerry and Bobbi and the Dead Senator: Doing Bad to Do Good

A Kerry and Bobbi Mystery

Auto-narrated audiobook available exclusively here: : https://books2read.com/u/bQNxeE

When investigative reporter Kerry McDonough finds double-dealing Senator Ralph van Patten dead in her bed, she can't call the police. Any investigation would paint her as suspect Number 1, putting her in an unwanted spotlight. Plus, if it gets out that she slept with an interview subject, her career would be blown out of the water. And she couldn't live with herself if people knew she was with a slimy Republican!

Instead, Kerry calls her jack-of-all-trades BFF, Bobbi, to help her dispose of the senator's body and uncover his murderer. But what should be two relatively straightforward tasks hit major speed bumps. The two besties have to dodge drug dealers, vicious assistants, an extravagant wedding, and the perils of suburbia, all while trying to stay ahead of a delectable detective in the race to find out who killed the senator.

Join Kerry and Bobbie on their caper to solve the mystery of the Dead Senator. Perfect for readers of Carl Hiaasen and Janet Evanovich. Watch for more Kerry and Bobbi Mysteries!"

Print and ebooks available here:

https://books2read.com/u/bQNxeE